SEASON OF ASSASSINS

Also by Geoffrey Wagner
Born of the Sun

SEASON OF ASSASSINS

GEOFFREY WAGNER

ISBN-13: 978-1-952138-04-1

Published by
Cutting Edge Publishing
PO Box 8212
Calabasas, CA 91372

PROLOGUE
THE PERMANENT SHADOW

The plumpish figure walked briskly up empty Edwards Crescent. This stately gentleman, incongruously clad in khaki, knew without consulting his watch that he was several minutes late for the Court of Inquiry, directly he hove in sight of that graceful Queen Anne house round the curve. But he smiled confidently. Prerogative of office. And he added sternly, Must get that salute better.

In actual fact it was difficult not to whistle on such a perfect London morning as this, the pavement tactfully freckled with sunlight in front of him and the consciousness in the air that the most devastating war in England's history was over at last. Won.

Ah, but that was the trouble really, he reminded himself. Won. Some tidying up to be done afterwards, of course. He felt fairly sure they'd get their man.

"Sorry, son."

Crossing the road he dodged a very small boy on a very large delivery bicycle.

A year ago he might have snarled at the nipper. Look where you're going, can't you? Something like that. No control. On the far side, approaching the house, he took care not to step on the cracks. A dead man. Oh delicate! Ridiculous really, still.... No, not for all it wasn't won. Not by a long chalk.

Up chaste stone steps. Well-polished brass.

Tingaling!

Deferential tread within. No butler. Instead, a lance-jack he hadn't seen before looked out, opened the door, fanned the peak of his cap.

"Russ-Sykes." The portly gentleman strove to produce his yellow pass and to return the salute all in one.

Miffed it, he thought crossly, and frowned as he bundled by the clerk in battle dress who had installed a deal desk, littered with Army orders, under a carved chimney-breast that always caught the eye. So he thought as he scampered, semi-kittenishly for a fifty-year-old, up. the first flight, up to the gilded Sam Paine door.

A sergeant stood there. Armed. Lanyard blancoed. Recognizing who it was, the sergeant smashed his feet on the perfect parquet, saluted. This time, a smart return.

"Everything ready inside, Colonel."

"Thank you. Mr. McCole arrived?"

"Come in ten minutes ago, sir. Yes, they're all inside now, I think."

"Thank you." He paused. One word. "I say, don't trouble to salute every time one or the other of us comes in or out."

Hastening away, faintly embarrassed, it seemed to him he virtually burst into the room, smiling oafishly at its sunny, graceful spaces.

"Good morning, gentlemen. So sorry I'm late again. Please sit. What a glorious day."

The laburnum-wood table, around which the uniformed figures now reseated themselves, glowed discreetly. Now the note of cautious (trust no one) confidence as they started chatting.

The desertion of the room was vividly emphasized by the mild sun pouring so gratefully in, playing onto the liquid surface of the table, practically the only piece of furniture there: for the rest, a few filing cabinets, wire trays, rubber stamps, with which the military struck modernity into those lofty absences.

"D'you know—" He loosened his Sam Browne a notch. "I do wish someone would invent a method by means of which one might read comfortably in the bath. It's most important to me in the morning."

"Celluloid pages, Charles," came a suggestion.

"Try a bed-tray, sir."

"Rubber gloves."

After more backchat of this kind the atmosphere relaxed and he threw open his brief case. "If I can find anything in this confounded mess." Hastily he buried a betting slip that had risen to the stirred-up surface. "Yes, I think we can resume in a matter of minutes."

The others were undeceived by the mock modesty, the paraphernalia of pseudo-inefficiency. Informal as he had made the Court of Inquiry, it already possessed a sort of inescapable logic. They knew old Russ-Sykes' peacetime reputation, long before the days when he'd been called onto the Judge Advocate General's staff halfway through the war. He was said never to have lost a criminal case, and precious little else either.

Looking up he quietly inquired, "Witnesses ready?"

"Yes." It was a Military Police officer to his left who answered. "Down below. In separate rooms. Sergeant says they're scared. If you remember, sir, I've got one of our men who worked in plain clothes for a while testifying. We laid it all on as you advised. They're waiting, all right."

"Thanks, Ellis. Well then," and he sighed, "I suspect we can proceed. All ready? First and foremost, do any of you feel we ought to go over any of that stuff from the other side once more? I mean in particular that German sergeant's story."

For a second the room seemed replete with silence. Outside a van drew up. An order was shouted. Boots clattered. Clang!

Charles Russ-Sykes was observing the man to his left, the only one in that gravely proportioned chamber wearing a suit. "And what does C.I.D. think, Alec?"

The man shrugged. "I don't suppose we have to see him again. I mean, we've got all the evidence we want here. And personally I think it's enough."

"Absolutely." The voice military, gruff.

Another: "There's no earthly reason why that jerry sergeant should be lying, sir. What motive..."

"You can trust a boche over something like this. No, he's got nothing to gain."

"Now, now." Eyebrows raised, Charles Russ-Sykes chuckled as he drew his fingers together. This was a signal of precision in his thought that had been watched with apprehension in many a peacetime courtroom. "No opinions yet, please, gentlemen. No judgments, no inferences, I thank you. Only, reports. First off, let's gather all the evidence we can. Time for the rest later." He smiled round. "All the same, I must say I'm glad none of you seemed to want that German medical sergeant back in here again. I'm afraid with that wound of his he made me feel somehow guilty."

"Novel sensation for you, what, Charles?"

"We'll have you swinging yet, sir."

"Thus it seems," he resumed, "that we have now drawn in all possible testimony from enemy sources." A trifle more hastily than normal he put in, "As Captain Ellis, our M.P. advisor here, suggests."

"One or two prisoner-of-war camps to be rechecked," the C.I.D. man interpolated thoughtfully.

"Quite. But barring that, and I recapitulate, gentlemen, we have our problem pretty well cut and dried. In 1942, a member of His Majesty's armed forces, engaged on active service in North Africa, or Central Mediterranean Forces as such troops came to be called, goes out on a special mission. During the course of this he disappears. The enemy suggest he escaped, though no one we've been able to find from their side so far seems entirely sure. In any case, they have no sign of him after the period we know about and they do appear to have been rather careful to take prisoners in cases involving P.E.D.G. patrols, where the personnel were valuable. To the enemy, that is, as to us. Further, we're all aware that the boche set-up in this case was composed of those fanatical, dedicated Nazis Rommel chose for such headquarters, and about whom we're hearing so much in the press these days."

"And who everyone now seems concerned to persuade us were just good clean sportsmen, at the mercy of orders from above."

"Hear, hear." A ripple round the table.

"Have you, Charles, by any chance seen that picture of the Gestapo thumbscrew they've just released? The amazing thing about it was that the manufacturer put his own damnable imprint on it. Proudly."

"Fiendish."

"I certainly trust they'll catch that missing general with the Teutonic torture ideas soon and that J.A.G. will deal with him according to his deserts. Human cement mixers, indeed. Ugh!"

"Merely methodical," came a dissenting opinion from down the table. "The German's a good fellow. I fought him on the Somme and again in France this show. The ordinary citizen there was simply led astray."

"Gentleman, please." Charles Russ-Sykes had closed his eyes. "These are theoretical considerations we can't indulge in now. I'm sorry I expressed myself as I did. I shouldn't have. Now then, let me restate the case to date. Our kind friend, this mysterious Englishman, fails to turn up on the known rosters of prisoner camps, or back in His Majesty's beloved service either. I think it'd be a helpful idea to run over the main outlines between ourselves for a few minutes before we call in our cardinal witness, who's evidently waiting down below or, for all I know, sitting outside by this time, under the watchful gaze of our N.C.O., on that rather nice chair."

"Sweating silly."

"So what we hope to find out this morning is no less than just what the devil happened to that bloke." He chuckled richly, "After all, we can't very well let him remain a permanent shadow, can we?"

PART ONE
THE MISSION

CHAPTER ONE

Philip Stevens lay on his camp bed and looked sourly up at the tear in his tent, through which the sun sliced down. A big man, his black issue boots lagging heavily over the edge this evening. Turning his head, he could see outside, with the flap drawn back like this; and what he saw took in a few dusty trees of an indeterminate color, a stretch of scabby earth, three or four goats, two wogs of indeterminate sex, and several other camouflaged tents the color of mold. There's North Bloody Sodding Africa for you all right, he thought. Roll on death.

He yawned. He'd slept less than he'd wanted to. A glance at his Rolex showed him there were still several hours to go. Too sodding many. Why did he suddenly feel like this? For the umpteenth time that day he looked at the dirty map. Dark House. Operation Cabbage. Beside the map, the plan of the building they were to enter.

Years ago—too bloody many now—he remembered how he'd entertained his fellow cadets at Sandhurst by doing the proverbial telephone book-tearing job. Yet though that was all so long ago by now, Stevens still felt as physically fit at thirty-three as ever he had. Fitter, perhaps. These past months in P.E.D.G.—the jolly old Personal Engagement Desert Group—did wonders for one's physical condition. Bags of training. No wine, women, or song. Just the odd shot of Haig and Haig if you had a friend in Q. Which made him think.

But no. In the act of reaching under the camp bed he hesitated, straightened. Been doing this too often lately. The men would smell it on his breath during briefing.

The desert. Stevens swore. Roll on almighty death. He'd got so boggering used to it all by now it was like a second life, really. Didn't know anything else. Years and years. Then he went and took on all of a sudden like this.

After all, he considered as he sat up and stretched on the metal bed, the men would get their tot on the boat. They all would. Himself included. Fair do's. But then again he didn't really like rum, he admitted as he began to clean his pistol, an old, cumbersome .45 his dad had had at Gallipoli and which he favored for these outings. Nasty greasy gas, that rum.

By a tightening of his spine he became aware of a series of electric splashes splaying the horizon to the extreme left. He stood up and looked out and saw that gnawing line bisecting earth and sky bruised by the distant explosions. Tank battles right over by Bou Rezit again, most likely. But again his skin prickled as the faint stitching of far-off machine guns carried through the air to the encampment. Spandaus, he knew, by their rate of fire. Brens slower. Too bloody slow. He didn't like the symptom. No, this time he was afraid.

Stevens examined the rounds for his .45. These were dum-dum, officially outlawed, and he slowly slit the soft lead of each chubby nose in a cross with his knife. He liked to be sure of stopping them, see. Brute Strength had been his nickname in the days when he'd boxed for Sandhurst and once, later, for the Army, short for Brute Strength and Ignorance, that was. Now he grinned at his reflection in the cracked mirror hung from the tent pole, as he ran the broken comb through thick brown hair. Why on earth, he wondered, had that wide-mouthed, flat-nosed mug of his proved attractive to the girls? Oh yes, he'd mashed 'em in his day. Again he swore. Girls. Skirts. As if you could find a wappy pussy in this godforsaken spot!

All at once Stevens noticed he was trembling. Nothing much, of course, but a definite shake-on of the left mitt. Cluck it, he cursed. The trouble was, he'd been in a sight too many of these confounded do's by this time of the war. Six jaunts in the past two months, to be exact. And they all said it—your luck didn't last for ever. Yes, that sodding feeling it wasn't going to hold up indefinitely. It hadn't for his dad. To get through the whole of the Gallipoli campaign like that and then buy it in the last week in France. That was how it went. Some people were winners, that was all there was to it. Some were losers. Bloody roll on.

"'Ere's your water, sir." A meager, grayish-faced and studious-looking soldier lugged in a brace of jerry cans and put them to one side of the tent. "I was hable to get you one extra, sir," he said with satisfaction as he began to sluice rusty water into a canvas bag slung from a tripod.

"Flogged it, eh?"

"Hacquired it, shall we say, sir."

Stevens smiled. "I'll bet you did." On the soldier's entry he had quickly folded up the maps, for though the batman knew his officer was out on a mission that night he had no idea of what it was, nor where Stevens was going. Nor should he have, by God. "Oh, for the day when a man can turn a tap and pull a plug again, Wright."

"Roll on, sir."

"I'm briefing the patrol in half an hour, then let's have some grub up before I dress."

"Right you are, sir. Grouse or caviar?"

"Make it an omelette. With asparagus."

"Sparrow grass, sir?" Wright grinned. "Lucky to touch it, won't we be." He hesitated. "Sure you won't be needin' your pack tonight, sir?"

Stevens laughed at that. "Absolutely sure, Wright, you inquisitive old basket. I told you, this is simply a training stunt. Go and ask Mr. Loran and he'll tell you the same thing. It's to get him into our way of working."

"I'll put out that dark battle-dress you wanted, sir."

"And make certain you've not only got the flashes off, but remove all signs of stitching, too. The jerries can identify by the shape and placing of a badge; they're no barmy fools."

This time it was Wright's turn to grin again. "Just a training jaunt, eh, sir? See, I sharpened your chiv." He pointed, loped off.

Stevens shivered as he saw the knife. He looked up after the man for a minute. He shouldn't have given the game away like that to Wright. Hell, it was always the clever ones who were the winners. Lack of gray matter had afflicted Stevens all his life.

Wright was a milk roundsman from Leeds, downgraded to "C" thanks to a hopeless stomach condition he'd had since a kid. They two had been sent to the unit together. Stevens had especially asked to keep Wright, despite the category, and Wright was now the only man in the group from Stevens' own regiment. There'd been one other, a corporal who'd gone out with them, but he'd ... some bloody wogs had ...

Stevens buried his face in the lukewarm water. He sloshed it round his neck to cut off his thoughts and wake himself up. Wright managed to find out far too much. Instinctive, almost. Was that another bad omen for the trip? Stepping out into the sunlight ten minutes later, he cursed that inability ever to get really clean in the desert. The sun was sinking, so that the parched landscape of flattened crags and wadis was starting to take on a menacing contour. Men's eyes were beginning to slide into their heads. You're scared, Phil Stevens, say it.

That was what he was thinking when he saw Loran. The young subaltern striding towards him had winner written all over him, Stevens thought sulkily. The lean, nearly girlishly graceful figure which would never look at home in uniform walked confidently, with the possession of class. Stevens had developed an instant dislike for the man directly he'd joined the unit a few weeks ago. Too many of his sort had made him feel too damn small too bloody often in the past. That's why at first he'd liked the desert, really, away from all those asinine mess taboos, and then they'd been sent this spindly drink of water. Drown in a shower. Now he was stuck with the fellow on a patrol of aggression. Wilf, the adjutant, had explained why Loran had been put on this particular raid. First, the man spoke German perfectly; second, he'd seen von Schultz. Just where, Stevens wasn't quite clear, but he understood the fellow was originally Norwegian.

Eton and Bloody Useless, was what he thought now, as he watched Loran draw closer. Harrow and Pusillanimous. The C.O. had said this constipated calf could get his first P.E.D.G. experience under Stevens. The Adj had added something about a perfect mixture of brains and brawn. And that was it. His alter ego all the way from Eton.

No, Stevens' dislike wasn't simply the usual regular's suspicion of the temporary officer; the fact that this Loran cove, say, kept his ink-black hair far too long for regimental standards and smelling of expensive dressings. Nor merely that he slept in blue linen sheets he'd brought out with him, so on. Nor was it a matter of Stevens never having been to Eton or the other place, although that did play a part in his dislike. Oh yes, he admitted that, all right. No, the real resentment was connected with another aspect of his own past, with his inability to pass elementary examinations like School Certificate, with having to "cram" in sunny holidays, spending blue clear days indoors over books other boys understood at first glance, then graduating—to put it at its politest—to the Army class at school, and squeaking into Sandhurst. Yet even all these things put together, he knew, couldn't wholly account for the rise of irrational fear he felt seeing the other come up, smile frankly, and hearing him say, "The men are ready for briefing, if you are."

Stevens said, "O.K."

Early, but why not? As he led the way he felt vaguely annoyed that Loran hadn't saluted him. Wasn't called for off parade, of course, though in the tent it would have been a moot point, to say the least.

"Well, how do you like P.E.D.G.?" he asked as they walked together.

"Rather fun."

Rawther fun—Jesus Christ, the fellow ought to have been in the Boy Scouts. A plume of darkish cloud could be discerned in the distance now.

Loran pointed it out. "What's that?"

"Tank brew. Or two, or three. Or possibly a boche diesel truck copped it, who knows?"

Yet although he said it casually he felt that queer glistening of skin at his spine again. He remembered his Signals man on one do getting hooked up with a tank operator and hearing the officer suddenly screaming and asking the gunner where his foot was.... Stevens stopped himself and began going over the C.O.'s instructions in "O" Group with Loran. He did it methodically, to clear his mind.

"And you did understand that fellow from Intelligence to say that the hallway was marbled, didn't you? I mean, rubber can slip on that. We'll have to tell the men. I don't imagine the garden is mined, do you?"

"Doubt it."

Again that adenoidal Oxfordese, that Ritz-Berkeley blah. Stevens turned and, trying to smile easily, stared square into the lanky, lantern-jawed face of that shambling schoolboy beside him. "Do you feel frightened?"

Loran looked surprised, perhaps even offended, at the question, then his whole face opened as he smiled in return. "Yes, I actually rather do."

"Good. I actually rather do, too. Very."

He was glad to have got it out. He would have liked to add, You don't look it. Had this lad ever seen bullets fired in anger, aside from some confection in a Curzon Street flickhouse?

"Patrol—patrol, Shahn'."

"Stand easy, Corporal Marrow."

Watching the wiry, red-headed corporal stand the men down, Stevens wondered if there was something different in the fellow today. Marrow, too? Surely it was just his imagination. But as he gathered the eight around him, he knew he'd also been unhappy at having had Marrow assigned him. Seconded from the Military Police, the man had been a Brighton bobbie before the war and Stevens had always had an ingrained suspicion of coppers. For that reason he'd never quite hit it off with Marrow. He didn't know quite how far he could trust him. Sort of an air of having secret info up his sleeve all the time. But possibly he was wrong.

The group had collected apart from the rest of the unit and as Stevens began—IIMAI—get it all in order now, he was thinking slowly, and at the back of his mind realizing how bloody far all these killers had come from Civvie Street by now. By and large they were typical desert commandoes (though disliking that term as over-dramatic), raw-faced but often enough with kindly seams in their teak-tanned skins. Ridgeworth, squatting at his feet, had been apprenticed in a book bindery, a peaceful trade. Goddard had been a circus performer, possessor of some useful tricks when it came to cutting up. On one mission last month he'd slit open a stomach practically from navel to breastbone. Stevens shut his eyes. Tranter—just what the hell had Tranter ever been in peacetime except sodding bloody hungry? Tranter had cut off a man's arm with a Tommy gun during some closish fighting in a street behind the German lines at Hamma'na only six days ago. On a Sabbath, as a matter of fact. He claimed to have watched it drop, studied the jerry's stare as he'd seen it, too. Information; it drummed through his brain: first Enemy, then Own Troops. Even this amount of thought caused him considerable effort. He gave the details out. Then Intention. He paused. He wanted the Intention para to come out naturally. "Patrol will capture General von Schultz."

The jaw-slacking silence that succeeded this remark was broken only by a whistled "Whew!" The men exchanged glances.

Tranter groaned. "I surrender a'ready, sir."

A stout youth called Stubbs put in reflectively, "I tole my best girl I oughta done 'er afore I left."

"Quiet there, pay heed to the captain," Corporal Marrow cut in sharply.

Stevens continued—Method; Administration; Intercommunication. When he reached this last he grinned. "Strictly nil. We're absoballylutely on our bloody own. Dropped by boat and picked up by boat. A minute late and we've had it. Shank's pony through the lines of one of the best divisions Rommel's got out here. Now, everyone realize just what the odds are?"

Ridgeworth rolled his eyes. "Did you say odds, sir? Weeping ruddy priest," he said under his breath. "Von Schultz in person."

"Gor bloody blessim," added another voice.

All the same, Stevens sensed that the task had subconsciously exhilarated them. For months now Intelligence had been trying to locate the rest house behind the lines the famous German task general used from time to time. All the men were secretly jealous of the brilliance of the Kreipe coup in Crete. After all, they had volunteered for P.E.D.G., if they had done so for varying motives—some to avoid the imagined or real persecutions of some company officer, others to get shot of bull, or because they were browned off. Undeniably this was a job which, if they clicked it, brought it off, would echo round the world. Stevens saw those patient, resigned eyes in front of him light up with the first excitement of that anxiety he himself had been sweating out all day.

"Let's get down to brass tacks," he said, settling his big frame on the earth in front of them. "Corporal Marrow has a copy of what we've nicknamed Dark House. If the info we've been given is accurate, and Intelligence is sure it is, von Schultz is back at this house on the coast at the moment. It's said to be lightly guarded since it's a secondary h.q. he uses and he doesn't want attention attracted to it. From the only photographs I've been able to see—aerial recce—it's a pretty bare and exposed place." ("It would be," came a growl from the men.) "But I want you all to memorize that plan for dear life. There'll be time on the boat there also. We'll have to work fast. There's rumored only to be a skeleton staff with him at the minute and if we can spring a surprise they may not put up much resistance. The main thing is to get to the general at once. Quickly as poss." He cleared his throat. "Mr. Loran and I aim to make up the main set of stairs while Corporal Marrow and his crew cover our retreat via the other set. We think he'll be asleep when we hit. You'll see from the plans what looks to be the main bedroom. Once we have him covered, we'll use him as a hostage. Naturally, our entry must be dead silent. There'll be guards, all right, of course, and they'll have to be dealt with silently."

His eyes flicked round the group. Again they crossed Marrow's. Damned if the old M.P. sweat doesn't look sort of suspicious of me, he thought. Was the fear he felt really something more than the ordinary anxiety? Showing, was it? Jesus, everyone had it, Loran had just admitted his, but after a while the sensation began to act as a depressive on the whole system. For the very first time in his life Stevens became frightened of cracking. He told himself that the next time he'd see Marrow and his merry men it would be in total darkness, thank God.

"Any questions?"

One hand went up. "Like if we're fired on, sir . . . I mean, you said as you didn't want a ding-dong."

"I don't. That's right, Tranter. Try not to fire back. We'll approach by the usual short bounds. Reserve retaliatory action till we withdraw from the place. And then only if absolutely necessary. Silent we come, silent we go's the motto. We don't want to give away the position of the boat, whatever we do. Now, you're all familiar with our usual procedure on these raids. I don't think there's anyone here who's not been out on a job like this before." He said it as a statement, then realized that Loran hadn't. The only one. The brain-box. The lingo-man. He went on, "So you know about making arrangements, I mean. Corporal Marrow will be in touch with me for all further details until weapon-testing."

Could it be as simple as that? No. Another hand.

"Yep?"

"Will there be any chance of a bevvy, sir?"

"There'll be a rum ration on the boat."

Stevens stood up and the patrol got with him.

"Trust the Nyvy," said a voice.

He smiled at them. "No looting, see. This is strictly a rapid job." Goddard hid a grin behind his hand. "All right, you can fall out now. I don't have to tell chaps like you what to take and what not to take by this time. Get those house plans by heart. Don't eat too much, especially if you're the seasick kind. Those motor launches can chuck you about quite a bit." Also, he added to himself, I like my scrappers hungry. "That's Operation Cabbage for you. Good luck, all."

He walked off, tailed by Loran, as Corporal Marrow drew the patrol up to attention and saluted. "Just plenty of cocoa," Stevens found himself saying, chiefly to himself, as automatically he scanned the sky for the boche planes that tended to come in at this time of day. Not a one. Another bad sign? "Plenty of mucking cocoa," he said again.

"I say."

"Yes?"

"Aren't we rather a small force for a job of this order?" Loran spoke as if we were about to enter Boodle's for a drink and was debating what to have.

"Just right. Two officers, one Corp, eight experts. Won't get in each other's way. I hope." He added to that, "Marrow's ex-M.P. He'll show you the ropes." He'd spoken without looking at the other, then he stopped and stared into those pale blue eyes which the evening sky had oddly darkened. Just a boy, really. The skull looked frail. "Do you like Marrow?" he asked for some reason. "What do you make of him? Frankly, I mean."

"I don't actually know."

"Notice anything odd about him just now?"

"I really couldn't say."

"I see. Right now, got your armament on you? Let's test our weapons, shall us? Tell that sentry what we're doing."

The two wandered off into the waste beyond the camp. Here there was an improvised range Lightly for his bulk, Stevens clambered into the wadi and set straight a sagging target. Twice he riddled that chortling cardboard with a fuzz of dust from the stone behind, then he watched while Loran missed. Only on the fourth round did the man strike the dummy and his bullet ripped low, where the genitals had been glossed over by the Army dauber. Stevens turned his head. The target rocked scornfully at them, it seemed. They went back to the camp. In the officers' lines Stevens thought, Well, our orders were to avoid shooting as far as poss. But God's teeth what a wet, what a wappy, sousy wet. He'd drown in a shower for sure.

He found Loran hanging by him. "Might I see your pistol?"

Stevens handed him the warmish Webley. "Handy. My pa's. That baby can blow a hole in a human being so big you can reach right in and feel around. Believe you me."

"I don't doubt," Loran said. He seemed paler than ever in the gathering dusk. "The target perforations looked distinctly rococo. The only thing is, I understood dum-dums were verboten."

Bloody cheek! Hell, you went to Balliol and thought you owned the world. "Look here," Stevens began hotly, then stopped himself. "That's my business," he said softly.

"It isn't really, you know. If one of us is caught breaking conventions of that kind, we're all for the high jump. I was thinking of the men."

"I'll do the thinking, Loran."

There was silence between them. Then Loran shrugged. "I'd better go inside and get ready."

"Better had."

Inside his tent Stevens fumed. It was all turning out wrong from the word go. So very wrong. But as he looked about him he saw everything neatly laid out as usual and felt faintly reassured. His dark battle-dress, carefully splotched with mud stains; cap comforter; new field dressing; compass; pan of cocoa; gym shoes. The bowie knife gave an evil glint. Wright had even drawn up the regulation Tommy gun and two grenades already. Nor had he forgotten the bottle of Scotch. All set out ready. Stevens especially admired order. Method. It was what had got him through. At that moment the bleak batman himself came in carrying a mess tin.

"Thanks, Wright. Put it down there, would you. I don't feel too hungry, as a matter of fact."

"You must eat, sir."

He began to peck at the stew. Outside, a dull crump. Although it shook the earth both men knew from experience it was a fair distance away. Still, Stevens shivered. He wondered whether Wright had noticed his doing so.

"Anything else you 'ave need of, sir?"

"Don't think so, thanks."

Wright hovered solicitously. Stevens wished he would skedaddle. He wanted to be alone with this new feeling he had. Examine it. British Army diet. Ginger put at over a hundred in the shade. He heard the firing outside. Patrol testing weapons. No, he'd never known fear quite like this before. A snake eating his entrails, sort of. Perhaps it was that mucker Loran's last remark. Got under his skin, as the Yanks might put it. Each mouthful he took of the stew made him feel sick. This was unusual. He generally had a terrific appetite. He caught Wright watching him.

"Anything you want, sir, I'll be right 'andy. You know my tent."

"Yes, thanks." Without looking at the man he said softly, "You know what I want done, should anything happen." He added hastily, "Never know what may turn up, even on training jaunts like this." He reflected that he only had one relative left in the world, an elderly aunt who lived in Durham and sent him a silk handkerchief of sumptuous proportions each Christmas. Probably thought he was battling the Boers, or something. He had one of her handkerchiefs in his pocket now and each time he took it out, the generous square of India silk looked intolerably splendid somehow, reminded him of Sulka's, the Burlington Arcade, places like that he never went into without feeling uncomfortable and conspicuous, places that young Loran would be at home in. . . .

"Ah . . . 'ope that won't be necessary hat all, sir." Wright was looking genuinely alarmed. "Yes, sir. Good—good luck, sir." He shuffled off.

If he didn't come back. So simple. If he never came back. Aunt Edie would receive a War House telegram, the usual one, and—Stevens wryly completed—would subsequently inherit a few hundred quid, the sum total of her nephew's "estate," saved from his pay month by month.

Distantly a dog wailed. Something chinked as he moved. The pistol pressed at his hip. His webbing smelt. The mess tin chattered at his teeth. A cringing desire for some form of softness, some syllable from another existence in the night, overcame him for a second; a form of life away from weapons and gun-pits and khaki cloth and ammo. Desert deserter. What a hope.

He remembered that sense of loneliness he had felt in the ring, but it was a creative loneliness somehow, not like this flaming. . . . No, he could eat no more. Stevens realized he was a being who had come to express himself almost entirely through hostility these past few years. What he liked was what he knew best, an ideal of physical and material efficiency. He hated slackness, sloppiness. Perhaps that was why he couldn't get on with a puppy like Loran. Always just on time for parade, and only just. Always with something on in bad order. And yet they drifted into jobs he himself would have had to fight like flaming hell for in Civvie Street.

He stood up now and stripped, egging his biceps to reassure himself, muscling the clean, shaved lines of his body. No slackness there, by God. That was why this fear he was feeling was sapping his energy. It was something altogether new, different, alien: Stevens was convinced it was a premonition. Like the men, he too was superstitious. He had never had it quite like this before.

Light was leaving the sky and soon the pitch blackness would fall abruptly over this northern strip of the great continent where they had been sent to kill. Darkness would come like the touch of a hand. For some reason Stevens felt an urge to cry. Darkness should be associated with comfort, sleep. He cursed himself as he soaped the soles of his feet, then sprinkled talc into a new pair of socks, fluffy from the batman's wash. Then the battle dress, gym shoes, trousers tucked well into the socks. Nothing metallic beyond weapons was taken at all. The smallest tinkle could carry for yards in that silent stretch of desert which awaited them near Dark House.

Tiredly Stevens reached for the cocoa paste and began smearing it on his face and neck. It was growing colder. Or was he simply feeling unduly chilly? The fabric of darkness gathering outside was rent again by another explosion. A nearby soldier swore obscenely. He hollowed his balaclava into a cap and drew it down over his head, making sure it hung unevenly, for proper camouflage. Almost before he knew it the negroid figure had slipped up to the foot of his tent and was saluting there.

"Patrol present and correct, sir. All ready to move off, sir."

"Is Mr. Loran there, Corporal Marrow?"

"Yes, sir. And I've checked over each man personal."

"Right. Be with you in a minute."

"Very good, sir."

The beaky-nosed wraith seemed to hang for a second, then disappeared. As he did so Stevens felt something irrevocable, a choking rush in his throat. He was going to be sick. No, he kept it down. For a second he tried to pray. But he had long ago forgotten the words. He wondered why he had always felt on his guard with Corporal Marrow. Now near-scared of him. He told himself that bobbies always had that effect on him, whereas a type like Loran would be able to say, "It's all right, officer," and it bloody would be. The snake of funk turned again in Stevens' vitals, and this time he did not deny himself the whiskey.

CHAPTER TWO

The dark-faced patrol was solemn now, as Corporal Marrow brought them to attention. Eyeballs glinting in the blackness, Loran saluted too, this time. Stevens was glad to see that. Well done, Useless. He had made up his mind to tear the fellow off a strip if he hadn't, and now felt ridiculously frustrated. What's more, it was odd how easily recognizable the long, lean face was, even under the blacking.

"I don't know if you're aware of it," Stevens said, "but these North African nights can be bloody cold. You've got a sweater on, I trust."

"Yes." Then Loran added, "What about the men?"

"You don't have to worry about them."

The men, by Christ. Listen to it! What cheek! Smiling drily, Stevens contemplated that silent rank of black-faced tragedians. They might have been a row of nigger minstrels, each Tommy gun a uke, or something. The only thing was, they'd been detailed to strum another kind of tune. What a rank of old soldiers, Stevens reflected, adding once again to himself, The men ye Gods!

"We aren't still at Sandhurst you know." Then he told Loran sharply, "Turn round."

The other hesitated, did so. Stevens examined the young officer to see he hadn't left any patches of bare skin showing on his neck, behind his rather cadaverous ears, underneath his wrists. The man fairly stank of a sweet hair lotion or cologne which reminded Stevens of the few times he had ever been into West End clubs. As someone's guest.

"Now do the same to me."

Out of the corner of an eye Stevens could see knots of off-duty commandoes watching the parade. "Thought I said I didn't want any spectators," he snapped, surprised to hear it emerge as half a snarl.

"Sorry, sir," replied Corporal Marrow. "It's the devil of a job an' all keeping the men from seeing their pals off." He turned and shouted and to Stevens his voice didn't sound natural at all—"Hey you! What're you on? Well, get a move on there!"

Stevens looked at Loran. "In answer to your previous question, laddie, all these blighters have been on binges like this before. They manage to look after themselves pretty well. When you're under fire, you tend to, you know. Bloody marvelous. Suddenly you find you can dig a grave for yourself in solid rock with a pen knife."

Then, in full view of the patrol, he bent and ran his hands up Loran's slender body. Through the cloth the bones felt hard beneath his fingers. He was aware how insulting it was to do this in public to an officer, but it would teach that clueless tick to tell him off about his dum-dums.

"Sorry," he said as he straightened. "But I have to make absolutely certain on these shows that no one's carrying anything that rattles in the slightest way."

"I knew that."

"Perhaps you did, old boy, but the lives of ten others depend on your remembering and carrying out our orders to the letter. You aren't with that chocolate-soldier outfit of yours any longer, you know. Corporal Marrow checks and rechecks the men. They also have a strong built-in sense of personal survival. You're my pigeon." He swung on the corporal. A tuft of red hair stuck stubbornly out of the man's balaclava and Stevens gave it a stylish tweak. "I'm sure that if any jerry saw you at fifty yards he'd take you for genu-yne Ayrab cactus, Corporal Marrow. You couldn't have done better if you'd been going on stage at the Palladium."

"Wish I was, sir."

No, despite the forced flippancy, Marrow's blackened face looked worried. Did he feel it, too? Was Loran going to be the bloody jinx or something? No matter how Stevens tried to smile, he couldn't keep down the growing sensation that this one had his name on. He wasn't coming back, none of them were coming back....

He swung sharply again. "Right. I'll inspect them now." He began walking in front of the single rank, thinking, Yes, bloody wonderful what an instinct for self-preservation could do for homo sapiens. All the men were perfectly made up, and well padded against the slightest noise. One he saw, however, was wearing glasses.

"Can't you do without those, Stubbs?"

"'Fraid not, sir."

"I didn't see you wearing them on parade earlier."

The soldier made no answer.

Corporal Marrow said, "Stubbs wanted to come, sir."

Stevens said nothing. What was the personal history behind that one, he wondered. He started round the rear of the rank. Tranter bulged fat with grenades. Goddard's chiv hung sleekly sheathed along his right leg. Where the blue hell would it all end?

He got hold of himself and drew straight. "O.K., Corporal Marrow. March off."

"Any last words to the men, sir?"

He lowered his head. "I don't think so, thanks."

He watched them right-turn, pad in single file to the waiting 15-cwt. A radio was on in the back of the truck and several other ranks had clustered round to listen. Stevens, approaching, heard a woman's soft-syllabled accents:

Vor der Kaserne, vor dem grossen Tor
stand eine Laterne, und steht sie noch davor....

A station in Cairo or Alex, probably. He shepherded the men into the truck. They got in one by one. Slowly, he felt. Loran stood beside him.

wie einst Lili Marleen. . . .
wie einst Lili Marleen

In the night air the tune was somehow unreasonably troubling; its sentiment plucked hard at him as he listened. He thought: nightclub, by Christ, think of it, muffled shoulders, a good deep female back, plenty of solid meat where . . . what the ruddy hell am I thinking of? Yes, the men were in. One or two of their mates were there to see them off. A voice said, "Yer look like a bleeding Eskimo in ter family way, Tranter."

Stab in darkness. A light flashed out. Stevens jumped. The Adj was loafing towards them, an immensely elongated figure who always looked wildly improbable in the desert, Stevens thought. That tall, gawky frame never seemed to be wearing uniform, but instead some hairy tweed of extreme antiquity, its hacking pockets heavy with twelve-bore cartridges.

"Phil? Shoving off?" He returned Stevens' salute. "All set?"

"Yes, I think so, Wilf." He tried to mask his too casual intonation. "You gave me a man with giglamps, you know."

"Stubbs? Yes, but Stubbs is very good."

"I know he is."

"Well, don't worry, Phil. You haven't got any foreign bods."

"Except for Loran."

"He's seen von Schultz. In the flesh. Don't forget to let the dog see the rabbit there, Philip. No, no, you're all tried and tested vintage P.E.D.G. I'm sure you'll have a very good shoot, indeed." Tapping his chin with his leather-shod stick, the Adjutant noticed Loran standing nearby. "Hello, Tom. Feeling peed-up?"

Loran laughed. "If you want to know—yes."

Funny, Stevens thought with a start, never really knew his name. Knew his initials, of course. Lieutenant T.A.C. Loran. Translated that one as Too Awfully Clever. Tom. Doubting Thomas Loran. Bloody roll on. He recalled that the Adjutant had been to the same sort of school as Loran, possibly the same sodding Borstal itself. Anyway, one of the posh ones. On ultimate issues they were bound to agree; that kind always did.

Stevens said bitterly, "I checked on every man's range average personally and then you go and do this to me, Wilf. I never thought to find out if any of them wore specs."

The adjutant was smiling and gracefully tapping his calf with his stick while he talked, knee crooked, to lanky Loran. The pair might have been at a bloody meet. Weeping Jesus. The Belvoir. Hounds will.

"We better get a move on, don't you think," Stevens cut in, "else we're likely to meet ourselves coming back."

"I was telling Tom here, Philip. He's dashed fortunate to be going out with you on his first spree. You have the luck of the devil."

"What kind of luck is that?" he asked harshly, then regretted his tone as he saw the other glance at him.

"Phil. Don't worry. You never have before. Look, knowing you, we have no doubts. You'll get our general. You and Tom. Frankly I think it'll be—well—a piece of cake." He took Stevens' hand and shook it with sincerity. "Good luck. Good hunting. Now I'll just say a word to the men."

He went to the back of the truck. Loran went with him. Stevens climbed into the cab. The driver, face unblacked, smiled at him. Why the deuce had Wilf gone and been and said just that? Surely it was bad luck. Then the adjutant was standing by the cab. "Good luck, Phil."

Stevens turned to the driver. "O.K. Lead on."

Seated in front with the fumes coming hot off the engine, Stevens knew that his breath might smell. They'd get to know he'd taken a swipe of Scotch before setting out, something denied the men. The word would get around that he was cracking. The dread ukase would go out. At Brigade a look would be exchanged. At Division the general would pick at his Pending tray, pass on a confidential memo concerning a certain commando officer drinking in the desert to a friend of his at Corps, who had a good friend in Stevens' own reg. Stevens would stay a captain. At the end of the war he would revert to War/Substantive Lieutenant. In regimental messes heads would be shaken, shoulders shrugged. Someone, somewhere, over just the right year of Dow's, would say the words, "Too bad. Just hadn't got what it takes, I suppose." A year later that dictum would have been converted into one word—yellow. They'd chuck him into Civvie Street with a rotten chit.

His head came up again. The road threaded towards the coast, then doubled back through some ack-ack batteries on itself, then serpented to the coast again through glorious, russet-colored rocks that plunged into a sea black as a bird's wing. Cold, that. He tried not to think. His hands were bothering him a lot. They seemed oddly conspicuous.

Aus dem stillen Raume, aus der Erde Grund
hebt mich wie im Traume dein verliebter Mund. . . .

He twisted and yelled through the ripped celluloid to the back: "Turn that bloody thing off, will you." Silence ensued. A few mutters. Some of them coughed and swore in the dust blown back.

Why'd he done that? They must never know he was jumpy. The feeling conveyed itself. Like riding a horse. And that was the awful sodding thing about it all. You not only had to screw yourself up to it, you had to do it so well you set an example to the others. Oh, they were watching, all right. The penalty of being an officer. Sometimes he wished he were an O.R. The smallest chink in your armor showed. Had Marrow noticed it by now?

The tiny white port came into sight ahead. The driver doused his already dimmed lights. A smell of aniseed hung in the air as they drove through the first winding streets and drew up at the jetty.

For a second after they'd stopped Stevens sank his head into his hands. Beside him the engine was switched off. When he looked up he saw a swarthy face within inches of his. Imagining it to be one of the patrol, he made an effort to pull himself together. Then he saw it was an Arab, burnous thrown back. He cursed and got down. As he did so, he saw that the wog had a gnarled stick in one hand and two children clinging to his left leg. The man stared at him with a perfectly blank look, a pure concentration. Stevens got out and busied himself giving orders.

The boat was bobbing at the jetty and the men were climbing in already. This part of the trip had to be accomplished as rapidly as possible. You never knew what hidden sets were maintained in these isolated villages. Even Ayrabs could be taught radio. Three transports had been sunk in exactly the same spot in a matter of months off Mersa Ageb recently; it was almost certainly the work of submarines receiving information from shore sources. Stevens hated that. Neutrals, indeed. The two officers got on last. Once more, as they pulled quickly out to sea, Stevens wondered why he was being so superstitious tonight, but the sight of that wog had again unnerved him.

Out in open sea a strong wind blew up. The men drew together in the stern and shivered. Stubbs and Goddard studying the map by flashlight under a blanket. Mustn't show boat's position. Stevens talked to the lieutenant in charge of the vessel and rechecked plans, synchronized watches, supervised every last-minute detail over and over again. Then the rum ration went round. Denied any ordinary access to liquor, barring the few bottles of beer that got forward to units like theirs, the men were immediately affected by the spirit and a few stagey jokes were exchanged. No one felt natural.

His huge frame hunched forward into the wind, Stevens sat facing Loran, whose thin knees pressed at his own.

"Don't forget," Stevens reminded him, "once inside the house, stick with me. I scarcely know a single word of German. And we may need to talk fast."

Loran nodded. He was rocking to and fro to warm himself against the night wind that now swept the small craft. They went over the last details again together. The boat began to toss.

"Muck it," Stevens said. One of the men, squatting on some planks at the bottom, started to show signs of uneasiness. Stevens tried to reassure him.

"Don't worry. We're going to pull in easy, give everyone a chance to get their breath. Besides, you'll find your land legs soon as we approach the house. Here, have some more rum."

"No thanks, sir."

Tranter now pressed his fists together in front of his chest and cracked his knuckles. Goddard was making a meticulous and motherly inspection of his knife. As the wind fretted his face Stevens felt two slimy fingers slide under his clothes, creep down his goosing spine. This was fantastic. He was freezing cold, yet pouring with sweat. Christ, his face felt wet too. He wondered if Loran had noticed it. Sure to have. He began to feign a mild seasickness, to keep his head in his hands. But the trickles of perspiration started over and over again. He'd never known anything like it before.

To show himself he was master of the situation as much as anything, he looked into Loran's face. "Know what I'd like to be doing now?"

Loran said, "I might guess."

"It's like this. I'd give anything to be in a garden, quite small really. My mother used to have a little house in Kent. You know the kind of thing. It always seemed to be warm in that garden. Nothing special, but the grass green as hell, and I'd give anything to be lying there in a hammock drinking beer. Know what

I mean? Ale. Younger's, in fact. The bitch of this stinking, cowing, sodding country is that you never see anything green."

"That must be wearing."

"It is. It is wearing. It's hard."

"Yes, it must be." Loran dropped his eyes, under glyphic lashes. "I wouldn't know, actually. I've only just come out."

"You see, it gets on the nerves," Stevens went on, surprising himself with his own loquacity. "It's as if you'd never known anything else at all. Frankly, Loran, there are times when I feel I've been doing this all my life. I mean I really wonder if I could—you know—behave if you put me back in civilized society, sort of."

The other laughed. "You get used to anything, even civilization. And some of the so-called civilized ones can be barbarians without much effort. Take our friend von Schultz."

"Are you a breasts or buttocks man?" Stevens asked him abruptly.

"What on earth d'you mean?"

Cupping his palms, Stevens joggled them upwards. "It gets on the frigging nerves. There are times, Jesus… See, I'd like a girl there, in that particular picture, I mean. Lying in a hammock, also. Course, we'd be a bit big to share one." He attempted a laugh. "Wouldn't we? No, you know the kind, thin frock, tight, very tight. Sort of thing a skindiver might find slightly suffocating, I mean. I'm a rear plaza man, I fear." He dabbed the sweat off his forehead, rather than wiping it and removing any make-up. "You married, by any chance?"

"Not, actually."

"Good. One shouldn't be in this racket."

"I gather you aren't, either."

"No, no." He shook his head. "Course, there were times when I nearly cut myself off a nice chunk of hearthrug pie back home but, ah, what's the use? I've told myself by now that bigamy and monogamy amount to the same thing. One wife too many, I mean."

Loran didn't laugh and neither did he. Together they stared at the leaden hills ahead. Getting closer. Much closer, sod it. Two sailors, Stevens noticed, had gone forward in the launch, each carrying an oar.

"What would you like to be doing right at this moment, Loran?"

The other smiled. Easily. (If only the bogger weren't so ruddy calm.) "Do you know, I rather think that most of all I'd like to be in an art gallery."

"Art gallery? I see. Sort of contrast, you mean."

"That, and the fact that I've always been more interested in art than anything, if you follow me. My father was something of a connoisseur."

"I can't understand modern art," Stevens said sullenly, thinking, Just the type, what did I say. "All looks boiled to me." Glancing down he saw that his hands were clasping and unclasping in his lap. "No, I've never known much about that stuff."

"Ah, but I didn't mean modern art. I was thinking of the Uffizi Gallery in Florence." Loran spoke with a different, wistful note in his voice, his blue eyes softening. "Or, say, the Prado. There's a museum." He added quickly, "I do hope they leave the Uffizi, don't you?"

"I've never been to those places."

"Our friend von Schultz has."

Stevens was concentrating on his hands. They seemed to be moving independently of his will. He stopped them, but they looked alert, like two pet dogs, about to go off into incalculable motion directly he wasn't watching. He breathed thickly. This time, when they moved, he sat on them. And as he did so he caught Corporal Marrow's eyes upon him. Had the fellow noticed? All at once Stevens divined somehow that the Corp was scared, too. He didn't know how, but he felt it with that prescience of ring rivalry he had. Now he wanted to lose Marrow, badly. He asked Loran, "Did you go in for it, then?"

"What?"

"Art, I mean."

"My last two terms at Oxford I did start taking drawing lessons. But I'm just a dilettante, I'm afraid."

"Nude models?"

Loran gave another easy laugh. "Well, yes, of course. But they're usually pretty averagely hideous, you know."

Stevens gazed into the sky and sighed. "Just so long as they had nice big pear-shaped octaves, that's all I'd mind about." Again he caught Corporal Marrow's close-set eyes on his. Definitely furtive. He himself was beginning to find it hard to know where to look. One of his hands had now turned itself palm upwards. The palm was pink and vulnerable-looking where the sweat had washed away the blacking.

"Actually my father had one or two rather fine Bosches," Loran was saying.

"Eh?"

"Of the later period, you know. Lucas Cranach and Bosch happened to be rather his specialties, you see."

"Here, take that thing off," Stevens interrupted him. On Loran's darkened wrist he had seen a watch. Of gold and wafer-thin, it stank of Bond Street. "Take it bloody off," he ordered roughly.

"Very well."

"See what I told you? You can't be too careful in this game."

"I'm sorry."

Loran removed the delicate, expensive thing, far too slowly in Stevens' own opinion.

"Who was that dauber you said your father collected?"

"Bosch."

"That's just what I think most painting is, anyway. Except for Peter Scott."

"Given your tastes in the field of feminine anatomy," Loran added thoughtfully, "I should have imagined you might have liked Cranach also."

"Ever meet the man? If he was so good, I mean."

"Bosch died roughly five centuries ago."

"My dad bought his in the First World War," Stevens said suddenly, thinking equally suddenly, Why the hell did I say that? Because I'm going to buy mine in the Second? Tonight? It was an unlucky thing to say, all right. And it seemed to him that his symptoms of uneasiness were becoming more and more apparent as they drew ever nearer their objective. He added mulishly, "Mother shoved off five years ago now."

"I'm sorry." Loran actually put a hand on Stevens' knee. "I know how you feel."

"Why? You lose your people recently?"

"No, my mother's alive. She's at our place in Norway, as a matter of fact. When the war broke out I was at home—it's up in the north of Norway, the Hamsun country, you know—and just about to go back to finish up my graduate work at Oxford. I was educated in England, you know."

"I knew that."

"I stayed with my parents till just after the Paget show. When my father died I wanted, I needed, to get out. A destroyer picked some of us up. Of course, there was a lot of red tape before I could get into a British regiment, owing to my parentage."

"But you fixed that all right, I imagine."

"Yes, though I did have to get naturalized first. Quite a business. Still, they hurried it all up for me."

"I'll bet they did."

"It does mean, however, that if I'm ever captured by the Germans they can legally execute me if they wish."

Stevens stared at him. "You serious, man?"

"Yes, that's the case. They don't recognize the naturalization and technically I'm an enemy national enlisting in another's country's forces. Highly illegal, I fear."

"Then, what the devil are you doing on this jaunt?"

"I'd like to see von Schultz again."

"Come to that, where did you see the blighter first?"

"At our place, actually. He requisitioned it. You'll recall he was G.O.C. German troops occupying Norway during the Paget do."

The boat had slowed. Stevens stared dully. Glancing ahead, he saw to his horror that they'd come much closer in shore than he'd realized while talking.

He heard Loran say quietly, "You see, General von Schultz happened to kill my father," then the motor cut altogether and in the sudden, uncomprehending silence the lieutenant made a signal to them. Utter quiet. Stevens slid forward the safety catch on his Tommy gun, whispering, for some reason, "Well, for the time being old Ma Thompson will have to do for the lot of us, I reckon."

Rowed, or rather poled, shorewards by the two blue-jackets for'ard, the boat slipped quietly through the calmer sea. All the men were sitting up now, gripping their weapons. Stevens pointed and they looked ahead: the outline of a two-storey Moorish edifice could be discerned down the coast. It looked miles away. Stevens muttered to the lieutenant, "Sure you can't get in any nearer than this?"

The man shook his head, then he too pointed. This time to a grotto in the rock where it had been arranged that the boat was to hide for the pick-up back.

As they slid slowly into the inlet chosen for the landing, Stevens felt appallingly vulnerable. One man overlooking this spot was all that was needed. One single Spandau. One tolerably brief burst and—*finito Benito. Bob's your uncle.* Jesus God, the icicles of sweat seemed to be streaking down his back now. He tried mentally to digest what Loran had told him. Poor mucker. Oh anything, anything. He couldn't even busy himself with giving orders now. There was nothing to do till they got in. *It's taking hours.*

"Can't you go any faster than this?" he grumbled at the lieutenant, but the other either ignored or failed to hear him.

A piece of cake, indeed. His hands began moving again, as if cut off from his body, independent of any volition from his mind. He forced them to grasp his Tommy gun. No, there could be no doubt about it now, he had never felt like this in all his life before, not even when he'd been sent in to box miles over his weight as a kid at council school. The curious depression he'd felt ever since the first "O" group had now crystallized into an aching void within him. He ducked his head, made himself—for these last yards at least—look downwards. And he saw an awful thing: a pair of brown canvas Army P.T. shoes writhing at each other in the bottom of the boat like two reptiles engaged in mortal combat. Horrified, sickened, he looked up to see who owned those slowly threshing feet. For a moment he had taken them for his own. Then he realized they belonged to Corporal Marrow. The fellow was simply in a blue funk. And so—let's face it—so, by God in heaven, was he.

"O.K."

The voice said it as a bump shook the boat. "Here you are. And bang on time, too. Good luck, all."

CHAPTER THREE

An aquiline country, under that shadow of darkness.

The almost limitless expanse of North African earth, with its outcroppings of rock and spindly trees, always seemed too wide to endure at night. Moreover, apart from this feeling he had of the continent being a kind of lunar landscape, too vast for human habitation, too total altogether for men to have to suffer any comparison with it, the land invariably seemed to Stevens disproportionately awake by night. The yellow stone and stunted ground seemed to await, exhausted, the next day's stare of the sun. And yet how creeping cold it was now.

They moved towards Dark House in strung-out bounds, exactly as planned, each section watching and covering the other: Loran with Corporal Marrow and four men, he himself with the other four. The place seemed a tremendous distance away. Their plan was to close on it from the far side in order to throw the enemy off scent in case they were prematurely spotted and pursuit were given. Stevens cursed as he stubbed his toe on the tough ground that fringed this barren stretch of coast. There looked to be better cover after they had crossed the road ahead. Far off, in the very distance, desultory firing could be heard, and a few red tracers streamed into the sky with the gossamer, fairy-tale effect of Japanese fireworks.

He watched the loping shadows of Loran's section approach the road, then suddenly found himself making a palm-down signal at the earth to his own men and simultaneously fell flat himself. A truck was bumping westwards up the road, its shuttered beams swinging jerkily. Loran hadn't seen it. Stevens' head throbbed with anxiety. The wind made his cheeks smart where he lay. Then all at once he knew that there was no one ahead: Loran's section had gone down and were hugging the earth also. Within inches of Stevens' outstretched right hand were some velvety flowers, he didn't know what kind, but that was typical Africa. The cruelty of it. So brutal and then, all of a sudden, so lavish on the senses. It was impossible to be prepared for what Africa meant for an ordinary Englishman. Meanwhile, the truck ground its way along the pocked surface of the road, passed the place where Loran's section had vanished, and Stevens hissed a sigh of relief. It was more than relief for his own hide; the poor bogger must have had it pretty hard in Norway, to lose his dad and all like that.

A second later he was fumbling in the breast pocket of his battle dress, from which he extracted a small pair of binoculars wrapped in a sock. Whipping them out, he put them to his eyes. By a stroke of luck he'd realized this was just what they'd wanted; the truck's blinkered lights would partially illumine Dark House and help to reveal where the sentries were. And so they did. The truck stopped, obviously at a challenge; a jerry came forward; the amber beam showed a helmeted head, another that came up to join it. Then went on. Stevens uttered a low whistle. A second later he'd dropped by Loran.

"See that? Two men behind the house. Probably patrolling that wall affair there and meeting at that point."

Loran said, "I'll work right round and take the one on the far side. It's set. You hit yours pretty soon after and we ought to be all right."

"Fine." He paused. Somehow he didn't want to leave the other. "Amazing how bright a completely moonless night can be in North Africa, eh?"

"I agree. I've felt positively floodlit every inch of the way so far."

"It's the air. Oxygen, I believe. Very clear." He added, "Join the P.E.D.G. and see the world." When Loran didn't respond at once he said, "You know, I'm sorry about your father. I hope we get that bastard."

"We'll get him."

"Well. I'd better be going."

Loran made ahead, this time without bounds. Stevens let him get right round—too far to the left, he professionally considered, to be strictly necessary. Understandable in a beginner. Over-keen. Then he lost sight of the section altogether and moved towards his side of the house. Ridgeworth was close beside him and Stevens hoped that the fellow couldn't sense his fear. Men could. Like dogs sniffing dirt, all that sort of thing. . . .

Tak-tak-tak-tak! Then, dead silence. Then, another burst. Dragon's teeth sown in that ringing sky. Sod it utterly. A booming crash. Then, one shot.

From the very first explosion Stevens had frozen. The firing had come from a distance in the desert. Still, it might mean that Loran had been spotted. Blundering idiot, was Stevens' first thought. He felt like weeping with exasperation. Why was I ever sent out on this scousy lark? Just my sodding luck. Dead ahead now, he could see the sentries in active confab, staring over the wall of Dark House into the darkness. Curse and confound it, then! They might think it wise to get another man out.

For several minutes on end nothing happened. He squeezed his eyes into the icy wind, noting what appeared to be a small woodshed affair to one side of the main building. About fifteen minutes of complete silence passed. The sentries padded cautiously out into the waste, then came back. This was ruining their schedule. Just at that moment he was aware of three shadows moving off towards the far wall of the grounds of their objective. In the darkness they seemed to be moving faster than normal human beings could. Stevens crawled forward, using his elbows and ripping his battle dress. Then when the sentry on their side had his back turned to follow a jink in the wall, he signalled to double forward. In this way they advanced in leaps and bounds until, half to his own surprise, the wall was right on top of them.

Flat on his belly behind spiny brush, Stevens floundered in an agony of apprehension. This time action was failing him. The only thing was to keep on doing things, however. He knew that. He felt petrified. Through a gap in the wall he momentarily spotted both sentries at the same time. A light went on in an upstairs window; all his senses reacted. A minute later a man smoking a cigar and carrying a drink in one hand strode out onto the long, white-plastered terrace, shouted something, went back in again. The sentries padded on.

Ridgeworth saw it first. Stevens always remembered that, for he really liked Ridgeworth. Always, whenever in his deepest dreams he was to recreate the nightmare of this drastic scene—the desert, cold steel, the Hun—he would remember Ridgeworth gripping his arm.

The sentry their side had vanished from view. This meant that, thanks to the arrangement the two guards had clearly worked out between them, the one on the other side was closer. Stevens distinctly saw a shadow rise up behind this far sentry. An instrument was raised—with precision, he had time to note, like a butcher about to chop into meat perhaps—and dully brought down. Certainly it made much less sound than he considered necessary to the realism of the scene. Presumably their elaborate testings had done that, at least.

The thing was, the jerry didn't drop. Instead, slowly, very slowly it seemed to Stevens watching with terror in his veins, he turned and silently, if not almost reproachfully, contemplated his attacker. Stevens even then realized the man must have been partially stunned by the blow with the billy which had been given him, stupidly enough, on the steel helmet, rather than across the neck. A flash later, however, and another shadow was over the low wall. The sentry galvanized into action, as if stricken with electric shock. That was certainly the only way Stevens knew of describing it to himself later. The man literally seemed to become contorted under his new assailant's attack.

Then he knew no more because he himself was interminably falling, falling, falling from the height of his higher wall on the figure of the alarmed sentry their side. With flesh beneath his fingers Stevens felt better. The world was restored. He closed on that convulsive windpipe and pressed with all his might. He scarcely knew what happened, he was so afraid. Steadily, however, he observed a kind of queer recognition in the German's ordinary face. A frown corrugated the brow, which creased more and more. The neck became a swollen eel. The face inflated. Stevens felt something wet on him—snot—as the man noiselessly fought for breath. Gradually, over the parted teeth, blood began to flow in spasms and a gargling in the throat made Stevens press the dying man hard against him. As he did this he realized he had exerted far more strength than necessary, that both his thumbs had in fact torn through the tough fiber of skin into the fellow's lower jaw and were, as a consequence, unpleasantly hard to extract.

Yet it was not he who had killed that unlovely boche. Stevens became aware of this with a sense of total frustration. All that effort. Ridgeworth, following up, had stabbed the jerry in the guts, it was now clear. The soldier was staring at his officer in a frightened way, as he wiped his chiv on his seat. "You didn't 'ave to 'aul his ruddy 'ead 'arf orf, sir."

Dropping the sentry with a gasp, Stevens doubled over to Loran. The first German's helmet had tinkled off, exposing a gash in the hair. Stevens felt fear like a pinprick in his palms now. What was strange was that the jerry appeared to be several yards from where he'd been standing. He was surely very dead.

"Loran? Well done, you. What happened?"

"Lost three men."

"The devil you did."

"Yes. By an amazing bit of bad luck we ran into a German who must have been paying some clandestine visit to that Arab village, or something. Whatever it was, he saw us first since he'd been relieving himself—rather Teutonically—in the bushes. He killed a couple before Marrow saw him. Had to fire, I'm afraid."

"Of course. Damage done already." Stevens wiped his brow. Loran's account had been so matter-of-fact, so calm. "All the same, it made a racket, you know. Hardly helps to have the boche tuning in on us from the word go, does it?" He felt the presence of the corporal and the other men behind Loran.

Someone said, "Poor old Dusty."

Softly, so that the others shouldn't hear, Stevens whispered to Loran, "Look, seems to me they've bloody obviously got wind of this inside. They're expecting us by now."

"I don't think so. If they'd really been suspicious they'd have put another sentry out. No, this looks as if it's going to be quite straightforward. But we'd better get moving."

"You want to bag that general, don't you?"

"I do."

"I don't blame you. Killed your dad, eh." Stevens remained with head bowed down for a second. He dragged himself up. "Oke. Loran, you come with me. And Ridgeworth and Goddard. Look slippy. Corporal Marrow, you take the others and move in from the terrace window to get that back stair as planned." Felt better for giving orders. He gazed round unseeing for a second. God bloody save me, he thought. "Hall flooring slippery, Ridgeworth. Easy does it."

"Easy does it, sir."

"We'll go easy, all right," said Loran with a smile, and the contrast in the calm of his tone, which seemed to mask almost muted jubilation rather than any hatred, weakened Stevens more than ever.

He asked, "Did you throw that boche?"

"Flying mare. It wasn't hard."

"I see."

"Let's go."

But at that instant there came a low voice calling with curiosity, "Erich? Erich?" A third sentry now prowled suspiciously round the nearest wall and came forward towards them, gun slung on one shoulder. Psychologically unprepared, Stevens felt his legs as if anchored to the ground with leaden weights. It seemed that the man was staring right bloody at them as they cringed behind their bank of rock.

"Erich?" he persisted, straight in Stevens' face. "Wo bist Du, nichtsnutziger Schlingel?"

Closer. Stevens gaped. He tried to ease his Tommy gun into position but for what seemed an immensely long period of time he was unable to move. The German appeared to be moving his legs in slow motion and the whole incident had the quality of a badly projected film. He could feel a runnel of sweat on his face, that seemed to proceed grotesquely, gradually, down his chin. Then Goddard did it. Half upright and studying the equally petrified jerry with great intensity, Goddard made a magical gesture, a hypnotic feathering motion aside his thigh.

Too low you fool you dozy hopeless detail!

That was Stevens' first panic-struck thought. The German bent at once as the ripple of light snaked him. He clutched his belly. Too low! But in actual fact Goddard's aim had been good—the man had been a circus thrower for years before the war—and the chiv had struck at the vitals. Less than a second later Goddard was on his man, and had slit the throat from ear to ear. Then for some reason, smitten with excitement perhaps, he began pumping the slimy knife up and down into the dead German's chest.

"Enough. He's dead," Stevens got out. He hated that. Mutilation. They did it back. No method. His whole body had gone clammy by this time. "Well done, lad," he whispered. He simply didn't know how he was going to get inside that house.

"Four-three." Loran smiled in the dark beside him. "That puts us one up. Good going." The bogger might have been on some well-mown green at St. Andrew's. "Ready now?"

"He shouldn't have done that." The whole of Stevens' throat was heaving. "All that stabbing, I mean. Reprisals. They don't like it. Army orders distinctly..."

"Let's move."

"No, you see they did shove a third sentry on. Understand? That definitely proves they were worried by those shots. They'll be right in there waiting for us. We're going to buy it properly, man."

Loran looked at him. "We haven't got too much time," was all he said.

Suddenly Stevens turned livid. Annoyance at once more being told off by this wappy runt crystallized itself into a kind of courage. "God's sodding teeth, Loran," he hissed, "if you aren't careful I'll go spare on you, I swear to heaven I will. I'll lose my ruddy top with you. Now I'm commanding this shower. Just keep that in your head. Follow me."

Bounding forward he realized his anger was really against the system that had bred him, in which certain men were winners, and the rest lost out, were victims, whatever rank they might tote temporarily on their shoulders during wartime. Together they swarmed silently over the terrace. Stevens saw Marrow and his men drop nice and loosely, one by one, over an open sill into a darkened room at the back. Any moment they might hear firing now. It was on. And as he, Loran and the two others worked round to the front, there was only the sound of dulcet music in their ears.

Schon rief der Posten, sie blasen Zapfenstreich,
Es kann drei Tage kosten. Kamerad ich komm' sogleich.

That ruddy tune again: they've got the same flicking station on. He whispered back at Loran, "Don't you think we ought to recce a bit more, see what windows are lit?" But few were, that they could all too plainly see. "It would help."

"Let's get on with it," Loran retorted crisply. "They can spot us moving about out here. Besides, someone is going to relieve those sentries soon. Corporal Marrow's in the place by now. Let's get on in ourselves, come on."

"Never have liked breaking and entering," Stevens tried to quip, but it was true, there was no alternative now. He entered the house through the hospitably open front door. The music grew much louder.

"Welcome on the mat," whispered a voice behind him.

Soft light swathed the main marble staircase confronting them and for a second Stevens gazed up those steps with a grave envy. It was all so much more opulent than the exterior had suggested. He stood blinking. Never had been at home in a place like this.

In starched white jacket a German orderly was silently carrying a piled-up tray down a passage towards them. For a moment Stevens imagined the man was actually going to pass by them. Then the waiter's eyes pingponged wide and—again—Loran moved. Stevens heard a sharp, stifled cry, saw the tray clean-swept of its crashing contents as if by some unseen hand as the jerry made a curving sweep upwards with it at Goddard going forward to help Loran. The tremendous smashing of the dinner plates and glasses drowned all but the mild grunt with which Loran dropped. Things skittered and skidded. The German seemed to writhe a little, then was still; twitched, then was quite still. Loran got off him.

It had all happened together so that Stevens hadn't been able to sort it in his vision with any particularly sequential logic. He saw Loran nodding as he rose from the body. At the same time Stevens perceived to his horror that by a fluke the wildly swung tray had come up behind Goddard and driven inches into the base of the skull. He lay there, motionless. Sickened, Stevens saw a bulge of brain under the cap comforter. A purée of potatoes, with what appeared to be a mushroom gravy, was being inundated with wine nearby. He turned away. He had never—ever—felt quite like this before. He realized he was heaving and panting heavily.

A guttural voice called from upstairs: "*Stefan, hallo*?"

A pause.

"*Wie dumm Du bist*, Stefan."

Footsteps receded. Clinging to the wall which now seemed to be palpitating in wet and steady rhythm behind his fingers, Stevens could see nothing at all except for the slow ooze under the dead man's balaclava. Wine or blood? He let his head fall back—*it might have been me*—and was astonished at how slackly it jarred. Somewhere, above the now muted music, a clock was ticking. The Tommy gun felt like a dead weight in his hand. Blue funk. Was that what it was? Was this what it was like? Did he know now? He heard further steps upstairs, someone whistling in tune to the song, but was unable to move off the wall. A distortion haunted his vision. Yet all this must have taken mere fragments of time, for now he could see Loran's blazingly white eyes confronting him in a worried way.

"You all right?"

"Let's get out of here, Loran," he mumbled thickly. "I told you they were waiting for us." The notion had implanted itself in his mind by now. The only hope. Loran had his hand on Stevens' battle dress blouse and was silently shaking him, shaking him remarkably hard for so slight a man. Stevens said, "I know this bastard killed your father. I know how you must feel, old man. But we can't make it. Not tonight. They're upstairs waiting for us."

Loran's mouth moved but Stevens couldn't hear what it was he was saying. He caught words only: "They buried ... quick lime ..."

They heard other, booted footsteps overhead. These went away, began to descend some wooden-sounding stairs at the back.

Emptiness scooped inside Stevens then. This was where it had to start, the dreadful action he was hopelessly endeavoring to arrest. He had a split-second's fiendish dream that Marrow was in reality a boche spy, who had somehow or other got himself in P.E.D.G., when the clattering steps at the back exploded into a deafening din.

The house awoke. Shouts, cries, answering shots. A thudding rush came down the passage. Corporal Marrow appeared swerving towards them, his Tommy gun smoking, blood welling from his right hand.

"He was armed, sir. He got the three of us, sir. Tranter bought it proper. And me, look, I'm hit, sir. Oh my Gawd, we can't do no more with what we've got...."

His terrified words were dragged down his throat by an enormous crash and he fell backwards to the floor. Whirling, Stevens saw a figure standing at the head of the staircase above them, dressed in pale mauve pajamas and holding in one hand a smoking automatic as casually as a cigarette. This elegant apparition actually took a couple of calm steps down the staircase towards them and Stevens saw that the pajamas were monogrammed on the left chest before he got his Tommy gun up and, as a bullet crackled past him, he riddled the whole area in front of himself. He'd moved quickly. Marble chipped and one arm of the figure who had fired turned suddenly into a bloody stump. But he couldn't seem to kill the man. Spitting and coughing, the pajama-ed German seemed to descend semi-buoyantly down the wide steps, while Stevens blazed and blazed, advancing as he did so. Nearly the entire magazine had sprayed wildly and inaccurately out, flaying the solid furniture to either side. Eventually, his chest a mess of blood, the man toppled down towards Stevens, carried forward by the impetus of his descent so that for one frightful second he was held erect by his assassin, Stevens himself.

"Here. This way."

Disengaging from the ghastly embrace Stevens tossed aside his empty Tommy gun and led the way into an unlit side-room. As they went Ridgeworth lobbed a grenade into the upper storey for good measure. A blinding explosion was succeeded by a single shriek that sent shivers down Stevens' spine.

In the half-light from uncurtained windows the room gave the impression of being luridly over-furnished with big fringed chairs and brass standard lamps. As one of these clicked on a voice said softly, "*Haben Sie doch alles, was Sie suchen*?"

Stevens found himself staring straight down the barrel of a very firmly held Luger. It was held by a fully dressed officer of senior rank. By God, Stevens suddenly realized, von Schultz himself. He saw the swastika flag beside the desk, and behind the blighter's shoulder the large photo of the Führer. Stevens squeezed the trigger of his own .45 but something went wrong. The pistol melted in his fingers and dropped with a plop at his feet.

"*Englische Seife*," said the German quite calmly as Stevens, seeing Ridgeworth raise his hands beside him, slowly got up his own. He felt stupefied. He realized he hadn't drawn his pistol on entry at all, but that in those ultimate, hallucinatory seconds after the light had gone on he had instinctively reached for some object of protection on the desk, which was littered with the general's impedimenta. The piece of soap he had grabbed now lay on the Moorish rug in front of him, where it had slipped out of his fingers. So von Schultz got us, he thought, but that was all he had time to think.

Later he was never able to recreate this action coherently either, though it was remarkable how deeply ingrained on his memory that face before him had become. The man smoothed a lock of thin grey hair back with his free hand, adjusted in a precise gesture the rimless *pince-nez* on his nose; and even in those instants Stevens found the pale, anonymous, and faintly clerkly features assuming character in front of him. It was that of the official fanatic, not the open-air Nazi like Rommel, but the indoor breed, the Streicher, the kind that killed old Norwegians and buried them in lime. All the same, Stevens couldn't help thinking, the sod must have had a damn good job done on that hair-lip of his lately. The photographs they'd seen back at camp ...

Nothing meant anything. It was as if the final pages of some book were turning over, when the German gasped and seemed to spring into the air. Loran had entered the room last and, for all his senior's superior training, with far greater prudence. Hence, hidden behind a doilied settee of Moslem design, he had remained unseen by the German. Springing suddenly out, he had chopped swiftly at the hand holding that Luger and thrown the fellow halfway across the room. When Stevens joined him a moment later, it was to find the man dead. Loran's hand was still pressing on a spot on the neck behind the jaw as Ridgeworth stood ready with his knife.

Acting totally on instinct, Stevens went rapidly through the dead man's pockets, fumbling with the few papers he found there and crushing them into the map pocket of his own trousers. Then with Loran beside him he glanced over the desk. Nothing much there. Swastika seal. Cigarette lighter in the shape of a tank. Calendar. Loran was bent over a small packet of postcards, photos, possibly five or six. Stevens looked. A naked girl.

"Mucky pictures, eh."

"Photographs of paintings," Loran said quickly.

"Well, we haven't got any time to spend on art work here, my friend," said Stevens, snatching them out of Loran's grasp and pocketing them also. "Get the light, Ridgeworth, quick."

Ridgeworth darted to the switch and snapped off the lamp. Shouts and cries were coming from the garden as well as from the house above them now. It was merely a matter of time before they searched this room, Stevens realized. But they'd accomplished their objective; they'd killed—even if they hadn't captured—their general. He felt an immense sag of relief all through his body.

"Now let's naff off, for Christ's sake, before they cop us." He turned to Loran. "Thanks for what you did. I had no idea you were a judo expert—Wilf never told me."

"I do know something about it, actually."

A shadow seemed to nod by the window outside and they stilled, dead. When it'd gone Loran whispered, "If we want to get upstairs, now's the time to move. They seem to be mostly the other end of the house. Come on."

Stevens stared at him wildly. "What the hell are you talking about? You're all full of balloons, man. There's the ruddy general dead in front of you, we've accomplished our mission. We can't do any more. I'm getting out."

Loran shook his head. "The trouble is, that isn't the general."

"What do you mean?"

"No, that's not von Schultz."

"Not... what are you jabbering about, Loran?" Stevens was staring at the dead German with sagging mouth.

"Staff Brigadier. See his epaulettes?"

There was silence. Someone shouted nearby.

"You're not... I mean, are you sure?"

"Certain. Let's get upstairs, quick. They mayn't be guarding him too closely if we hurry."

But this time Stevens wagged his head. "It's no mucking use, Loran, I tell you. There's only three of us left. They got all Marrow's lot, see." It seemed the ultimate, the most exhausting cruelty of fate that the general was still alive. Stevens felt desperately weary. "We can't do anything like that now, I'm afraid."

Loran said sharply, "Of course we can. If we can get up there and cover the general, we can still escape by using him as a hostage. It's been done before. You yourself said so."

"Look here, Loran," Stevens said in a quavering voice, "I'm in charge of this show, not you. I'm ordering a retreat." Yet it was—he had to acknowledge in his heart—an order to a superior, to one of the winners, those who always stayed on top.

"No, sir." This time he heard Ridgeworth's anxious tone. "We can still do it, sir. I'm sure we can. Like Mr. Loran said."

"Shut up, Ridgeworth," Stevens cut in unsteadily. "You don't know anything about it at all."

Boots banged down the marble stair. Together they'd hauled the German officer under one of the plush settees, Ridgeworth had closed a cupboard on himself, and Loran and Stevens had gone to ground behind a desk—a question of seconds. The footsteps approached, paused; someone listened at the door, then it opened and a light went up. They saw spurred boots only.

"Siegfried?" inquired a cultivated voice.

Then the light went out; the man left the room, slamming the door. Stevens heard himself give a great gulp, like a pardoned schoolboy. Absurd. Gross blots of darkness were swelling at the edges of his eyes; he wondered if he were ceasing to be able to see. He dabbed at his face with the back of his hand and thought, Christ, I've been hit, then saw by the light from the window that the blood on his hand was from a nose-bleed he'd started. But the whole front of his battle dress, he saw as he got up, was in a mess from that appalling dance in the hallway. Loran had taken his arm.

"Come on now."

"Let's hear the hue-and-cry settle down a bit, eh? Then we can clear out."

"We aren't clearing out," Loran muttered in his ear. "Not until we've been upstairs."

Stevens felt weakly infuriated with the man. "Look here, Loran, don't you try to swing that sort of thing with me."

He saw Loran frown. "You can't get out of it. Our orders were to bag the general. So far we haven't seen him. He's still at large."

"They've probably got him miles away by this time, I tell you it's hopeless going on."

"Let's move."

"Listen, Loran, you take your orders from me, understand?"

Footsteps again, and everything wavered in front of Stevens; he couldn't make his limbs move properly while Loran stood beside him there in the dark. Stevens' body shook in a rigor of fear, he saw nothing in those seconds, he found himself actually hugging Loran to him. A voice bawled, some lights giving onto the terrace were extinguished, and the steps went away.

"Thank God for good boche blackout training." Loran laughed softly as he extricated himself from Stevens' clasp. "Now let's get going upstairs, shall we?"

Sweat streamed down Stevens' face. His shirt felt plastered to his back. "Listen to me for the last bloody time, Loran, or I'll punch your ruddy tab. Now then. Get this straight. I'm your senior officer and I'm giving you an order. We're going to run for it, all three of us. If you say anything further I'll report you when we get back for disobeying orders in the face of the enemy." Loran didn't speak. Stevens whispered, "Got it?"

"I won't argue."

Stevens became aware of Ridgeworth's aghast eyes. He added hurriedly, "That goes for you too, Ridgeworth."

"But, sir, we can't cut an' run like this now. There's still a chance..."

Stevens struck him. Then nearly wept. It was the half-heartedness, the dramatic falsity of the blow more than anything that sent the sense of disintegration coursing through his frame. Yes, he truly wanted to weep. For a moment he gazed glassily at the soldier. Then with a sob he got out, "The whole place is obviously bloody seething with boche now, and you two start ordering me about. You don't seem to understand. We haven't a bleeding earthly. It was a fatuous mission in the first place."

Neither said anything. Both examined him with an identical stare of meditated calculation. As if they were coming to some decision about him. He began to panic. It's them or me, he thought wildly.

"I'm doing this to protect you," he said as evenly as he could. "This is my appreciation of the situation, got it?" But he'd known all along this show had his name on. Now, even if they did get through, Loran could report this; Ridgeworth could see the Adj. Of course, it would only be their word against his—and he was the senior—but there happened to be two of them, one of him. And he'd just struck a man.

"We'll get out by the front, the way we came in," he found himself saying. "So far as I can hear, they're all out combing the grounds—they think they've searched the house O.K. We'll make singly for that hut affair we saw on our way up. I'll go first." The final word emerged from his throat as little more than a moan. He thanked God he had make-up on so that they couldn't see the true complexion of his skin. Loran had lowered his eyes but Ridgeworth was still staring helplessly at his officer. Don't look at me like that! he wanted to bawl at the man. But he knew they knew. Oh yes, they knew all right. It was his duty to go last, not first. The first man would have the best chance, of course. If he attracted any attention the others would fairly cop it properly. No, Stevens said solemnly to himself, there won't be any living with this pair again.

"Look." Loran spoke quite without the urgency he himself felt. "I'll go last, but I think we ought in duty bound to let Ridgeworth go first."

Ridgeworth protested. "No, sir, it's quite all right. As Captain Stevens says, sir."

"You do what I say," Stevens snapped.

"Age before beauty," Loran mildly interjected. "Give Ridgeworth a chance. You know we ought to."

Stevens raised his hand to hit him, too. For a second they stared each other in the face. Then the big hand dropped, the eyes dropped in front of that so confident regard. Stevens stalked swiftly to the door. Opening it a crack, he looked out. The music had stoped. The clock ticked madly, so it seemed. The pool of blood Marrow lay in was now visibly lusher than the wine. His carroty crop was all awfully twisted. The dead German lay sprawled in his pajamas in front of the pomegranates and other African fruits, like some titanic sacrifice to Mars. Goddard and the waiter farther down. The stench of hot gravy. What a godawful shambles. Enough to turn anyone's stomach, surely. Averting his eyes from all this, Stevens forced himself to scan the passageway to the back. Surprisingly enough, the coast was entirely clear. He motioned with his head at the others.

A minute later all three were standing just outside the house, looking down at the body of a jerry officer. Stevens himself gazed at it in perplexity. There had been no transition in his mind. What in God's name had happened?

"It's daylight," he exclaimed. "Something's wrong."

The night was still wrapped round them, however. A flare had simply gone up, from some searchers the far side of the house, as they huddled closely behind a boulder. From what Ridgeworth mumbled it became apparent that he—Stevens, no less—was responsible for having hit the man such a colossal blow with the butt of his pistol that the face now gave the impression of having been squeezed under a great weight. For a second that bloody mush fascinated him, then he pointed, gasped, ran hell for leather over the low, low wall, and away.

Stevens had never been especially proud of his speed. Rugger and boxing had been his forte, and at both his fault had always been a certain slowness of the pins. He'd always tried to make up for that with some of his celebrated Brute Strength and Ignorance. Twice he tripped on the uneven earth. Twice he swore foully, as much at himself as anything. When finally he lay on the floor of the wooden shack some two hundred yards or so from the house, he felt as if his stomach had slowly been pulled out. He retched for breath. A horrible sensation assailed him—something was being pushed down his nostrils from right inside his head. A nightmare, by God.

Only after he'd recovered did he see through a chink in the woodwork just how phenomenally lucky he had been. The jerries seemed to be all over the shop, but somehow or other they hadn't seen him. His mouth stifled on a rush of vomit, but he managed to swallow it back. He openly admitted to himself by now that his morale had collapsed and he even began watching his own actions with a kind of terrified apprehension, like a man furtively picking his scabs.

He saw Ridgeworth vault the wall and come running awkwardly towards the hut, pumping his arms. Why oh why in blue blazes didn't he leave his Tommy gun behind, Stevens wondered as he saw him. Dump the thing, man. And as he watched in the surge of that irrational anger he realized the subconscious truth of his own feelings—he didn't really want Ridgeworth to make it to the hut.

Within ten paces of the shack there came the crack of a shot and Ridgworth fell. Again, that immediate shameful sensation: the one that got him won't get me. Watching from inside, Stevens saw the lone German who'd fired start towards the body, rifle in hand. He knew that his own chosen hiding place would now be discovered and, leaping to the broken hut door, he plugged the oncoming Hun high in the chest with his .45. The weight of lead carried the man backwards, with a contorted expression that widened all his features. Stevens stood panting, staring at where Ridgeworth writhed some ten yards from the hut. Though groaning fearfully, the man seemed to be alive, and Stevens knew he ought to go out and pull him in. His eyes scanned the ground to try to observe the disposition of the searching Germans. Some seemed to be firing into total darkness in the general confusion; they hadn't noticed the one isolated shot.

"Sir! Sir!"

The stoically suppressed cry sent a shiver down his spine. He tried to pay no attention to it.

"Please, sir," Ridgeworth was grunting. "Christ, aaah, it hurts, it hurts so, sir." Doubled into a ball now, he had begun whimpering like a child. His words terrified Stevens. Then he saw Loran running.

Loran moved fast, steadily and absolutely silently. Again Stevens absorbed the realization that these two men were the only ones left alive of the whole patrol, beside himself. And they were both in his hands. He could shoot Loran down like a dog, now, at this very minute—if only Ridgeworth weren't staring at him like that.

He saw Loran make for Ridgeworth and in little more than a single fluid motion stop in his tracks, gather the wounded soldier up under his armpits, and begin dragging him—heels bumping—towards the hut.

"Don't... sir... huuurts!" Stevens heard Ridgeworth imploring like a baby.

When he reached the hut Loran laid Ridgeworth down. The man had been badly hit in what seemed like the front of the upper right thigh—Stevens couldn't bear to look too closely—and his chest was rising and falling rapidly. "It's my... am I gin' be orl right, sir? D'you think... my..."

"You'll be all right, Ridgeworth." Loran was untwining a field dressing. "We'll get you out of this."

Stevens said, "We can't carry Ridgeworth out of this shack between us, any more than we can take off and fly. For Christ's sake be your age, man. You know that perfectly well. Where the blithering blazes do you suppose we are, larking it up on Aldershot Plain?"

"'Sright, sir," gasped out Ridgeworth from the floor. His face had greyed under the blacking. "I'll be O.K. They'll look arter me, the jerries will. You two shove off, sir. I would quick." At the same time he was twisting and squirming in his agony. It was horrible. Just like a cut worm, thought Stevens, appalled by the sight. It was all Loran could do to get the field dressing anywhere near on.

"Here, hold his legs, would you."

"We haven't got all day."

Sweating with fear Stevens knelt and held still those threshing limbs. Loran bandaged the man. Stevens tried not to look but he could still see. Ridgeworth had bought it all right, cop in the spot where every soldier was most deeply scared of being hit. It was dreadful. Foam sprayed out of the fellow's mouth as he gasped; he hadn't a single earthly chance. The poor mucker's dying, Stevens realized with sullen dread.

Loran had wound a pencil up into a passable tourniquet. "Think you could stand?"

"Ah no, sir." Ridgeworth spoke with a kind of wistful effort now. "I've 'ad it. You two push orf."

"We can't take him with us," Stevens whispered. "Don't you see?"

"Then I'm staying here with him," Loran answered.

Stevens stared at him, sick with fury. That soddy top-dog accent again. "Look here, Loran, I'm giving you a direct order. Got it? There does happen to be a war on, you know, in case you hadn't noticed. You don't know.... I've been in quite a few of these shows just lately, believe me, and I..." His voice momentarily broke. "Dozens of 'em. If I was hit as bad as this, then I'd expect to be left. I'd ask to be. Unless you bloody think you can work miracles, I mean." He sneered slightly. That was better. "Didn't they teach you back at the depot that commandoes are costly? It's our code, see. You can't afford to sacrifice two for the sake of one."

Loran said simply, "Sorry."

Stevens fisted his fingers. The winner. As Loran bent over the mortally wounded man Stevens caught the smell of the West End barber's shop again. The field dressing on Ridgeworth's lap—on what had once been what the wog called a man's qalaoui—was now nothing more than a dark pulp. And the fellow had started foaming and writhing again—"God, it huurts," he was pitifully whimpering.

Stevens firmly considered he was going to die, but somehow or other—though he'd seen enough of them kick the bucket by this time in his Army career—the idea of watching Ridgeworth croak became too much to bear.

In a low tone he told Loran: "Look, his nerves are starting to wake up. In a few minutes he won't be able to stop himself from screaming. It'd be a mercy to leave him. After all, the boche may have morphine here. In any case, we'll be found. We've got to get out of here fast."

"I'm sticking here."

"Remember what you told me on the boat. That if they do take you prisoner, they'll probably put you up against a wall. Almost certainly will after all the killing we've done here."

"I know, but I'm staying."

"O.K., Loran, have it your way." He tried to alter his tone. "O.K., then. We'll get Ridgeworth out of this somehow. Only, it's useless the two of us trying to carry him. We'd be spotted for sure. You start first, see. And I'll put Ridgeworth over my shoulders, feet up, you know, I've done it heaps of times on training and it's the only hope for a man hit in that spot. Come on now, it's our last chance, I'm twice the size you are, you couldn't begin to do it so don't pretend you could."

After a second's hesitation Loran agreed.

"Very well."

Stevens said quickly, "See that line of bush? It leads the way we came in. Over the road. You run for it, hell for leather, mind. Once I see you've got there safely I'll join you. With Ridgeworth. Like that we can use the wadi we came in by." He added softly, "Good luck."

Loran went.

"S-sorry, sir." Ridgeworth was struggling behind him. Stevens turned his head. Convulsions. The soldier tried to throw up a smile. "See you in Leicester Square arter, eh, sir?"

"Leicester Square," Stevens said vaguely. He was watching Loran go. Ten paces. Fifteen. Twenty. Without thinking he cocked his pistol. "Hang on, Ridgeworth," he said quietly. The man gave a sobbing choke. He was dying for sure, Stevens thought as almost abstractly he covered Loran with the .45. Nearly twenty-five. Getting difficult, but still possible. He could bring the wappy mucker down easily enough. And with these dum-dums... Then suddenly hell erupted in front of him.

That was how he put it to himself much later. Loran walked into it. Bought the whole bloody shop. Stevens saw him hit and for a horrified second imagined he himself had completed his little fantasy, actually closed his finger on his own cold trigger. And killed him. The strike of shot seemed to lift that scant figure right off the earth altogether as Loran still inhumanly ran, ran, then he was in the dust and scrub while the jerry lead poured straight into him. Tracers, too. Point-blank shots. Loran had run slap into a knot of boche, a group which Stevens hadn't seen, in evident consultation after their search.

He felt possessed of an unearthly calm. Some fatality had interpreted his wishes. He found himself shaking coldly. He never would have pulled on Loran, of course, but bogger it, it was bloody well as if he had. And now the poor devil had drawn their fire, and he himself could make it the other way. Where the road was clear. Or seemed so, at least. First, however, he had something to do. He turned methodically. Outside the firing had momentarily stilled.

"I'm sorry I struck you just now," he said tenderly, kneeling in the blood beside Ridgeworth. The hut seemed to be swimming in it, it was appalling to think of so much vital fluid coming from so relatively frail a human form.

"That's all right, sir. Know you didn't mean it—arter all, you bin in all these do's lately, the terrible pressure, we all..." The man spoke between bubbling moans and shivers. "Sir."

"Yes?"

"I'm going now."

"You'll be all right, Ridgeworth."

"Na, sir. I'm dying. 'Ad it."

Stevens wanted to say No, you aren't, old man, but how could he lie before those so final eyes?

"I'm sorry I hit you, Ridgey. I shouldn't have done it. You put your head back, cop. Yes, like that now."

"Proper do, wannit, sir?"

"It was, indeed."

Into Stevens' mind had come the realization that now he was all on his own, the last of the patrol left—except for the soldier so painfully dying in front of him. Loran had been killed. Of that he was certain. Even if he did, by some fluke of fate, live on with all that lead inside him, it was a ninety per cent cert the jerry would execute him out of revenge. As a Norwegian. As Loran himself had said. No, there was only Ridgeworth left. The fellow gave a lurching plunge, a short anguished cry. Stevens shut his eyes.

"It's getting bad now, sir."

"It won't be, lad, not much longer."

Lying back in his officer's arms Ridgeworth felt the cold steel at the nape of his neck, however. Stevens hadn't intended that. There came into the soldier's eyes a stare of naked comprehension. Seeing it, Stevens squeezed the trigger with a grimace. The shot made a great bleak crash, a deafening black echo, like a hole in hell itself. The body jerked; it was horrible. Stevens had time to see that all that was left in his arms was a sort of mess of wet velvet where Ridgeworth's head had been, then he felt the ground pounding hollowly underfoot as he himself was racing into the African darkness in the opposite direction to the one Loran himself had taken.

He was meaning to circle back widely towards the road and then, once over it, back to the shoreline which he could then follow on to the boat. There was just time—if only it hadn't gone.

Trust the Nyvy, my eye. He had paused, fighting for breath in the blackness, when he saw him. The German was lying down, taking what seemed to be most careful aim and the whole of Stevens' frame cringed within its skin.

"Don't shoot!" he screamed. "Nicht schiessen!" He cried it piteously as he went forward with his hands held very high. The Hun had got him after all.

CHAPTER FOUR

But he hadn't, you know. Stevens had run a long way round from the house. Farther than he'd thought, and probably dangerously far. Actually what he'd done, he subsequently realized, had been to follow the route taken by Loran's section coming in. The German he'd imagined in the darkness to be covering him was dead. He saw him lying there, a stick grenade protruding from one pocket, gun stuck out in front of him. It was exact. The area of the skirmish Loran and Marrow had had. Stevens saw the dead bodies of two of his men at twenty paces distance, one of them, on closer inspection, seemingly untouched. Yet very, very dead.

He lay down deside this last corpse—Stubbs'—for a second and indulged in a sort of crooning moan. This turned suddenly into spasms of heavy laughter. Uncontrolled. Uncontrollable. He knew now he'd broken. Another flare went up behind him from the direction of Dark House and he clung, cringing, to the bitter earth. All this brutal death, on the fierce rim of a feelingless continent. He was not a complicated man, and he had enough savvy to acknowledge when the light had dimmed once more to that pitchy, hunted black that after this fiasco he'd never be the same again. Never again could he lead a raid with any kind of confidence at all. It simply wouldn't be safe to send him out with men. What he'd done to Ridgeworth rose to an enormity that beat monstrously at his mind. He had not merely infringed a code, it now seemed to him, although that would have been bad enough for a regular; no—he had killed a fellow-soldier on active service. It was inconceivable that he could calmly go back and serve in the commando after this. He'd never know a bickering moment's peace in his mind. And if it were ever suspected … even if nothing official were ever proved, God—what had he done! Christ alive, the men themselves extracted their revenge for deeds like that. Let alone the brass. One bullet in the back of the neck on their next patrol, that's all that'd be needed to settle for Ridgeworth. God!

Stevens' mouth felt scaly, tongued with salt. The night gave him an icy clutch. His body shook feverishly. That's it, he thought, I've got a fever. Thoroughly understandable, that. Only, what the hell did I do to clobber that jerry outside the front door? Can't remember clearly. His bruised eyes seemed to burn with blades of piercing light in the blackness and, from their corners, yield a brackish ooze. He rolled towards the dead soldier's gun.

He was quivering and his head was drumming as he removed his right gym-shoe and sock. It was difficult, lying along the ground like this. Might blast his bloody head right off, you never know. Not the .45, old scout, he told himself, not the cowing Colt. I mean, just in case the bullet might lodge. And blow off your whole bleeding arm too, eh. Carefully he set the boche rifle to fire single shot, engaged it in a nick of rock, felt for the trigger with his big toe.

At first, in the shock of the close explosion, he imagined he had indeed blown his whole left arm off. But as the warm sense of fluid traveled to his fingers and the hurt began, he saw that he'd done exactly what he'd planned, nicely notched the flesh there. Lucky he was a methodical type, really. He'd had to get his arm close to the barrel to avoid smashing the bone for good.

Now it was hard to get the plimsole back on. His foot seemed to have swelled up. Leaving the lace undone he started running in the direction of the road, left arm limply hanging. Soon the searching army seemed far behind. He could feel it somehow. But he remained cautious. He crossed the road, hit the coast. No sight of the boat. Again he panicked. Didn't fancy the idea of trying to get through boche front lines in the state he was in. And as he drove himself onwards, hardly caring now what target he made against the sea line, he developed a crazy sensation of wading through a field of high bright flowers. The night was growing colder and colder. His arm throbbed violently.

Suddenly, the dip to the inlet. There!

But to his horror he saw the boat some fifty yards or so out from the grotto where it'd lain hidden. They were about to clear off, it became plain. While Stevens stared down at it, hopelessly wondering if he should risk a cry, he imagined he saw a balaclava-ed form in the stern. For a hideous second he surmised that one of the patrol had—miraculously enough—survived after all, and got back before him. Then the seated figure made a motion, he saw that he'd been wrong.

"Got 'im, sir?"

The call from the brush made Stevens start. Two of the tars had come up here, it transpired, to help with the embarkation of the general.

Stevens shook his head. He panted out what had happened. "They were all there ready waiting for us, see. We forced the house all right but jerry was there all teed up. Every man jack of the patrol bought it except for me. And me, I was winged." He tried to hold up his bloody left arm but suddenly, to his surprise, found himself unable to do so above the shoulder. What's this? he thought with alarm.

"Christ!" exclaimed one of the soldiers, deeply shocked. "Suffering jack-up, sir, every one of 'em but you, eh? Christ, what luck."

" 'Ere, let me give you a 'and, sir," said the other.

Somehow or other Stevens stumbled down to where the boat had now been poled back in. The naval lieutenant, who'd been playing Russian Bank in the interim, commiserated with

Stevens, white-faced. The result of the action was too shocking for anyone to want to talk much.

"Let's get cracking," Stevens said.

"Good idea. They've started sending up flares."

With a nod from the lieutenant the boat, which had hove off shore to catch flashlight messages from the sailors it had landed, was now once more poled out in silence. Only when the engine broke into a tidy bumping note did Stevens relax at all. His left arm was like an iron board. A sailor bound it for him after Stevens had recovered a little and taken off his battle-dress top. Then he lay in the back of the boat, wrapped in a blanket, shivering. He didn't want to talk to any of them. He was terrified of that frightful laughter starting up on his lips again. Somebody gave him rum. They drew quickly out to sea.

CHAPTER FIVE

From the village jetty a truck roared him back to the unit. He was sitting up now, his left arm held as high as it would go on the advice of a Medical Orderly with a scared expression who'd been among the small reception committee. They'd radioed back No General from the boat.

"Better take him strite to C.C.S."

However, Stevens insisted on returning first to the P.E.D.G. forward bivvy.

When they got in he hurried to Wilf, waiting in the tented orderly room. A young Picquet officer was there also. They both stared at Stevens with set faces. The blood from that bounding figure in the mauve pajamas had covered his trousers in front as well. The adjutant listened silently to the news of the wiped-out patrol, and the young officer escorted Stevens solicitously to the M.O., a mild man with faded first war ribbons who'd been waiting up against their return. Inured to death and bloodshed all his life, the doc listened to the story over a pipe while he inspected the wounded arm. A clean cut.

"This beggar must have got pretty close to you."

"He did. It was in the hallway." Must remember that one, Stevens thought.

"Hurting much?"

"Yes, well it's coming on a bit now."

"Swallow this." The M.O. put a thin pill under Stevens' tongue. It tasted bitter. "Phil, I'm going to send you back with this little puncture. It could get better in our sick bay here all right but frankly for some time I've thought you needed a rest. You've been out on quite a few of these ding-dongs lately. Probably too many."

"Frankly, it did get a bit harrowing tonight, Doc. Worst I've been in, as a matter of fact."

"It must have been a nasty crack if they got the whole lot except for you." Speaking in a muted murmur the M.O. was wiping the blacking off Stevens' face with a piece of dampened lint. "We might as well try to clean you up a bit before you go."

"Yes, it was a pretty unpleasant scrap, all in all. Can I collect what I'd like to take with me from my tent first?"

"Course. We'll just have this cleaned out and dressed for you and then you can charge over and get Wright to pack what you want." While an orderly began cleaning the wound he went on, "I'm sending you back as Walking Wounded, Phil. Eight A General."

"Christ, do I look that bad?" Stevens grinned at this hint of heaven. Now it was all over he seemed to have lost any kind of faith whatsoever. He felt hollow with exhaustion.

A fingernail of light was nudging at the darkness of the African sky as he walked over to his tent. He realized he looked much like a wog himself, still wrapped as he was in the blanket. Wright was there, apprised of his arrival already, so it seemed. He was setting things out on the camp bed and he, too, looked up with an expression of distaste at all the blood.

"Glad you're back, sir. An' all."

"So by bleeding George am I."

"Not 'urt too bad?" he asked as Stevens shed the blanket. "I see they done you up."

"Not too bad." But this one knew him too well. No questions. Wright knew. Somehow he always seemed to find out everything connected with his officer. "Return that blanket to Q some time. Don't flog it. Listen, they're putting me in dock with this thing. I didn't want to go, but M.O.'s orders are orders."

"Yes, sir."

"Heard already?" Yes, by that mysterious grapevine through which the private soldier in a British battalion learns of everything before it happens. Stevens realized, in fact, that Wright was now diligently setting out a haversackful of precisely all his officer would require in hospital or in dock.

"The rest—then they've definitely 'ad it, sir?"

"I'm afraid they have."

"Corp, too?"

"Corporal Marrow, too."

"Two pairs of drawers, cellular," Wright counted sternly. "I darned them socks, sir." Stevens now wished he would go. "Can't say it's invisible mending exactly, I'm afraid."

"I'll be back soon," Stevens said.

"Well, I reckon I've put out hall you need there, sir." The batman straightened his flimsy frame. Outside the tent Stevens could see a few men walking about and chatting—obviously in discussion of the wiped-out patrol. His patrol. "Han' they sent over your battle-dress blouse, the Nyvy did, sir, you left it in the boat. I've put you up a clean 'un." He turned abruptly on his heel and went out.

For a second Stevens lay back on his bed. He closed his eyes. His arm was still stiffly throbbing but the pain, thanks to the morphine pill the M.O. had given him, was far less localized. A general ache possessed his whole body, however. When he opened his eyes again the sky outside had lightened several degrees. As he moved, shedding his binoculars, he wondered if he ought to turn in the papers he had taken off that jerry staff officer now rather than later. That would at least show evidence of having entered the house. But he was in doubt. Might such a step somehow yield hidden testimony of how he had shirked? He couldn't seem to think properly any more. He was debating the problem when he saw the battle-dress blouse Wright had brought back for him. In the silence of the camp his being awakened. Sweat pearled at his forehead and his scalp knit tight with sudden spidery fingers.

For the left sleeve had been torn in two places by the entering bullet, and in the growing light Stevens could now see that the hole in front was charred with powder burns. This itself was no direct evidence of guilt, he knew, for it was possible that in the melee a jerry might have shot his arm as close as that, but the sign had become so well known in the desert by this time as a symptom of a self-inflicted wound that he felt petrified. Had Wright seen it, suspected the same? Surely it had been too dark for Wright to have seen it. But the batman had been unnaturally brusque. What could he do? Turn in an officer? While Stevens tossed these questions hectically through his head he began rending at the soft cloth in a panicky fashion. Yet that, he realized as soon as he'd started, was perhaps only going to give the game away worse. And it seemed impossible to remove the blackened edges entirely with the fingers of just one hand. Finally, sweating profusely, he started biting at the cloth, eating away the tell-tale burns.

He gasped. At first he spat out what he chewed off the blouse. Then he thought, Christ, Wright will spot the flicking pieces. Confirm the bogger's suspicions. Worse than ever. He picked up the khaki fragments and retched as he tried to swallow them, but succeeded. In a complete panic now, he tore at the stuff round the bullet hole with his teeth until it was frayed sodden with saliva, as he chewed and swallowed the strands of cloth that he was able to bite away. Then he managed to get his left arm into the sleeve and do himself up after a fashion. Must wear it now, despite the blood. He hurried out into the first raw light of African day. Bloody fatal if he bumped into Wright again now; if the batman saw what he'd done to his sleeve and rumbled.

The last of the coolness was rising as Stevens tried to saunter as slowly as he could to the waiting 15-cwt. He could feel it under his legs, that thin mist that made the coming sunlight somehow all the more hostile and painful. He was determined now that, come what might, he would never again return to this unit.

Couldn't. A cruel radiance from the sky illumined the bumpy track ahead as they started off, back towards rear echelons deep in the inscrutable desert.

The driver finally left him at a row of long, low, straggling tents. Inside the nearest of these were lines of stretchers, mainly occupied by wounded men, some of them—though not many—groaning with pain. Quickly Stevens lay down on an unoccupied stretcher. Surreptitiously he shifted the dressing on his arm so that the blood began to well out in soft throbs. Soon his left sleeve, and the stretcher underneath, were covered by it.

The tent seemed to be in pretty average confusion—which was what he'd expected and hoped for. M.O.'s and orderlies were milling up and down, and there was the constant sound of trucks arriving and ambulances pulling off.

"Got a fag, cop?"

"What?"

"Yus, a burn."

Stevens rolled his head. A Kosbi with a neck wound lay next to him. He tried to read the label attached to one of the man's battle-dress buttons.

"Sorry, old man, you're out of luck." He hadn't taken smokes on the patrol, and anyhow it probably wouldn't do the beggar any good to have one in his condition.

As if reading his thoughts the man said, "Better to smoke here than hereafter, as they say, guv'."

Two stretchers away plasma was being administered.

"In the El Ala do, mate?" The man was unable to know Stevens' rank because of his lack of identification badges.

"No. I'm in P.E.D.G."

"Ah." A second while the information sank in. "Hurt bad?"

"Well."

"What are you—orficer?"

"Captain."

"Ah."

The next time an orderly came past, the soldier called out, "'Ere. There's a P.E.D.G. job caught it, mate. Capin'. Hurt like friggin' 'ell. Better bob this one back quick."

The orderly bent over Stevens. "Din't they give you nothing at C.C.S., sir? No ticket, nothing, I mean?"

"I came straight through from my unit. We're on special reconnaissance. Closish. Secret missions." He added, "I'm not permitted to tell you any more, I'm afraid."

"Arm wound, sir?" He saw the orderly eye the blood.

"That's right."

"Dressing seems new."

"M.O.'s. It may have slipped a bit."

"Well, we'll fix it up in a jiff. Can you walk?"

Stevens drew a breath. Was it really going to be as easy this? So far the first steps had been so simple, the path opened ahead to grander perfidy with no difficulty however. "Not too well," he answered the orderly calmly. "The M.O. said I wasn't to, but I'll try if you like."

"Oh, no need for that, sir."

"Feel a trifle weak, as a matter of fact. I think I was to be sent back to Eight A."

"O.K., sir, we'll get you out of here just as soon as we can."

Stevens was lifted into the top left bunk of an ambulance. He considered making a moan or two, but rejected the idea as melodramatic. The stretcher beneath his was filled with a man dying of gas gangrene. The sickly stench, compounded with desert dust flying through in a steady stream from in front began to weary him as they got under way. They were going to have to drive for hours, so it seemed. He learnt that General Hospital 8A was in a small town near Mecheli called Beda Wat. The groaning ambulance kept toiling on and stopping in the heat. One of the stretchers carried the former loader-operator of a brewed tank who maintained a monotonous flow of obscenity until Stevens felt his nerves fraying to break-point. Fantastic. Once he counted off eighteen four-letter words in a single row, followed by a string of fourteen, followed by twenty-two. Harsh, consonantal words. And the man didn't pause to conjugate sentences since his obscenities could be inflected to include any part of speech, it was plain. It just went on and on and on in a doggedly steady rhythm, like the lingo of a lunatic.

"For Christ's sake shut up," Stevens got out at last, his eyes shut. "Shut up and get stuffed, man." And the fellow was so surprised he did so.

That night Stevens tossed between sheets in a bare, calcined chamber with four other officers. The hospital was a former school, and the officers' wards were on the top floor. Ah, those sheets had an impossible texture of peace, and the four forgiven men, all back from the line, passed the single urinal bottle to and fro voluptuously. They had been told not to get out of bed and where they came from men by and large obeyed orders.

Next morning Stevens was allowed to use a small lavatory at the end of the hall. The appointments were minimal, but tiled. And although no water came out of the taps, you could still turn them gloriously on and off and play at being civilized. He strolled about that lav like a pasha.

This hospital was still staffed with male orderlies but, when Stevens had been there five days, there was an intake of wounded from an unrecce'd infantry attack, and he was entrained for 13C, placed some distance back at Akhdum, a coastal town just over forty miles from Alex.

Here he found himself in a more organized ward with fifteen other officers, all cursing the climate, and being looked after by English nurses. The wound in his arm rapidly recovered. Soon the dressing was left off. But he was careful not to lift his arm any higher than shoulder level. Since he in truth hadn't been able to for some time, this proved easy enough and, when a doctor first asked him to have a try, he was able to fake stiffness with an almost genuinely puzzled expression.

For several days, however, he was not allowed up for another reason. The fact was that, by way of some reaction from the sequence of dangerous missions he'd been involved in and, especially, the consequences of the last one, Stevens found his mind sinking more and more into a stupor. He slept continually and, when awake, watched the rectangle of window in front of him, the blue sky like a blazing flag hung up just outside. He listened to the wog chatter drifting up from outside—all Insh'allah and Ou 'allah and stuff like that—and then the frightful tuneless playing of their flutes. The wog played his flute in the streets as a series of notes, undecipherable, meaningless. It got on the nerves. And as the light faded at evening, life seemed to ebb from the airless dormitory and Stevens knew a solemnity, a deep sadness. Nothing, it seemed then, could ever mitigate his guilt. Not even oceans of tears could wash away what he'd done.

Sometimes he watched the ward sister make the beds with feminine efficiency. He lethargically refused most of the meals she brought him on a tray. Mainly he ate Marmite on dry bread, washed down with weak tea. He liked that. The days passed by in a blank. A padre would come in with a trolley of books and ask him what he'd care to read. He tried one or two classics he'd found difficult to finish at school, things like War and Peace and The Galsworthy Saga, but to his annoyance found them even harder to get into now. As for modern novels, it seemed absolutely inconceivable to think of people actually catching trains, going to cocktail parties, walking to church on Sundays. He put such books down after a few pages had passed vacantly in front of his eyes. The officer in the next bed asked him once what he was reading and he had to think for several seconds before replying.

To tell the truth, he avoided talking to the others there. His terror was that one day, rolling his head to the door as the bakelite trays were wheeled in on the luncheon trolley, he would see someone from his own outfit standing there. He still hadn't formulated any clear plans for the future. The future required enormous effort; it belonged to Allah. Whenever he tried to think ahead his brain turned muzzy, a drifting sensation took him.

"Stare, stare like a bear." Sister Matson was smiling at him. "Tell yer ma to cut yer hair."

He realized he had been gazing at the well-rounded rump of the ward nurse as she busied herself making the bed across from his. He shook himself awake. It was certainly a pleasantly upholstered podex. Odd that he hadn't noticed that before.

"Sorry, Sister. I assure you my mind was on higher things."

"They're also excellent," said the officer in the next bed.

"Now there's an honest man for you." The Sister flushed and laughed. "And that's just why nice girls like me are so suspicious of them."

"Am I a dishonest man?" Stevens asked her.

"Oh, I shouldn't think so. But I'm definitely a nice girl."

"With very definite higher things," put in the other officer.

The nurse ignored him. "Now then," she addressed Stevens, "like me to make your bed?"

"What do you think?"

He lay like a prince while she moved about him. Once she bent and he caught the drift of costly perfume. Under the starched cap her hair was softly fair. Cut off for so long from the sight of anything more female than the oddly sexless wog women, Stevens began to feel his pulses pound. His senses awoke. He was getting better, all right.

Perhaps something of this communicated itself to the nurse for she rose, warm-faced from stooping and tucking in the bed, and left the ward without saying anything further to him, one hand adjusting a strand of straying hair. Under the belted linen her flesh moved elastically. The contrast with the world he'd come from, that Arab universe without security or comfort, was all at once overwhelming. By God, he could still give the girls a treat, couldn't he. Which was more than that poor sod Ridgeworth ... if he'd lived. ... Stevens sank back and shut his eyes.

"Marvelous, isn't it?" The officer next to him, leg slung ceilingward in a dirty cast signed with a dozen nurses' names, grinned cheerily across. "Hell, I haven't seen a rear elevation like that since the Mack Sennett comedies."

Stevens smiled too. "Dead right. She's exhausting."

"Every throbbing inch of her, old cock."

For a while they began swopping limericks. Stevens soon ran out. They tried making them up, based on the perennial *There was a young lady of Niger.* The other chap was extremely fertile in the most excruciatingly recondite eroticisms, but Stevens himself, after vainly sucking at his pencil for minutes on end, could seldom get beyond the second line. The change in meter simply floored him at this point.

That afternoon his bed was one of those wheeled out onto the veranda for half an hour or so of fresh air. Through the blind dazzle of sun outside he was dimly aware of the usual honeycomb of cubes that made up the average wog town, blocklike patterns of white houses relieved here and there by colored mats hung out on terraces. Bloody human quarries, that's what they were. The hospital itself was a big new building and, although it was patrolled by sentries, crowds of Arabs made clusters outside until dispersed. Dogs hung around. But always there was from somewhere that aggressive, pointless articulation of the city wog—with never a laugh in it anywhere—to which he simply couldn't grow used. It was so sharp, alien, reeking with contempt for other people and the lack of result to anything. And then the silence, and the djenoun. Only, then, the screaming distant cattle, the braying mules, which were just as depressing anyway.

At the end of one spell on the terrace Sister Matson appeared beside his bed. She had no make-up on and her soft, bee-stung mouth was adorned with two beads of perspiration on the upper lip. Her blonde bun was straggling undone and the sunlight streamed through her thin uniform, defining a pair of disruptively slender thighs practically to the sturdy body junction.

Stevens found his throat swelling. Then he saw a doctor beside her. The latter was holding a sheaf of X-ray pictures in one hand. Still wet, they reminded Stevens of cool places and blissful darknesses.

"I was just wondering, Captain. I mean, you didn't by any chance receive a blow on the head in this mission of yours, did you?"

"Well, I don't think so. That is."

Stevens struggled rapidly to think. Possibly his case had taken on some new slant. He fought for time. "See, Doc, as we were getting away, so many things happened, then I picked up this blighter in my arm, I may well have been clobbered for all I know."

"At the time you were shot?"

He thought quickly. "Perhaps. In that hallway."

"But surely you'd remember. You were conscious all the time, weren't you?"

"Yes, I think so."

"You only think so?"

"Well, yes, that's right." He felt the doctor studying him closely, even with compassion, and here, he realized, he held one advantage. P.E.D.G. missions were classed as "highly secret." Every commando was instructed to keep his clapper shut, and even hospital doctors weren't supposed to winkle out more than was needed for immediate therapeutic purposes. By and large, the medical staff more than respected this secrecy. And in the ward, in fact, it had already given Stevens a certain prestige. Now he was the only one, he had told himself over and over again, barring a possible captured boche prisoner, who would breathe a word about the particular show known as Operation Cabbage.

He said carefully, "I don't know if I could be altogether sure, Doc."

"You didn't report a bruise on the head. We found no lacerations of the skull."

"Granted. But ever since I got concussion at school once, playing rugger, you know, well, I've really had a glass head, I'm afraid."

Stevens contrived a "painful" smile. But how much easier it was—the second patent lie—after the first. He was surprised at how little it bothered him, much less than he'd expected by far.

"Concussion." The doctor's brows went up. "I didn't know that. That's the trouble over histories in military hospitals." After a pause he said, "By the way, what school were you at?" When Stevens gave it the other grinned and gave his in return. "Used to play you. But I'd have been before your time, I fear."

"Still, you might remember Oldham, though. He left before I got there but he was quite a legend as a wing three."

"Scott, yes. Fellow was like greased lightning in his day. However, in the scrum your Venman was hard to beat. Now Venman and Rice…"

They reminisced amicably for a minute, comparing notes from a sporting past that seemed centuries away. Arabs squawked below. They got on to tactics—wingers, the pack. Stevens was always glad his dreary little school had played the rugby, not the association, code. It made after-dinner chat a bit more bearable in the mess. No school that amounted to anything except Winchester and Charterhouse, and it was quite obvious he hadn't been there, played soccer these days; it just wasn't a gentleman's, a winner's game.

"Well, I think we'd better take this pretty easy, you know." The doc placed a sympathetic hand on Stevens' shoulder. "You're sure you remember everything, all the time?"

"Sort of."

"I see. And still you can't lift your arm up higher than the shoulder?"

"'Fraid not, Doc. Wish I could."

That one was easy, too. Frankly, it was getting easier all the time. Behind the bed the nurse laughed gently. "He's quite enough of a handful as it is with one arm, Doctor."

"Right. Well, we'd like to keep you under observation a bit longer here."

"No footer, eh? And still c.b.?"

"Still confined to bed, I fear."

When the doctor had gone Sister Matson wheeled him back into the ward. There was some lusty applause at her more categoric movements.

Stevens smiled at her. "What an insinuation out there just now. Really."

She ducked to tidy his bed. Then she straightened with a slip of paper. "Don't try to play the innocent Amy with me, Captain Stevens. You ought to be ashamed of yourself."

"What do you mean?"

"The poet in you, I suppose—well, I'm afraid I simply haven't got any time for that sort of thing." She stalked superbly out of the ward, flushing furiously, yet—Stevens could not help noting—with a sly smile curved on her lips. He examined the limerick she had just picked up and replaced on his bedside locker. It was one of his neighbor officer's juicier imaginings, concerning the athletic activities of a one-legged lady from Gatwick.

It was three weeks before Stevens got up. Then he was permitted to stagger to the washroom for his morning shave. Already, however, he was growing used to the amenities. This more elaborate place looked infinitely less luxurious than had the little loo at 8A. Already there'd been complaints about the brand of soap supplied.

In the mirror his own face, tanned now from afternoons on the verandah, was thinner and somehow different. A different image. He felt glad of this. A new issue of battle dress waiting for him when he got back one morning. Too tight across the shoulders as per bloody usual. Then out of the window he saw the group of jerry prisoners swinging up past the hospital. They were singing their song:

Die Fahne hoch,

Die Reihen fest geschlossen ...

The old fear nagged at his vitals. Would he never get away from it, then?

A week later he became a day-room patient. It was only a matter of ten days or so now, he suspected, before his discharge. Sister Matson had mentioned that he'd have to go before the routine board. Soon, jolly soon, he knew, he'd be forced to think up something. Something pretty damn good. And finally, one blazing, aching, empty morning, Stevens began to formulate his plan.

CHAPTER SIX

It was after lunch that he strolled over to the sisters' mess, a marquee in the grounds. Several nurses looked at him with inquisitive smiles, but he was not allowed in. Sister Matson had to come to the door. She appeared, frowning with a surprise that was clearly pleased.

"And since when have day-room patients been allowed into the sisters' mess, Captain Stevens?" she asked in a mock-scolding manner.

After his constant contact with those coarse, lined faces of the desert—faces not given much water to wash in—Stevens found the one in front of his now sheer cream in the sunlight. It appeared to be fairly gurgling with hidden mirth.

"Look, Sister. The doc says I'm allowed out today. There's a truck into town at six. I know Akhdum's supposed to be a godforsaken hole but wouldn't you come in and have a slash with me?"

"Oh, I couldn't possibly."

"Why not?"

"Well, for one thing I'm on duty till seven."

"Get someone to exchange, or relieve you early. Listen, I'm sure you can do it." He persisted since he could see that the invitation was making her glad. "A dicky officer needs an escort his first time out in a wog dump like Akhdum," he urged her. "Come on. Say you'll do it."

"All right," she decided. "And thank you very much."

"You'll have to look after me, you know," he replied.

"Somehow, Captain Stevens, I have an inkling you're fairly good at doing that yourself."

Why had she said that?

A khamseen came up that evening. She sat in the front of the truck and he in the back, with three other officers and some orderlies going in ostensibly to pick up supplies and actually to get plastered as rapidly as possible.

As soon as they came in sight of the sea Stevens breathed in like a new man. There was a sense of freedom about the sea. He insisted on her getting down with him outside the town and walking in along the shore. She took off her shoes.

"Why don't we go in and bathe?" he asked her.

"Because I didn't bring my costume, that's why."

"Neither did I, but it doesn't matter."

"Ah, but it does, you know." That sly smile again. "Anyway, I'm absolutely positive you shouldn't go in your first time out."

"Ah, come on."

But he couldn't persuade her. She shook her head. "I'm also positive it wouldn't be good for you to see me starkers—that's something I'm certain of."

"Think of me as a doctor, then."

"You breathe too hard. No, really. Let's sit here, you mustn't overtire yourself first time off like this."

Such maternal solicitude was marvelous, and he readily yielded to it. He lay on the sand while the hot air rolled down off the hills. Lying there beside her, he felt the furtive rustle of papers in his leg pocket. Soon he'd have to examine properly what he'd taken off that jerry officer in Dark House. He'd put off doing so since he didn't want to be reminded … Ridgeworth's brains …

The wind began to blow more and more strongly and they strolled along the sand with it behind them into the town. Barefoot, she looked even bigger than before. Stronger, by God, in all the right places.

"Sister Matson, I fear you've been incorrectly dressed," he pronounced as they reached the road and she put her shoes back on. A few shapeless bundles watched them with hostile eyes, squatting on the dunes. "I'm afraid I'll have to turn you in to Matron."

"Do call me Lucy," she said.

"My name's Philip. Most people call me Phil. When they're not calling me other names."

She put a hand on him while she balanced to shake out a blancoed shoe. "Thanks."

They took a meal at a mess run by the Red Cross. Steamy soup. Diced beetroot beside a mysterious mound of "shepherd's pie." Lucy chose a fish whose fried crust broke at a touch to disclose a core of white flesh within.

"Ah, a fly," Stevens exclaimed. "Shall I send it back to the manageress, do you think?"

In fact, he was at home with this kind of grub, which Lucy considered just awful. She was still ridiculing the diet when they emerged again into the fetid African night, Stevens finally gorged on spotted Dick and she sated by two small prunes lurking skittishly under dollops of custard.

"Good old England," Lucy gasped.

Stevens felt weak. They sat down in a café of sorts and waited for the ten o'clock truck back. He ordered arak and she beer. The drink hit him right away.

"Christ! This would make a stevedore gag."

"It's only because you haven't had any for so long, you know. I'm quite sure you shouldn't be drinking it, Phil."

"I'm quite sure I shouldn't have done a lot of things," he replied quietly. He felt very close to her in this alien dump stinking of aniseed. Out in the street dogs cringed by. He thought: In some of these wog villages they still stone women. In the dim light of the bare bulb Lucy's face had loosened perceptibly. She was perspiring again, thickly, and began dabbing at her face with a handkerchief the size of a postage stamp. In such a setting, the "classy" hankie and her strong perfume excited Stevens profoundly.

"By the way, Lucy, you wouldn't happen to know when I'm going to be discharged, would you?"

"I did see. But—confidential information, I fear, Philip."

"I know. Have another glass of beer." Glad to look away from her, he bawled at the gyppie waiter. "What a hell of a race. Don't give a single damn about anything except their own skins. Now the boche you can respect, I admire them, and the eyeties too after a fashion. You can love them. But these sods would bash their grandmothers for the gold teeth in their clocks."

Lucy was right, though. After so protracted an abstinence the cheap arak was affecting him. He growled vaguely. "'Bout the only relationship I've ever had with the gyppie in all these years has been to tell him to get me something or beggar off." She laughed. Her hair shook. Within the uniform shirt her body moved. "You've been out some time, then?"

"Yes," he said slowly. (He was thinking: I mustn't give anything away.) "Yes, I'm a regular, Luce."

"Sorry. Nearly forgot myself, didn't I? I mean, no names, no pack-drill. How many times have we poor girls been told that everything to do with P.E.D.G. is highly secret?" She rolled amber eyes. "Won't do again. Promise. Honest injun."

"When's my board, Lucy?" The waiter—if you could call him such—had shuffled up the new round. "Come on now, it won't do any harm to tell me, will it?" The soapy beer slopped out of its suspiciously anonymous brown bottle into her glass. "Listen, I'm not going to give the game away to anyone. I just want to know, that's all. Frankly, I'm dying to get out of dock."

She paused, sipping her beer. A ring of froth clung as if gloatingly to her upper lip. She wiped it off with movements that seemed in very slow motion. Stevens could see that her handkerchief was soaked. "Week from tomorrow, then. I shouldn't have told you. But, there. And you absolutely mustn't tell, else they'll have my hide."

"And you do have such a very nice hide, Lucy. No, you needn't worry, I'll keep it to myself." He lowered his eyes. Method, he was thinking. It always wins. Objective one accomplished without loss. "You don't attend the board in person, do you?"

"No. It'll simply consist of the ward doctor, you know, Surgical, and the other one from Administration."

"Yet you send in my report."

"I most certainly do. In triplicate, no less."

They laughed. He turned the conversation. Once she got up to see if the truck had come. Patches of moisture made the linen cling to her. Standing in the doorway of that stage-set café, holding aside the beaded curtains, she looked out of another world. Stevens was reminded of a Somerset Maugham story a master had read them at school. A placid, bigboned English girl "doing her bit." But he had to be careful. Still waters sometimes ran deep. His head dropped suddenly into his hands. Would it work—with Lucy, would it work? A camel yawed by. She returned to the table. In a pimpled mirror he saw he'd slipped his right arm round her back. The flesh was firm. He felt her sigh.

"Behave, Phil." She pushed his hand away. "Remember, I do the ward report."

"This isn't the ward."

"I know. But."

"You're very glam, Lucy."

"Well, the truck's come, Captain S. We ought to go."

"Time, gentlemen, please."

He paid. They got up to go. But he hadn't bargained on feeling as weak as this. He had to hang on to her in bloody earnest now. Ducking the ancient flypapers, they made for the door.

"What a hole."

The smashed street, that rotting beggar pressing his tin mug at them in such a cringing way that it seemed put-on, fake, though undoubtedly wasn't, the savage lack of reality struck at Stevens. The twisted pepper tree at the corner personified agony. He clung to the mockingly old tree for a second, thinking, I've got to. I can't go back to P.E.D.G. Whatever happens, I can't do that.

"Phil! What did I say? You've had too much to drink."

"Sozzled, eh? No, I'm all right. Mush do this again, Lucy."

He was helping her into the cab of the truck. All at once, as he did so, he realized that he had extended his left arm well above the shoulder. He recoiled with a gasp. She didn't seem to have noticed it. The driver started up. The officers in the back were all but dead drunk. On the way Stevens joined in the unprintable, also virtually unspeakable "Ballad of King Farouk and Queen Farida" they all struck up. He hoped Lucy couldn't hear the ditty too clearly. Or did he? *Stanna shwayeh! O desire!* the chorus drove up appropriately brutally into the blank black night outside. Behind. *Quais ketir, King Farouk, let the swaddies have a look*! But no amount of filoos would help him, Stevens knew with a sudden bursting rush of loneliness and despair.

Back at the hospital he saw Lucy into the sisters' mess without more than a few muttered words. She too seemed to have gone quiet, uneasy. She simply thanked him and squelched strongly off in her nurse's shoes.

CHAPTER SEVEN

Finding himself alone in the day room next morning Stevens decided to examine the papers he'd taken off the dead German officer. His fingers shook as he began to handle them. And he cursed. When would he start to forget the nightmare—Loran's face, Ridgeworth's eyes, Marrow dead? They kept on rushing back at him, unexpectedly, like shades out of hell. That was why he'd never got himself to examine these papers thoroughly before. And he was surprised to find how much it meant to him to do so now. The baking Nissen hut began to throb before his eyes.

There were the usual letters. Photo of a girl? None. Receipt for some goods bought from a German depot in Sfax, it seemed. Methodical, the boche. Stevens tore these into methodically tiny fragments and chucked them in a waste-paper box. Then he found himself spitting on them. For a moment he retained the only item that seemed of any consequence, a driving license or *Führerschien* for the dead man whose first name was appropriately Siegfried. Taught as a commando to value and preserve such documents of identification, Stevens read the man's birth date and *Standort*. Under *Truppenteil USW* he learnt that he had indeed been, as Loran had correctly identified him, a staff brigadier. One of the winners who'd lost, muck him, thought Stevens bitterly. And he tore the license into tiny fragments also. Only the photographs were left.

Since he'd felt better Stevens hadn't studied these again and it was with more than the expected shock of recognition that he did so now. Five in all, somewhat crushed by this time, but all clearly photographs of paintings. Three showed no more than the painting and the frame. Two had been taken further off. One revealed the arch of a doorway and a long corridor lined with plaster casts and adorned with the insignia of crabs, either cut or painted on the wall. All but one were portraits of young women. Or of one young woman. Portraits all the way, definitely in the round, and abso-jolly-lutely starkers. Quite porno, in fact, thought Stevens observing the meticulous treatment of the lower regions. But although these front views frankly excited him, it was the nymph as she appeared in reverse, going not coming, that glued Stevens to two of these paintings. What a b.t.m., he thought, his throat thickening with desire. The buttocky little beast, she looked bloody sloe-eyed to the soul. He repocketed the photos with a chuckle. Then he went for the waste-paper box again, spilt its contents into the unused stove, and set fire to the papers with a match. The license crackled in the growing flame. He was streaming with sweat when a thin subaltern with a virtually Fu Manchu mustache and a patch over what had once been his right eye strolled into the Nissen some minutes later.

"Quite a pong," said the youth, sniffing the stove. "Been burning some smutty pictures, or something?" Stevens stared at him sharply. But placing his narrow bottom on a chair and his slippered feet on a table, the other settled to one of the two battered *Tatlers* which were the day room's reading matter, besides a copy of *Whitaker's Almanack* for 1937.

It was as Stevens began his last six days that the ward doctor, who had grown increasingly well-disposed to him, decided to lend him his own P.U. With the wounded pouring into 13C at the rate they now were, the doc himself had less and less time to use it. Stevens started driving Lucy into Alexandria in the evenings.

"Lovely eyes you've got, you know. Such a deep gold."

"They change to gray when I feel sexy."

He laughed. "Cat's?"

"That kind of thing."

"I'll remember that."

"Don't you dare."

Such stolen occasions were altogether different. Working overtime as she now was, Lucy was tired through and through and really felt in need of the brief breaks. He spotted it by the first drink she took, an ice-cold martini.

"Why do they serve these things with a petal floating in them here, do you suppose?"

"Dunno. And the veg." He indicated the olive. "Think it's buckshee? Nothing in this bloody country is. Down the drink, old scout, and I'll consume the rose." She laughed as he actually did so. "By Gor, that's the best bloody rose I've ever eaten."

"You know, Phil, I feel just like that young lady of Niger tonight."

"With the smile on the face of the tiger? How about the monopede from Gatwick?"

"Well, not quite yet."

Later. Driving back in the dark.

"Please, Phil, use both hands. These roads were strafed last night."

"Wish I could. Only, I've got to steer with one."

Now they were sitting on a terrace filled with flower-pots and dark faces while the soggy *plunk* of well struck tennis balls came up to them.

He said, "Lucy cat, can you imagine, are people actually queueing up still at Victoria Station?"

"I imagine they are, you know."

"I can't picture it really. It's another world. I'm going to be lost when I go back."

"You won't be the only one."

He took her hand. "Tell me what those pills are they've been giving me."

"Phil, I'm not meant to. Please don't ask me that."

"You might tell a pore old wounded Tommie, Sister."

"No, truly."

"O.K. No names, no pack-drill, as you put it to me once yourself." He clapped his hands and an immaculate, soft-skinned waiter wearing a ruby fez came up. "Do that again. Mine was Younger's."

"So's mine this time," Lucy interrupted. The "boy" bowed off, a look of supercilious scorn on his face. "I've been drinking too much of late. Gin puts on the poundage, and it always seems to end up on the back of my lap." She smiled. "To be honest, pretty well everything I do these days seems to be immoral, illegal, or just plain fattening."

The drinks arrived. "Here's hoping," he said. "Heave ho." They chimed glasses and drank. Swiftly. That was another characteristic of North Africa he'd noticed. When you had the opportunity you didn't waste any time getting pickled. "Hell, I'd almost forgotten what the good stuff tasted like. What all this..." He waved his big hand. A band was playing Strauss. Someone was swigging rum nearby; he was certain he could whiff it. "Dance, Luce old thing?"

Her breasts almost shoved him off, they were so hard and deep. Fantastic, he thought. Bloody grapefruits. Later, back at their table, he returned to his topic.

"See, you happened to be there when I told the doc I'd had concussion at rugger once. Frankly, I did black out on that particular mission during which I got hit."

"You did?"

"Yes. But I didn't tell the doc so because I want like anything to get back to my unit. Just as soon as I damn well can."

"Tell me, Phil. You were hit over the head?"

"Bloody hard."

"The X-rays showed nothing."

"Well, I was clunked all right, believe you me. I didn't know what happened for quite a while. Only," he put up a hand, "for Gawd's sake, Luce, don't give on to the doc, will you? Promise?"

She was biting her lip. "I ought to tell you something."

"For heaven's sake," he protested, "you mustn't tell that doctor, whatever happens. Christ no. Only reason I mentioned it to you was because I'm partially shot away, see. And I trust you, cat. Why I've not even told . . ."

"What?"

"Well, you know. I bump into things still in the day room. Drifting spells. I mean, things get out of focus."

There came a pause between them. She said softly, "You really oughtn't to be driving yet by rights." She shook her head with a troubled expression. "Phil, I want to tell you something too. Confidence for confidence. Promise me you'll keep it to yourself now. I mean it."

"I promise," he replied. "Honest injun."

"You see," she said, making rings on the table with the bottom of her glass, "those pills you've been put on are Benzedrine. The doctor was afraid you had what's known as narcolepsy. It happens sometimes with a head wound. If there's the first possibility—no, I'm serious, Phil—of your having been concussed in that business, you owe it not only to yourself but to any man you might command to stay out of it."

"Stay out of it!" He produced the exclamation with exactly the right shade of disgust he'd been rehearsing. Disgust was an emotion easy to simulate after a period of active service in North Africa. "What the hell are you talking about, Luce? I've got to get back to P.E.D.G. Don't you understand? I'm a regular. That's all I know."

Again she shook her head. "It may be hard for you, Phil, but there it is. You've just told me something that might be very very serious. This blacking-out story puts me under a genuine obligation. You simply can't go back to command men in action if there's the first possibility of narcolepsy. Oh, hell," she concluded wearily. She sought his hand: a real need. "Here I am jawing away. I've hardly been out here any time at all and look at the way I'm behaving. Anyhow. Just anyhow."

He squeezed her fingers. "What made you go into nursing, cat? You don't look the usual type."

"I was a V.A.D. at the start, then one or two things happened, and I switched over." She smiled. "Now, like you, I'm a regular. Rough, isn't it?"

"But I've got to get back to my men."

"No, I really mean it. Quite serious. I'll have to report what you told me."

He looked down. She mustn't see his eyes. Luckily she abruptly excused herself at that and headed for the ladies' room.

For a moment he watched her rhythmic gait as she strode on her rubber-soled shoes. Yes, Lucy was built like one of those pretties in that brigadier's "art" photos. Nothing too big but, sure as peaches were sweet, absolutely nothing too small. He flicked up a waiter.

"One gin and no mafeesh." As far as Stevens knew, mafeesh was the wog's convenient way of saying, There ain't none.

"Geen, sah'b?"

"That's what I said, you fathead."

When it came he poured it into Lucy's beer, then gave the jigger to the waiter, who removed it poker-faced. The gyppie had got beyond scorn with this foreign dog, this Christian filth, it was clear. The band had changed its tune and Stevens, mouth ajar, suddenly paled.

Deine Schritte kennt sie, deinen zieren Gang,
alle Abend brennt sie, doch mich vergass sie lang…

He hated that tune. Oh God, how he hated it!

"Mos' unsa'sfactory. And you know what," a voice was belligerently cawing across the adjoining table, "you know wha-at, old man?"

"No. What?"

"Never saw a drop for a month. Vair vair unsa'sfactory. Not a drop. One whole month. Fact I'd go so far as to say two months. Nothing out of Alex, nothing out of Cairo."

"Vair vair unsa'sfactory, agree."

Stevens shifted his head. The man had a small face with the baked cheeks and pale forehead of so many in the desert who wore peaked caps. His eyes popped angrily over the table at a youngish major in perfect Sheapherd's rig—faded khaki, lanyards galore, chocolate suede boots with crepe soles of caricatural dimensions. The band stopped.

"An' thar we were," the voice now nearly bawled. "*Without a drop.*"

"Vair vair unsa'sfactory."

"Mess sergeant told me it was hopeless."

"Rotten luck."

"Useless to indent."

Idly listening to the fatuous back-chat, Stevens suddenly realized that what this shower of base-wallahs were bleating about was a shortage of bottles of Worcester sauce. Bloody marvelous. Christ Almighty, he thought with sudden savagery, I'd like to stick the Worcester up their jacksies and put those twerps in the line. Maybe they'd learn how to get corns on their knees from crawling about a bit.

Lucy strode back, moving past the tables with an easy motion of her hips that didn't disturb the carriage of her upper body at all. Her shoes made that curiously exciting sound like sponges being squeezed out. She sat down and crossed her legs with the special rustle indicative of silk, rather than the still scarce nylon—Stevens preferred silken leggings for his ladies.

"Feel awful, cat."

"Why so, Capitaine?"

"Tell you all that. 'Bout my dizzy spells, so on."

"And I'm jolly glad you did. Where other people are concerned…"

"What's the worst that can happen?"

"Oh," she retorted cheerfully, "you can be court-martialed for a self-inflicted wound, I imagine. There's a man in Ward 18 who's going to be, so you won't be alone." Stevens shut his eyes. Give nothing away. Then he heard her laugh. She was scoffing the beer he'd spiked. "Oh, this is bitter." She made a wry face.

"I know. So's mine."

"I'm sure Younger's isn't usually like this."

"Everything tastes different out here. I.e., worse."

She smiled. "Bolo, Phil? I mean you are, aren't you. You must have had a rough time out here. Just so long as you haven't doctored this brew."

Across the room, over the scarlet fezzes of the waiters, Stevens saw that some joker had struck up an English pub sign. WYBMADIITY. WHICH BEING INTERPRETED—*Will You Buy Me A Drink If I Tell You?* AND IN REVERSE—*You Thought I Intended Drinking A Mild But You're Wrong.* Stevens stared at it, intrigued. Variation of the usual IYB-MADIBYO—*If You Buy Me A Drink I'll Buy You One.*

Lucy was saying, "You ought to know that after what's happened, with that gammy arm of yours and all, they're practically bound to category you."

"Downgrade me!" Stevens managed to get the stare of horrified opposition into his face again. "But that's absurd. I'm as fit …"

"As a fiddle, I know. But this is different. Try to get used to the idea, my dear." She spoke muzzily. "In ease it happens. For I'm afraid it's going to."

"But I've got to get back to my unit."

"Now stop." She was right, he mustn't go too far. This time when she drank she made a proper face. "This is funny, Phil. You're certain you wouldn't have laced it while I was away, would you?"

"Me!" he laughed loudly. "Let's try another. May taste better." He made to signal the waiter, but she stopped him.

"No, really, this is more than enough. I feel squiffy as it is." She stood up somewhat uncertainly. "Don't you think it would be nice to leave this place? I mean, it is pretty much blue death and ivy, isn't it?"

"Is it?" Apart from being unable to believe in the place, he'd thought it vaguely posh. The gilded carvings, the palms, the ferns. "O.K., let's drive out to a beach and bathe it off."

Clearing the chair behind her he felt that spider down his spine again. Far across, on the other side of the room, not far from the WYBMADIITY sign, was a familiar face, an image from Stevens' past. At first uncertain, he suddenly placed the beggar. The M.O. who had patched him up in camp was part of a group of four, chatting away with a pipe in one hand.

Hurrying out after Lucy, Stevens realized this most likely meant the unit had been pulled back from special patrol duty for a while. About time, too. There had been the usual rumors of a rest going the rounds for months. In the evening outside he shivered. He got in the P.U. beside Lucy and drove as fast as the old bus would allow. You had to drive fast here. Thank God, he thought, there weren't so many days left now before his board.

Lucy had her costume on under the uniform this time. The jersey clung to that really first-class flesh. She was remarkably generously endowed, and in prime condition.

"Come on, race you in."

He caught her, of course, as she'd intended he should, and dragged her squealing into the surf and suddenly, as they plunged in and he was about to lash out in a crawl ahead of her, he heard her cry—"Watch that arm now, Phil!"

His body tautened under the water's grip. She'd have seen. "Thanks."

He subsided into a genteel breast-stroke, left arm low. Lucy swam powerfully, with a methodical concentration. He let her get out to change first. The sopping costume had rucked up those superb buttock-cheeks and she tugged absently at it there as he followed behind her. A perfectly slung pelvis, he considered almost professionally, the fat padded firm and high and emphasizing the waist. Not to mention those outstanding gifts above.

"I like you wet," he said.

"Wet inside and out today, I fear. But that sobered me muchly, thank heavens."

With her head bent as she toweled her hair her neck was the traditional peaches-and-cream, and he noticed—with a kind of inexplicable apprehension—that it seemed perfectly round. A nape that made you regret not being an executioner, by God. Just the job to chop off. Her back was strangely long. And there was that splendid innocence about her belly, too, as if she'd suddenly grown, so that he was almost surprised when he went up to her and found that in his arms her head only came up to the middle of his chest, scarcely above the solar plexus, really. The place where it hurt most to be hit. She shivered when he kissed her, then proved unexpectedly expert in the clinch, working her tongue inside the corners of his mouth, seizing the back of his head very strongly, and snorting through her nostrils in a satisfied rhythm. They motored back in comparative silence. The doc had been firm about his taking a Benzedrine pill before he drove, so he slipped one into his mouth on her instructions first.

The next day Stevens heard that his board was set for an afternoon early the following week. Lucy was tied up all evening and he couldn't seem to get to see her at all. He wondered if he'd gone too far and cursed himself over and over again. But the day after that, he collared the P.U. once more, and she accompanied him willingly enough into Alex.

The city was more elegant than Cairo, of course, but still far too much a summary of the wog temperament to be bearable to Stevens. To be despised, to be made to feel futile, all by a shower of flaming, cowing sods, a race who lived in a kind of exasperated peace with the present. With absolute apathy. All for Allah. Id est, for Jack. For the moment. No future. It was a sin to plan for the future in their flaming code and to a Westerner, Stevens dimly reflected, this came through as an absolute aimlessness, a devastating lack of purpose or "drive."

It rained and they went to a flick. Gangsters snapped out of the sides of their mouths, all about "dahls" and "dahlars", guns duly "spoke," and a Venus in lamé writhed on a sofa while a Latin lover smacked her face. It was a pretty enough fantasy but one that seemed somehow more substantial than the one they went out to after the picture gave up in the last reel. The wog proprietor was lying asleep across the entrance door and they had to step over his body into the aggressive banality of the Rue Nebi Daniel.

"Look, Luce. You hungry?"

"Not muchly. You?"

"No. Let's get a bottle and shove off onto a beach somewhere."

They drank the warm Scotch in the back of a truck overlooking a deserted, dirty beach. She relaxed visibly after the drink.

"All I could get." He lied easily now. "That Naafi I tried didn't have any beer."

"Guaranteed to make you see double and feel single in a climate like this, I'll bet."

He kissed her ear. It smelt of soap. He had picked up, too, after the drink. Lucy had come in uniform as usual; her collar was starched and it felt very good holding her close to him like this. All his sense of collapse faded. The linen she wore had a much-washed quality that made it adhere with especial femininity to the curves of a body ready to burst exuberantly out of it. Dammit to hell, if one could only stop that monster Time. He moved. She moaned, pushed him off.

"Mustn't."

"Come on, then. Let's go in."

They bathed for hours and, when the sun sank, retired to the car and drank some more. Dusty fronds lined the road behind, along which a few mangy asses were occasionally prodded by filthy wogs.

"The way they treat their animals," he said to her. "It's nothing short of bloody criminal. When I first came out I beat one of those bastards up for assaulting his mule. But what's the use?"

A donkey driver came into view just then, passing a house with yellow jasmine and calling out "Aieee!" to his animal.

"*Khallih*, you bastard," Stevens shouted half-heartedly at him. "*Khabayuh*, you mucker." Vaguely he wondered who lived there, envying him. "Since everything's decreed by Allah in this godforsaken hole," he explained to Lucy, "you're completely free to do anything you flaming please, you know. Notice how the wog is a man of immediate decisions, unattached to anything else. Except banging up some more cash for himself. And of course morality in our sense of the word simply doesn't exist for them." He stopped at that. The Arab donkey driver went by grinning, calling, "*Ou 'allah'*?" shyly and derisively.

When darkness fell Stevens laid two Army blankets out in the back of the P. U. "Be more comfortable like this, Luce old girl." He didn't look at her as he put the backboard up. "That sodding khamseen has started again."

While the light leaked painfully out of the pitiless, foreign sky, they sat like school children at a "treat," sipping their Scotch. He pulled her to him suddenly.

"Phil, I'm really and truly unsure how wise this is."

"Your eyes have gone gray." A tawny fleck in the depths of one.

"Well, let go of me for a moment and I can help."

When she was half bare he said, "There. I knew you had a lovely hide, what did I say. I'm sorry about this arm of mine."

"You seem to be doing quite all right with it, my man."

"Keep that on," he pleaded. "Don't take any more off, please."

"Want to tear away the last shreds yourself, is that it?" She gurgled as she slipped out of the final garment. "Well, I want to be nude, nude, nude."

She gave a vigorous, a victorious, wriggle under him and he felt her cold skin. The sea-bathing had iced her nipples which prodded strong as thumbs, wrinkleless and tough on their darkly raised aureoles.

"Cat," he groaned.

"I say, I do feel awfully single. Is it very wicked of me, d'you think?"

"No."

"The trouble with you, mein Kapitän, is that you're too sexy by far. Bet you could kill a girl like that—I mean a little girl. . . ."

Kill, kill! He tried to take her but she held him for a second.

"You know what virgo intacta means, don't you, Phil?"

"Yes."

"Well, I'm not."

He didn't know what to say. "That's all right, Luce. I didn't think you were, actually."

"Mind?"

"No."

"Good."

He entered her well-nigh brutally. At the moment of satisfaction she again held him from her while an oddly anxious expression crowded her features.

"What's up?" he asked.

"Promise me one thing."

"What's that?"

"Don't do this unless you really love me, will you? Promise me that, please."

"Yes, Luce, I promise, cat." But it came out as if he were begging. "I love you, soft catness."

She was cold-skinned, but perspiring. The combination piqued him enough to let him forget his usual sense of sin. It seemed only moments later that they were driving away, off down the dusty path. The blonde beach had turned into a cruel platinum behind them. Dagger color, really. As he drove he was aware of Lucy's placid profile beside him. The lashes lay heavy on slackened cheeks. Once, drawing at a cigarette, she said, "Odd, how randy this country makes you feel. You were very delicious, you know, Philip."

He said nothing. He'd got what he'd set out to achieve, hadn't he? He'd accomplished his plan, his mission.

It was just after ten that he left her off at the sisters' mess, parked the car back near the doctor's quarters, gave the key and distributor arm to the good medico's batman, and went back into the white building that housed his own ward. In the corridor a tall dark sister accosted him.

"Oh, Captain Stevens." She gave a pointed smile. "I did wonder when you'd be coming back in. I went over to the mess but Mattie wasn't back.'

For a second he was forced to think who that was. The nurse lowered her lids. She can see it all over me, he thought hotly.

"All right, I've returned Sister Matson," he said testily. Should he add, Bright clean, and slightly oiled?

"You see, there's someone wants to see you."

"See me? At this time of night?"

"Yes. It seems they only have a short time. In fact, they only arrived ..."

"They!" Blood drained from his head in spasmic faintness. Physical satiety had weakened him; he could feel it through his bloody bones.

"That's right. Some officers came in a quarter of an hour ago. I understand they know you." She added coyly, "Of course, seeing the P.E.D.G. flashes, I didn't ask any questions, I know how secretive you people ..."

"P.E.D.G.!"

"Well, one of them wasn't."

"Where are they?"

"They're over in the day room now. There's no one else there, naturally. Please be careful of the blackout, won't you. I told them you were due back in the ward by ten and they said they'd like to wait."

He tried, "Oughtn't I to go to bed, Sister?" But that was only giving his fear away. He'd have to face the music.

She shrugged. "You've time." Her eyes gave a brief twinkle. "Don't worry. I won't report you."

CHAPTER EIGHT

Swinging on his heel, Stevens went back down the corridor, down and out again, across the day room. He mopped at his forehead with one of his aunt's silk handkerchiefs. The sky was now a deep indigo and a dog out of nowhere prowled at his feet as he walked. One isolated wild fig tree seemed to emanate a feline odor as he passed. It was still far too hot.

Through a chink in blackout felt the Nissen lanced out light. A feeling of weakness so strong that he really began to wonder if he were genuinely narcoleptic overcame him for a second. Those godawful African stars, bright as bloody fury, just like so many little diamond chivs all prodding at his flesh—they seemed to bear down at him now from overhead with a relish of renewed malice. It was as he'd thought. Looking in, peeping through the chink, the nerves tightened on separate wires in his big body as he identified the man in the aluminum chair facing the window. Stevens clenched his fists, closed his eyes, raised his head back on his neck. The great thing to do was keep his story straight. He opened the door. Three figures rose.

"Phil!" exclaimed the lengthy adjutant with a kind of hesitant concern as he came forward, extending one hand.

"Well, Wilfred." Stevens forced a grin. "Welcome to Thirteen C. 'Fraid I can't exactly offer you gentlemen a round of bubbly. We're not allowed near the bottle, I fear, but what else can I do you for?"

"This is our Major Taylor." The Adj still spoke worriedly as he introduced Stevens to a short, bustling major with almost blue lips. "He's just joined from the Rifle Brigade." A well-built captain stood on Wilf's other side and Stevens now saw what he hadn't previously seen from outside, but which the sister sending him over had presumably caught, namely that this officer was wearing the insignia of the Military Police. Immediate dislike registered in Stevens' mind—why was it he'd always hated coppers? "This is Captain Ellis," the adjutant was saying, the anxious expression deepening as he spoke (Stevens had seen a similar expression on the face of a schoolmaster instructed to cane him). "Well, I've told Captain Ellis just how very highly we in P.E.D.G. regard you, Phil, but—I mean, let's all sit, shall us?"

He drew Stevens into the semicircle they'd made round the monstrously redundant stove, the same one in which Stevens had burnt the staff officer's papers. Their boots made much noise on the flooring of harsh concrete. And how frightfully dingy the day room looked, all deserted and ill-lit like this.

"Back from Alex?" asked the man called Ellis.

Stevens said, "Yes." Grudgingly. It was already hard to fight off three.

"Not a bad burg. You feeling better now?"

"Fine."

"Look after you all right here?" asked the major gruffly.

"Yes, O.K., thanks, sir." Especially the ward sister, he supposed he should have added. A bit more of this back-chat went on, then the M. P. bloke spoke up.

"I hear that arm of yours is none too good."

"Been having a word with me poor old doc?" Stevens mildly inquired.

"He seems like a stout chap," cut in the adjutant. "But I'm sorry to say he told us—keep this under your hat, mind, Phil—evidently there's a good chance of your being downgraded when they let you out of here, old boy."

"Ah, over my dead body, Wilf."

Ruefully the other shook his head. Somehow, Stevens thought, the beret he had on only made him look more than ever like a country squire dressed up for some house-party charade. "It's on the cards, Phil, and you ought to know it. Frankly, that's why we dropped in to see you."

"Chin-wag, eh? Glad you did."

Flash of light. Lit cigarette. "The er ... group has moved. And is going to again." He added, "Major Taylor here and I are actually returning from a rather protracted recce for a new site. Ellis met us by prearrangement at Alex. Sorry we're so late."

Ellis in Alex, Stevens thought swiftly. "How can I help you, Wilf?"

"P.E.D.G. draws its personnel from a variety of outfits, I don't have to remind you of that."

"I know." This Ellis sod was watching him avidly, no less.

"In the normal run of events the C. O. and myself would simply receive your report. Unfortunately you had to be sent straight back here and we've never really heard all the ins and outs of what happened on Operation Cabbage, have we? The C. O.'s temporarily hors de comb' with jaundice. Major Taylor is our two i.c. and thus personally standing in."

How frightfully nice, Stevens thought. "I understand," he said. He looked slowly round at the M. P. officer.

"Captain Ellis." the adjutant went on to explain, "has requested to be present. I felt sure you wouldn't mind. A mere formality, Phil. M.P. are fussy about their blokes, as I'm sure you know. And one of 'em bought it with you."

"Marrow was killed," he said coldly.

"Captain Ellis simply wants to know everything you can give us on Corporal Morrow."

"I tell you I saw him shot."

"I know. I'm sorry." The Adj's tone grew kindlier. "Frankly, I couldn't hate this more, Phil. I know just how you must feel after a show like that. Losing all your men and all. By the by, you did hear, didn't you?"

"No. What?"

"Von Schultz was recalled to Germany. Some top-level stuff in case of projected Atlantic or Channel landings, so I gather. All the same, we can say it was a damn good shoot, what. One of their staff, a brigadier, copped it properly, so we found out later. You got him nicely, it seems."

"Loran got him," Stevens said thickly.

"Poor Tom."

"You put up a—a damn good show," mumbled the major through darkish lips.

"Look here, Wilf," Stevens broke in urgently, "I'll be getting back to the unit in a week at latest. There's absolutely nothing in this business of my being down-graded and seconded to something else, believe you me."

"We've talked to your doctor, Phil."

"Muck him, I'll get back, I say. I will, Wilf, I swear it. And when I do I'll tell you blighters all about that dizzy mission you saw fit to send me on. I'll bumf it in umptiplicate for you how we didn't stand an earthly from the start, how's that now?"

"I know just how you must feel." Uneasily the adjutant stared at soot-hued boots, gleaming under the whacks from his leather-shod stick. "But we have Ellis here. We do have to ask you to go over the whole thing with us, Phil. From start to finish, if you would."

"But I won't remember everything. That's the point, Wilf, don't you see? Blanks in my memory, man. The think-tank not connecting quite. I mean, I was smacked by a jerry getting away and I bloody can't remember everything." His voice lowered to a pleading whisper. He was glad to see them exchanging glances. "See, I've been hiding it from the doc. If I told him how much I'd forgotten, he'd category me for sure. Think I'd had concussion, all that sort of rammel."

For a second no one spoke. Heart heaving, Stevens wondered if he'd gone too far. He added hastily, "I was concussed at school once. Rugger game. You can check."

"I played rugger," interjected Major Taylor happily. "Please believe me, Stevens, we do regret this being in any way necessary. But it is. Take all the time you want. However, that mission did represent rather a serious loss of life, as doubtless you realize."

As doubtless he ... Jesus Christ, the chump. Had he ever seen a man with his brains on display? "I know," he went on, with a nod. "The whole crowd bought it. As a matter of fact, sir, there's not much more I can say than that."

The Adj was now frowning most unhappily, and twirling his stick prettily over one knee. "That's the odd thing, Phil. We've never had a show quite like that before. Now please don't think we're being nosey. Needless to say, we all have complete faith in your ability and integrity. Still, the fact remains that we've never had a patrol go out and lose every man, barring its officer in command."

Stevens managed a wry smile. "You mean, it doesn't look too good, eh, Wilf?"

"We're not insinuating anything, Phil. Simply that for formality's sake we've got to go over the ground with you personally. Brigade are interested."

"They would be."

"It'd help an awful lot, old man," piped in the little major. "I mean, if you could."

CHAPTER NINE

If he could. Was there any bleeding choice? Luckily he had by now rehearsed this moment (how many times?) lying in that torpid stupor of the ward day after day. So that when the adjutant added, “You can speak quite freely here, Phil, just as you wish,” he sighed and pitched into his story.

Indeed, it was no story as such. The best way to fib, Stevens knew, was to twist the truth as little as possible. School taught you that, if nothing else. In any case, the M.P. mucker watching him with that bastard look, as if he were about to jump out of the window or something, was only interested in Marrow. And Marrow had been killed, very dead, in action.

When he got to that part, in fact, and began to describe the pajama-ed German who had potted Marrow tumbling down the stairs, Stevens felt his skin tingling and he realized he was giving these blighters a star account, a graphic recital that would ill accord with his supposedly blank spots later on. He fuzzed over the scene in the room with the brigadier as much as he could. Then came the lie. He braced himself for it.

Major Taylor was gazing at the concrete floor, his lips sagging. He had listened in silence, commenting every now and then in a high-pitched voice, “Poor feller,” or “Damn luck,” or “Rotten shame.” Stevens guessed the man hadn’t seen much action and he was tempted to lay it on thick.

“When we left the room I all but skidded in that blood and muck. You know, wet brains, so forth. Yes, damn near took a purler. Loran was coming behind me. . . .”

"This was in the hall, right?"

The sodding M.P. type again.

"Yes. I seem to remember that Loran and I both stood there for a sec, listening hard and wondering what we ought to do. Have a last bash for the general, see if any of the other fellows were still all right, or..."

"Or?" cut in Captain Ellis.

"Well, pack it in. You know, clear off."

There was silence for a second. It was broken by Ellis following up, "Until this point you yourself hadn't actually been hit?"

"No. I was bumped about then, I think. See, I was moving across the hall, stepping over Marrow's body, when a big Hun coming in... or something... Anyhow, all I can remember now is being outside with the other two holding on to me. There was a jerry there too, and he'd also had it. I think I killed him." A further lowering of his head seemed to resurrect that smudged mess where the face ought to have been. "The whole cowing, frigging, sodding place had woken up... I'm sorry, forgive me, what I mean is that then Loran, I think, suggested it was no earthly use, we'd have to skedaddle."

He stopped to gulp in air. It felt thick and hot. Go easy now. He'd drunk too much in Alex. Making love to Lucy had sapped his vigor, that was for sure, he felt all tom up, blast it. The others remained silent after his outburst. Then the Adj said, "He was new. It was his first outing, you know."

"After that," Stevens completed, "I believe we decided to run to a hut some distance away from the house. I got there first."

The adjutant held up a hand. "Let's just get this straight now, Phil. For the record, I mean. There were the three of you left, correct?"

"That's correct. Loran, Ridgeworth, me."

"Then why did you, as senior officer, go first?"

He didn't falter. Ready for that one, all right. "Wilf, it was for their safety, man. In the darkness there none of us could see for the life of us where the jerry was at all. Just weaving away somewhere out there in front of us, swanning about, that's all we knew. I thought if I went first and they were waiting, why then I'd draw their fire, see, so that the other two could escape in the opposite direction. As it happened, the way I chose was probably the clearest."

"Might have sprung a nice little pencil-mine for 'em, too," Major Taylor added gravely. "One of their nice little debol-lockers, thank you. No, I think you were perfectly correct in your appreciation of the situation. You cleared the path."

"Well, that's what we did," Stevens said.

"Phil always was the methodical kind," put in the adjutant kindly.

"What happened to Ridgeworth?" asked the M.P. captain.

The adjutant laughed. "We don't want to turn this into an inquisition. Please don't feel that, Phil."

Not much, he thought. "It's all right," he said. "Ridgeworth bought it getting to the hut."

"So he didn't reach the hut, is that it?" Ellis pursued.

Stevens would have liked to take the man to that hut and wrap the bleeding place round his cowing M.P. neck. He perceived a trap. If ever a boche P.O.W. were taken, one who'd been present at Dark House that night in person, this story of his might be shaken. Once again, he realized, it would pay to stick as damn close to the truth as he possibly could.

"No. Ridgeworth was hit on the way there. He couldn't run very fast, you see. He was clipped in the groin."

"And killed?"

Stevens simply stared at the banana martinet. "What do you think?" He was grateful for the adjutant's muttered, "Oh, my God," at that moment, and he himself added, "No, he wasn't killed outright."

"So that he may still be alive?"

"I fear not. Ridgeworth got it in the guts, to put it as mildly as I can, and as he lay there Loran ran and picked the poor devil up and dragged him into the hut. To be frank, I'm not too clear about that part of it."

"And then?"

"After that I believe we decided that we'd make our getaway, Loran first, myself carrying Ridgeworth the best I could after. Unfortunately Loran ran into a hail of fire some fifty yards from the hut, and was killed; then I ran out in the opposite direction and almost at once felt Ridgeworth struck as I lugged him on my back. I dropped him and found he'd been hit in the head. He was obviously dead, or dying fast, so I left the poor bogger and ran for it. On the way, as you know, I was winged."

There was another silence as he finished.

"Thanks, Phil." The adjutant said it with respect. "I rather thought it must have been something like that." He turned to the major on his left. "Anything further to ask, sir?"

The little man cleared his throat and clenched his eyes tight together. "I don't think so. No, I don't think so at all. We'll just have to recommend a verdict of Missing, eh?"

"Missing, Presumed Killed, sir."

"Yes, I think that'd be kinder on the next-of kin," Stevens said. "It's pretty certain everyone bought it all right."

"Then I think that's all we need to know. As you can see—" the adjutant glanced about him—"Operation Cabbage was an unpleasant do. Captain Stevens acted according to the highest traditions of our force. As a matter of fact, Phil, the C.O. wanted you to know you're to get a mention in despatches for the way in which you've conducted these very hazardous missions over a considerable period of time." His stick slapped. He turned to the M.P. wallah. "Now then. Have you anything further to ask?"

"Yes."

"Please remember that Captain Stevens has been through some pretty rough scraps with us. It's no fun to lose a whole patrol, not to mention getting clipped yourself into the bargain."

Ignoring the adjutant's tone, Captain Ellis slowly straightened. "You take any papers off that staff officer, by any chance?"

Stevens said, "You aren't by any chance suggesting that this thing was fishy, are you?"

"Phil!" Wilf's exclamation was punctuated by Major Taylor's again hoarsely clearing his throat.

"No, but are you?"

"I do think it's going a bit far, pressing a chap like this," said the adjutant.

Ellis showed no embarrassment whatsoever. "You P.E.D.G. people are taught to bag all the papers you can. You must have gone over a relatively high-ranking officer like that, provided there was any time at all, it'd have been the first thing you'd have done surely. And nothing seems to have been turned in." He added, "So far."

At that moment a rhythmic buzzing, a note of irritation in the air they'd noticed, crystallized into an aggressive drone; this, in turn, ceded to an angry, ascending low. Stevens stood up. The adjutant went for the lights. This evil din increased. There was a scuffle. The bombs, when they fell, created a dragging air in the Nissen hut and were followed, after an interval, by an animal rending of the leaves of a tree outside and a clanging, furious and bitter, of shards of metal against the tin of the hut. The plane could be heard receding. For a second Stevens thought it was recircling, then knew instinctively it wasn't. Someone could be heard shouting, quite calmly, outside. The adjutant put on the lights. He and Stevens were standing. Major Taylor had remained in his seat, where he maintained a perplexed expression. The M.P. officer, however, had gone to ground under a rickety bridge table and could now be seen, very red in the face, brushing at his knees.

The adjutant smiled at Stevens. "Sixty yards, would you say?"

"Nearer eighty, Wilf."

"Miles away." He added, "All the same, too close for a hospital."

"I imagine it was that ack-ack battery nearby. The blighters play whist most of the time anyway." As he spoke, however, the battery got belatedly into action, pumping frantically into the sky. In a pause in the firing, which shook the Nissen to its core, Stevens said, "To be fair, Wilf, they lay off as much as poss for the patients' sake." When he turned to the M.P. captain it seemed that those photos he had on him burnt through the cloth of his pocket. "In answer to your question," he pronounced patiently, "I didn't nab anything off that jerry. I'm afraid that in the rush we didn't stop to buff up our bleeding nails, you know."

"Well, that's all then." Major Taylor spoke cheerfully, indeed with relief. He extended a hand. Stevens took it. (Very small.) "Dash it, sorry you got hit but these things, well, they happen, don't you know." The new two-in-command produced this hesitantly, out of wobbly lips. "You're a big man and a fine target. I should take it easy for a while, if I were you."

"Yes, I intend to, sir."

They all walked out to the jeep. The guns were still intermittently banging.

"Too bad about Tom Loran," said the adjutant.

"I know. He seemed to have a real gift for judo."

"Yes, we knew that when we took him on. Also that von Schultz occupied their house and killed his father. Beyond removing a deal of portable property to Germany, I gather. No, I'm sorry Tom didn't bag the general, he wanted to awfully, you see."

"It's tough to buy it on one's first outing like that."

"That Brig you got was one of his henchmen. Notice any Norwegian service ribbons on his chest, by any chance? Oh yes, both of them came up through KRIPO."

"What's that?"

"Kriminalpolizei. The toughest of the tough. Torturers, really. You know, the irony over Marrow was that we were thinking of pulling him in. Yes, indeed," and the adjutant chucked long legs over into the tiny vehicle, "as luck would have it, that was probably going to be Corporal Marrow's last patrol. We'd had a report that he'd been showing signs of nervousness, possibly beginning to crack up. Speak not ill of the glorious dead, but you didn't see any signs of that sort of thing in the man, did you, Phil?"

"To tell the truth, yes, I did."

"In what way?" asked the M.P. captain sharply. He seemed to have got himself together by now and had seated himself in the back of the jeep.

"He looked scared stiff in the boat. I noticed he was trembling."

"Is that all?"

"It's quite enough in our outfit," rapped the adjutant decisively. "Oh no, someone like Phil knows the symptoms all right. No aspersions, mind, but Marrow was undoubtedly going. And who can blame him, poor lad, he'd done more than his stint with us. Our sort of life, Captain Ellis, can play merry hell on the nerves, let me assure you."

"Poor feller," added Major Taylor.

"By the way, Phil," Wilf now went on, "we'll be sending back your gear."

"I see. Will Wright be bringing it here?"

The other shook his head. "Since you left, we've had to return Wright to regimental duty. Your regiment, of course. He left a week ago."

Stevens pondered. "Speak to him before he left, Wilf?"

"Oh yes. Usual thing. How glad we were with his work for us. Etcetera. He very much wanted to see you again, actually. Told me to let you know he hoped to catch up with you one day. Funny thing, he put it just like that." The Adj laughed heartily. "Since he was about the only bloke seconded from your particular lot, Phil, perhaps he will at that. Good-by, and—good luck."

Major Taylor's lips parted. "All the best, old man." Then in a confidential undertone he added, "Hit 'em for six, mind."

The M.P. officer also shook his hand. "That's one hell of a big pistol you've got there, Captain Stevens. Must be almost a .45."

Stevens looked down. Compulsory to go into Alex armed these days. The unlovely wog. "It is," he said.

"Well, I shouldn't care to get in the way of that very much."

You keep out of my way, son, Stevens would have liked to answer, and you won't. He bade them farewell, watching them tear off down the track to the gates, where the tail light—after the sentry had passed them out—gimleted to an eye and then vanished out of sight, as the ack-ack battery steadily recommenced its pounding of that implacable sky overhead.

CHAPTER TEN

Mention in despitches, by Christ. Anger blinded his mind as he paced the day room all next morning like a caged beast. For a second his useless fists pawed the flaming air: he'd have liked to knock the bastard teeth down that M.P. mucker's throat. Tear the bogger in two like one of those phone books at Sandhurst.

Lucy wasn't free. But she got off again the day following and he made love to her with rage in the back of the P.U. But somehow this didn't do any good, either, his nostrils were filled with Army odors—blanco, webbing, burning metal. He buried his head for a second in the khaki blanket.

Lighting a cigarette she didn't see his shaking shoulders.

"Phil?"

"Um."

"You really love me, don't you?"

"You know I do." He was beginning to tire of the relationship, of course. He'd almost accomplished his set objective in it. "Don't worry so," he said.

It happened then. He'd put on some swimming trunks he'd bought in Alex—probably made from flogged Army burlap—and without thinking swung himself out of the back of the truck in a lithe vault. The sun struck him like a blade and the hot sand made him literally dance.

"Hey, come on in," he called.

But Lucy, clad too in her costume, was staring at him in a strange way. "Phil," she pronounced gravely, "you realize that's wonderful?"

"What?"

"You can extrude your arm above the shoulder now."

Christ sod it! he swore at himself. Damnation, you couldn't think of everything, could you. And just such a little thing as that, he knew, could catch one out completely. His face must have shown his thoughts, for hers became more solemn than ever.

"Great Scott," he tried with false hilarity, "I can get my arm up now, you're right." Tentatively he raised it a little. "Bloody marv. Now they can't downgrade me at the board."

But it wasn't any good, he could see that all right. He wasn't born to be an actor, not with Lucy at any rate, not after making love.

"Let's go in, Phil." She walked into the brackish water with her head bent.

That evening he took her to a Bar American in the Rue Bab-el-Mandeb.

"*Irish 'Allah'*," said the grinning waiter. "You lak?"

He took arak; he badly wanted to get tight. He wanted to forget everything, Luce included, sitting there opposite him like a sphinx. Exactly. What the hell was she thinking precisely? Cat after cream. Hell's bells, he felt like punching himself in the bloody clock; anyone could slip up, couldn't they? He was only human. Human, he thought acidly, gazing out at that street of Moslem brick and muck, that world of baksheesh, and surrender, sharp sensual apprehensions, and I'm All Right, Allah. Resentment welled in him like a tide.

"Phil?"

"Yes." He saw down her chest. White where the tan stopped. Whoppers, really.

"Tell me one thing, I mean."

"Anything, Luce." Terrific chubbies. Sort of dugs, as a matter of fact.

"You will be straight with me, won't you?"

"Yes, cat, 'course I will."

Just a colossal cat in the lion sun. Turning then, he saw her eyes were wet. Creeping Judas but this one really loves me, he thought. The sudden sight of her face, all relaxed with drink and innocently concerned, supplied him with a quick idea.

"What I wanted to know was just whether, well," she shrugged, eyes hanging on the table, "I mean, did you know all along you could lift your arm like that?"

"Of course not."

"But you must have known, Phil. Patients develop sensitivity to things of that kind. You'd never have let yourself swing over the back of the pick-up like that if you hadn't known it wasn't going to hurt. I mean, *instinctively* you wouldn't."

"Look here, Lucy, are you seriously insinuating that I've been swinging the lead?"

In the silence she pressed wildly at her eyes. "Sorry, Phil. Please forget it. I just wanted to be sure, that's all. Out here it's so … what I mean to say is, I've come to care for you rather a lot."

"Then put it right out of your block, would you," he said gently. "I hadn't a clue I could lift my arm up properly till this afternoon. And I'm delighted. When I get in I'm going straight over to tell the doc." But as he said it, and they got up to go, he knew this was another person in his life he'd have to lose. On the way back that evening she again asked him to forgive her—"One gets so wrought up out here."

"Doesn't one."

Kissing her goodnight, one of his buttons brushed a nipple and she winced. Back in his narrow bed, lying next to wounded men, he closed his eyes and again his mind filled with those unvarying images of affliction, those utter shades of the half-world, Marrow going down, that bastard's head, Loran chucking the staff officer, lunatic Nazi, the Streicher breed, those porny pictures, a jerry coming in to search the room, Ridgeworth's eyes, his cowing, sodding, mucking eyes.…

The officers to be interviewed waited in the ward. A young gunner lieutenant returned having successfully disguised a bad case of nerve deafness from excessive exposure to gunshot—viz. from having his block half blown off.

"For one 'orrible mo'," he grinned at them, "I really thought the blighters were going to have me back arse-bashing in the shop for the duration. Phew!" He fell on his bed. "I guessed brilliantly while they whispered like a bunch of old biddies from different corners of the room. Frankly, I didn't hear a thing, but my more recherché replies seemed to impress 'em."

"Captain Stevens, sir."

Stevens got up and followed the orderly over to the day room that had been selected for the board. Lucy had been wrong. At least, the two hospital docs were there in force all right, but they were presided over by a father-figure, an R.A.M.C. colonel reeking of senility and of that kind of medical practice that had "won through" in the Crimea. The Lord God "mighty in battle" was behind this one, for sure. Hatless, Stevens did not salute. He simply sat down and pressed those hands of his between his knees.

The ward doc smiled in a kindly way. He asked a few questions, then ran rapidly over the case. Listening in a cruel calm Stevens realized that Lucy hadn't told them he was able now to extrude his arm above the shoulder. She'd hidden that particular info. His big body relaxed a fraction on the chair.

The Admin medico made copious notes. Bumf wallah. The colonel kept up a continual brittle cough throughout the proceedings. As he watched them, Stevens felt a kind of envy. Winners, these. And after what he'd done he'd be permanently on "the other side" of the tables he sat at now. Never again would he rejoin that friendly respectability personified by these three dutiful, even rather doggy, figures beyond it.

"You're still having trouble with your arm, I understand." This from the ward doc, after completing his record.

Stevens hung his head. "Well, you see it's like this..."

The doctor swapped a smile with the colonel. "Come on now, Philip Stevens, I think all of us here know just how much you people want to get back to the line. There's a different kind of life there, I know. But only this morning I had a word with Sister Matson and she told me your arm was still giving you quite a bit of trouble."

"She said that?"

"Yes. Now—like to raise it for us, please?"

Oh God, it was so easy. Then suddenly Stevens thought: Careful, son, these blighters have minds like bloody adding-machines. He got his eyes fixed to a gleaming tongue-depressor on the table by his dossier.

"I'd hate to, really." A rueful grin. "Must I, doc?"

The doctor released a guffaw. "There you are. What'd I say?" He swung on the others. "Well, colonel, I think that's the slander sheet in toto for you. The deltoid was badly lacerated and this, in conjunction with that calcium deposit on the bone," he slanted an X-ray plate into the light, "has considerably reduced the leverage."

"You a games player at school?" inquired the colonel with a smile. "What did you do at school?"

"Captain Stevens boxed for Sandhurst, sir."

"Did, did he." The smile of satisfaction on the colonel's features widened. "Well, if I've seen one of these plates from a scrapper, I've seen twenty. Always that same calcification in the left arm." He coughed luridly.

"And on top of those -er other symptoms he showed at first. I think you'll agree, sir. The floating sensation. On page three. Sister Matson's report is very detailed there."

"Ah yes. M'see." The colonel glanced up quickly. Stevens anchored his hands again. "I'm sorry to say there's no question in my mind as to your returning to regimental duties, Captain. You'd better make up your mind to that."

"But, sir..."

"You look pretty done up still, if I may frankly say so. And if I know anything about the P.E.D.G. you've been dashed lucky t'have stayed in one piece for as long as you have." He paused to cough again, then added bluntly, "If I were you, I'd thank me lucky stars we're going to have to downgrade you."

A piece of cake, Stevens told himself as he endeavored to saunter as slowly as possible back to the ward. Somehow it had all been too damn easy. Looking back on his life since the raid he seemed to have been involved in a perfect string of fakes—from the moment when he'd feigned seasickness in the boat over, from the moment someone had said at the unit, "Eh, got hit, old man?" There was something suspicious in this facility.

In the ward they asked him—"What did you get?"

"Permanently C," he got himself to scowl in reply. For a second the cunning chatter of wogs in the courtyard below became bitterly audible. I'm part of that world, he thought suddenly, with a sort of hopeless panic, the world of give-up and grab, the world of obey nature and say it's all Allah whenever anything happens at all. Sickening, really.

"I say, I say." The gunner bloke was strolling over with a truly comical expression of commiseration on his face. "That's too bad, old man. That's too bad."

"Rotten luck, old boy."

Just then Lucy walked in. Squelchy shoes and jouncing rump and all. Her amber eyes fell filmily on Stevens' and as they did so the springy step momentarily faltered.

Die Fahne hoch....

They could all hear the bastard song. Advancing column of boche P.O.W.'s chanting as if they were bloody winning the war instead of losing it.

"What did they give you, Captain?" Lucy quietly asked. "Ten years or a life sentence?"

He paused before answering. "Verdict of C."

He walked out. The others didn't know he'd been rogering Lucy silly these past few days and he didn't want it to show. It could, all too easily. Under a eucalyptus tree he scanned the papers they'd given him.

Die Reihen fest geschlossen. …

Would it never be over, then? He read his posting. First to the Convalescent Depot and then, after two weeks, to an I.R.T.D. or Infantry Reinforcement Training Depot. He knew those dumps. Initials. Square-bashing. Bumf. Perhaps, though, he could start life all over again as an initial, a bloody cypher in some wappy base office, where no one had ever heard of such a thing as a stick grenade that blew your balls off, never to have to meet. … Very far off something bumped, thumped, as if an unseen hand had faintly shoved at that texture of cerulean overhead. Gunfire. Whose? Jesus Christ, to get out, get shot of the whole bleeding shower of shite, the day after tomorrow now. …

The doc was walking cordially across to him.

"You were our last customer. Now for once in a blue moon I've got an evening free and can try out that old P.U. of mine you've been so kindly running in for me."

"I'm damn grateful to you for lending it to me, you know."

"Glad to have been able to. Transport's tight as hell, and you deserved to enjoy yourself after what you've been through."

"Doc," said Stevens quickly, "I mean, did Sister Matson by any chance in that report of hers you quoted … ?"

"Oh, highly confidential." The grinning Mr. Bones wagged a finger under Stevens' nose. "Seriously, Mattie's one of the best ward sisters we've got, isn't she? No more lie about a patient than take off for outer space. No, she was quite definite about your arm, old scout. She even went so far as to express an opinion that your extrusion was less than it had been. That could be. The deltoid contracting as it mends. I've seen ... well, just try to keep extending it as much as you can, won't you?"

"I'll do my best."

"Fine. You've been a first-class patient. Most co-operative. I'll be tickled to death to let you have the P.U. tomorrow after four. Just make sure you still slip one of those pills down before driving, however." He strode cheerfully off with a wave of his arm. The man in the white coat for you, all the way.

At first Stevens didn't recognize Lucy when he met her in the Rue Fuad. She'd taken the entire day off—his last, after all—and gone into Alex ahead of him with an ambulance for supplies. In that way they hoped too to dodge the gossip that sprang up in sisters' messes like fungus round quite ordinary, banal lives. Also, she wanted to do some feminine shopping first.

She had on a pastel summer frock, very English indeed, and he realized this was the first time he'd seen her in civvies. Bathing costume, yes, but not a dress. It made a difference somehow. A distance was placed between them. He thought of Maugham again.

So far as he was concerned the set-up ruined her allure, converting her as she stood against the backdrop of a Coptic church to a rather large girl of a kind he'd never have got to meet back home. Without the belt the body looked all but flabby. Yes, he'd tired of Luce all right, he wanted to get her out of his life, and fast. And of course, though he'd noticed the accent thing before, it'd all been blurred by desert life. There'd been the sexual bliss. For it had been bliss, stoating with Lucy, he had to confess. Yet here she was, as if about to visit a village fête in a vicar's poncy garden. Clearly she'd played hockey for Cheltenham Ladies' and there was that assurance of her kind that was like a red rag to Stevens. The mark of the winner, again. George, he could just see her in some winter Wiltshire village, in tweeds, with a shopping basket, and babushka-ed. Her shoes alone, filmed in heavy dust as always in North Africa, were real, reassured him a little.

She came and kissed him without a word.

"My dear cat," he got himself to say, "my very dear."

Her eagerness in the embrace was unusual. He made himself think: I don't owe her a bleeding thing, cow it, everyone knows women get twice as much out of the mucking business as men do, she asked for it all along. He drove into town and then out past the Bacos bus-stop. After they'd bathed they returned to Alex for dinner. She was completely permissive, let him do anything he liked with her. Yet he felt inhibited.

"Keep in touch with me when you leave, won't you, Phil?"

Jesus, she'd be expecting him to marry her next.

"Lucy," he said, "there's something I want to ask you."

"Yes?"

"Why did you tell the ward doc I couldn't extrude my arm when you know I now can?"

Her face, to his surprise, turned gently radiant. "Phil! Don't you understand? I'm terribly in love with you. I'd do anything for you. When I spoke to the doctor this morning I knew you hadn't told him, as you said you were going to. So I also knew you wanted to get out of all that hell. You didn't really want to go back, did you? And I don't blame you. Not a whit. Far from it, my darling. I realized how awfully much, actually, I wanted you to be safe. Yes, I suddenly wanted you to be. A quite different person in me wanted you to be, you see. No, I love you too much to let you go in again." She concluded quickly, "Now order me another drink, Phil."

A cramp twisted Stevens' side. Was Lucy insane? Her duty as Ward Sister was to.... He drew himself short. Didn't know what he was thinking of. She'd helped him, hadn't she? What the hell had her duty got to do with it? But as the new drink slopped a little over one of the corners of her lips he knew that somehow or other he'd spread his corruption, made her lie too.

"I see, I get it," was all he said. Then, "Thanks."

He was delighted when the time came to take her back to the hospital. The kiln-dry air was blowing off the desert to the south.

He kept telling himself as he drove that he didn't owe her a thing, not a single sodding thing.

"Kiss me, Phil," she breathlessly said and he had to call "Steady, there," as she lurched against him at the wheel.

"No, kiss me. Do anything... kiss..."

He almost ran for the ward when he'd parked the car.

The next day he left without saying good-by to her. The truck from the Con Depot came earlier than he'd expected and drove him off at once.

He sat in front beside the driver, watching the vista of sand, bat-dung, and camels, that land he loathed yet loved, pull under him like some ragged magic carpet. Africa—the world of the losers, the ruled, the "lesser breeds," without whom of course the bastard winners wouldn't have much to do, would they now?

In the last streets he sensed, rather than smelt, that combination of coffee, ouzo, anisette. He saw the gutters full of brittle melon seeds, heard the clack of tric-trac in cafés. By Jesus, it was a way of life that had driven him nearly stark staring ravers. Yet it was a way of life. Then they pulled out into the country where the wind whipped over withered yellow grass and thorny bushes and sand.

"Can't you move this crate any faster?" he snarled at the driver, but he noticed a whine in the timbre of his voice. A new world, he thought, I'm leaving the sons of God, the ibni Illahi, right behind. I'll frankly never see any of that lot again. Ever. Starting from now. You're clear, laddie boy, he told himself, no furtive images, no faces from the past. And he believed it too, with all his heart.

PART TWO
THE INTERVAL

CHAPTER ELEVEN

In the evening sun the crowd moved densely, their bronzed North Italian faces shadowing in the tortuous Loretta streets. The dark glasses of the men flashed like pennies in their skulls while the vigorous women walked more slowly, often arm in arm, with serious, absorbed expressions.

The hefty British lieutenant-colonel shoved slowly through this vital throng, a head taller than most, the large body somehow opening a path as if it knew it were confronted only with inferior beings. A band of youths with heavy black curls watched him with exasperated hatred under a poster stuck on a wall and showing a charging soldier, his face calmly noble. *Guaglioni.* A French WAC in thin tight denim trousers. Two Yank airmen with their high soft boots and that phony relaxation of theirs. The British officer knew most of this population by sight by now and trusted got one of them further than the end of his nose. But he invariably enjoyed this time of day, after he'd finished what was called work, or chucking things in his OUT tray, and this late sunlight lanced through the narrow pagan streets with their blistered shutters, their active shops, full of gleaming cheeses and straw-colored bottles, if precious little else. Yes, it was good to get out in the open air again. He wasn't much good at chair-bashing.

At the curb he stopped by a staff car on the window of which a sticker said CAMP COMMANDANT. The easily translatable second word seemed to mean a lot in Iti and the short freckled driver, who now jumped out and saluted, kept it nice and conspicuous.

"Hello, Evans, you may fall out now. No, I won't be needing you any more today, thanks."

"Very good, sir."

He watched the car start and, honking imperatively, if not imperially, nose its blackout lenses through the throngs. A right chap, Evans. Knew absolutely nothing. Kept his mouth shut, too. All the staff at the Loretta HQ could be said to do that, as a matter of fact, since they knew jolly well how cush their wicket there was, and they weren't going to spoil it if they could help it. In seven minutes Evans would be in the murky arms of Marisa, for whom it was all as easy as chewing gum.

He turned off down a cobbled lane to a bar. A more uneven ragged side-street over which the swallows wheeled and screeched in the last rays. A boy pushed by him on a bicycle. He settled the Ayrab wallet deeper in his pocket. He felt like celebrating today. Ever since the Normandy landings, in fact, he'd sensed that tide of jubilation rising inside him. Like coming at long last to the end of a journey. It was going to be possible, it was all going to be possible. He would, as they put it, "make good" in the end.

Outside the bar he paused and looked in before entering. In doing so, he realized how used he had grown to this life of subterfuge and deceit.

Fiorentina was at the receipt of custom all right, good as gold and twice as natural, overflowing her stool behind the cash register. One British officer drinking with cautious movements. No other military about. And just then Vincenzo himself, a tiny man with a face that went out at the bottom, and across which the mouth was chiseled in a harsh line, spotted him from behind the bar. He went on in.

"Double Campari," was how he answered Fiorentina's hushed-out "*Sera, Signor Colonello.*" For a second he studied her colossal mammalian structure, bloody marvelous really, all four feet of it caressing the keys of the cash register over which the small fingers proudly pianoed. Tring ensued—"*Ecco, Signor*!"

Moist lips burst like a fruit in season. Bloody marvelous. Only thing was, he himself preferred the podex, to tell the truth. And for a moment he remembered those photographs, now there you could see a proper hindquarter or two, whereas Fiorentina's South-southwest was altogether too much of a good thing. Anyway, he happened to know she was a wise virgin and didn't let any married soldier bang her for nylons every second night.

"What a nice big grin." He patted her back, took the slip she gave him and went over and placed it on the bar where it wilted in some spilt muscat. Vincenzo poured the bitter. The other officer mooched off. When he'd done so the old barman extracted from his waistcoat pocket a white metal watch, which he proceeded to wind up.

At this signal Stevens removed from the inside of his battledress blouse two cartons of State Express, one tin of plum jam, and a couple of tins of Kiwi. They vanished behind the counter in a flash. Beside his drink lay a pile of lire notes.

"Your change, Signor."

"Somebody been careless with his money, eh, Vincenzo." Stevens came from the chronically worried middle class and, although it was probably unwise to do so, he counted and recounted the notes, frowning to himself as he did so. "Yes, I'd say that's about right. Just so long as there aren't any duds."

The minute barman was screwing himself up—"*Signor Colonello.* A great battle. They say. . . ." He underwent a mime of exploding bombs. "*Choum! Choum!*" Then some unintelligible stuff which concluded, "Paris—taken—finished."

"All nonsense, Vincenzo old lad," Stevens tranquilly replied. "Put it where the monkey put the nuts." He glanced behind him into the street. It was growing darker. "No, don't you believe a word of it, old fruit. We're no more than ten miles inland as yet at the most. Ten." He spread up his fingers. "I'm likely to be stuck here in Loretta for some time, never you worry. There's been a big tank do near Bayeux and Tilly, if that's any help to you."

"But—the Ruskians?" Vicenzo's expression, with his slit of a mouth, was one of comically aggressive reproach.

"God knows. Can you credit any of their despatches? No, this thing may take years yet."

But he didn't really believe it himself. No more did Vincenzo, wily old owl that he was. The barman poured more Campari into the emptied glass without asking. By her cash register Fiorentina was eating sliced tomatoes, which every now and then she anointed with olive oil from an old beer bottle. She was also missing nothing of what went on.

"Mind if I use your telephone?" Stevens bagged a *gettone* and crossed to the antique instrument.

"*Pronto.*" Dulcet soprano.

"*Giulia*?"

"*Sì.*" Dubiously.

"*Qui*"—he struggled with his dreadful Iti, a language he really despised— "*qui è Phil.*"

"Pheeleep?"

"None other. Phil Stevens, lassie."

There might be, doubtless were, other Phils in that sweet seagull's life.

"See, I feel like celebrating tonight. Feel like joining me at the club in an hour?"

She agreed at once. Giulia was a hungry whore, though high-class and worth every cent of her *solde*. The best part about her was that you could take her out to places like the so-called Lansdowne Club. As a matter of fact, she often looked conservative beside some of the off-duty nurses and John's Ambulance types the other officers brought in with them. And the best part about the Lansdowne Club was that it hadn't, yet, acquired the shibboleths, the mystique of the average home mess. All that awful bull about what school you'd been to, whether you'd made the first fifteen, what college at Oxford or Cambridge (you might as well have not been there as have been to some). By God, he was professionally competent, wasn't he? What the hell had his social lack of grace got to do with it—in the Army, of all places? Anyway, at the Lansdowne he felt all right. He went back and finished his drink and with a farewell "Finito Benito" to Vincenzo, and a pat to Fiorentina's arched back, he walked out.

Once out in the street again he found himself pleasingly slack-limbed. On the stone of a wall opposite a swastika, inscribed with charcoal or some burning substance, still writhed like a spider. A very small car, filled to bursting with a number of very fat, fairly frightened-looking elderly Italians, sped by, nearly touching him. He felt he could have bowled it over with one hand. God's teeth, he thought suddenly, it's over at last. With this Normandy thing, it's merely a matter of time. The bloody past is bloody well dead for bloody good.

The Lansdowne was originally an Italian Air Force club, by far the ugliest, most pretentious and comfortable building in Loretta. The brownish flood of the Adige flowed in front of it and on the other side, since it was situated on the edge of the town, the view to the mountains was superb. It was now requisitioned for Allied officers. None of whom knew a nick about the past of one Phil Stevens, he thought as he pushed past the hag selling Eighth Army newspapers and entered the hallway over which the statue of a Roman boxer presided by a meekly trickling fountain. And no wonder. What a giant. The Iti was said to be genital conscious, in any case. The English nurses hardly knew what to do with themselves when they went past the brute, of course. Stevens stared up at the cestus round the fist and wondered if they really used to load them with iron or lead as was rumored. Kill a man like that. Kill...

Abruptly he turned and went up and out onto the terrace where evening aperitifs were being served to the mewing strains of a string quartet. He caught sight of himself in a mirror. Putting on weight. Several British officers there. Stevens parked his bulk at a tin table and ordered gin and orange. It came in a mush of suspect ice and, on top of the Camparis, affected him strongly. He stretched out his legs and ordered another. The big pistol sagged at his belt.

In front of him clusters of pine trees in regular formations dropped into the plain. Stevens saw briefly the debris of the ruined jerry vehicle still not cleared up in that nearby ditch and again worried whose responsibility it was, have to call up the town major about that tomorrow, sharp. Then, looking up, almost level, came the mountains of what had once been the Gothic Line. Like the track of a murderous cat this immemorial earth was imprinted with the marks of war. War, war, war. His eyes picked out two blackened tanks, ruined equipment of the Panzer Lehr, in a cornfield the wheels of some overturned truck, and near a group of those nice round Iti haystacks a number of whitewashed crosses, all neat and acrid—Dreck of an Army in retreat. Poor bloody boggers, there lay a good few who wouldn't be late for St. Peter's reveille, but all the same he felt it here as in the desert—the one that got him can't get me. Even now faint flashes splayed that distant horizon, yet they only had the effect of fireworks, comfortingly harmless. Stevens thought over how he had become what he'd once considered the lowest form of animal life, the base wallah. It'd been remarkably easy, all in all.

First, the Con camp. Lots of P.T. sergeants who'd have fainted on a firing range bulging their jockers at him and bags of initials on their nice clean sweaters, too. Stevens had been good at P.T. But not too good. A tented waste by a clashing sea in between Cairo and Alex. Remembering not to play volley ball, for instance, show he could lift his arm up properly. Then the I.R.T.D. Then, posting. Yes, posting by heaven to a mule transport team reorganizing in Cairo. Getting to know the ropes, the intricately knotted ropes, of all that idiotic, senseless, wasteful base life. But he'd breathed again.

The mule transport outfit, a relic of the old Cairo Cavalry days, hadn't had any mules since 1941, but a number were still "on strength" (or weakness) somehow or other, and evidently it took two fairly distinguished-looking officers to supervise these non-existent quadrupeds, so fictitiously on establishment, pay out for their fodder weekly, and hand over the whole racket when disbanded. Very funny, indeed. Stevens had joined those clever jokers, the mule transport officers, past masters of procrastination, and like Dad he'd kept mum about it all.

Weird and often neurotic eccentricities appeared in these base officers. His so-called C.O., an R.A.S.C. major with superbly inauthentic Kaiserian mustaches, made a point of collecting wooden coat-hangers, which were at that time in short supply.

"My dear chap, what do you say to this?" He'd come into the office, puffing, after a sortie into the blazing Cairo side-streets, and waving two cheap metal hangers. "Made quite a bag, what. Found 'em in a shop near old Si Benar's, won't tell you just where." He twinkled. "They're only metal, still they have a genuine Marks and Spencer marking on them, you'll find."

It was a triumphant moment for Stevens when he found he himself, by accident on purpose, had packed a noble specimen of British craftsmanship from 13C. Until the major turned it over and discovered that the wise orderly in charge of the officers' ward had burnt OW 34 in the back.

Evidently the major hoped to sell his collection of coat-hangers for a handsome profit when he got back home, "at the end of it all." As he often told Stevens, "You see, there's hardly any left there at all by now. Old country's quite run out of stock. It's perfectly true, dear boy. Hotels etcetera will all be badly in need of. Oh yes, you'll be able to cop the devil of a business in this line at the end of it all. Only like to let you come in with me, Phil."

Lucy had arrived on leave. Once. And for three days only. He explained that he hadn't said good-by that last morning at the hospital because he'd been "too moved." He knew that shortly after that, with the advance of desert forces, 13C had gone forward. The Sisters were given a roster of a few days off each. Lucy put up at a Red Cross hotel in Cairo and Stevens felt terrified every second he was with her. But he needn't have worried. This was a new Lucy, slackened, weary from weeks of foul ward duty, a Lucy longing to hit the bottle too. For he couldn't make love to her sober in those frightful days. Only when he saw her off did he know she knew. Her huge eyes misted over. Poor cat. He had to lose her.

From the mule transport outfit, to the tune of a pythonic party at the end of '42, he found himself posted to a branch of AMGOT outside Algiers. He watched his step now, in palatial offices next door to a first-class restaurant at El Biar. What's more, he went up to Major in the bargain—"Major Stevens showed initiative and determination in all phases of his activity with us," he read in the transport team's report. But he was tired of Africa, its acceptance, the wog assent to arbitrary laws called Allah, the craven submission, the animal-like women, the scornful self-satisfied men with their beaten beasts of burden scarcely able to drag one leg after another.

So it was gladly he moved on to Sicily—terrace flat in Catania, staring straight up at Etna. Here he sat tight till No. 1 District moved on to Perugia. Now he was sub-attached as Camp Commandant to a shower of odds and sods in Loretta. The location was far from ritzy but he'd gone up to Lieutenant-Colonel in the move without a squeak of protest from the reg. Today the war was finally ending, so it seemed. . . .

He sucked sweetly at the ice-cold gin and orange. Then he ordered another. Good. He was getting drunk.

"Yes?" There was a figure by his chair. Then he shambled to his feet, grinning oafishly. "*Come sta*?"

"*Non c'è male.*"

It was Giulia. Slim, dark, and bloody quivering with sex. The first thing he thought was how nice it was to see an Iti girl who didn't have to dress out of old curtains. A trifle magenta-lipped, ear-rings a spot too large, but otherwise O.K. Giulia was *formosa*, right enough. Derrière with just the right amount of overhang, too. Perfect.

"I'm damn glad you rolled up," he said. "Take a pew, *carissima*." He hauled back a chair. Giulia folded her really abnormally long legs, parked her pouting posterior, and he slouched back, eves glinting, into his wicker seat. He called up more drinks from the waiter.

They stayed drinking for some time. Stevens grew maudlin as the light faded from the sky, and the red trees below them, around which a few iron-cropped infants played, turned black. Briefly he sank into one of those sludges of self-pity he'd been indulging in lately: never very clever, always did my best though, our Upper Fourth damn stiff at school, should have been made a prefect, always picked on me in the mess. They came all too easily, the items of evidence against the code.

From this mood he turned surly. Giulia looked at her watch, a man's timepiece whose head-aching assembly of gold dials adorning her thin brown wrist was doubtless the result of some hard work. Evidently she wanted to go in to dinner.

"All right, eats," he said.

The room was all tapestry battles, red plush, and giant vases of artificial flowers. Giulia shuddered. For her it was "sad." Stevens thought it "rather posh."

"Eats" revived his temper. Powdered egg and bully was washed down by an Istrian Cabernet chosen by Giulia—vino was either red or white for him—and this turned him quite tight. Across the wavering table he could see her face becoming more and more discontented. She was toying with a bottle of aqua minerale, a water from some Livorno company whose label was thick with the prize certifications of various spa hotels. He leant over. "You get into that dress with a shoehorn, ducky?"

"You're tronk, Pheeleep."

"Shut up," he said, spilling egg out of his mouth.

Nearly everyone else had left the dining room by this time and the Iti boys were doing the tables.

"Bring me some gippo for this horsemeat," Stevens said. The wop waiter didn't understand. "Gippo, blast you. And presto, see. Good Heavens, even poor old Wright would have understood that." And he started to giggle slightly. Eventually a mess sergeant, English, brought him what he wanted, namely a large bottle of tomato ketchup. He lathered his meat and Giulia's with it. "Pomodore, pomodore," she shrieked, "no, Pheeleep, we get too much." He spattered it thoughtfully down into the warmth between her breasts.

Giulia rose, hissing like a snake. She said two words in dialect and to Stevens, convulsed with mirth now on his tilted chair, they sounded bad words.

"Ooo!" he gurgled, between tears and laughter. "Ooo-er!"

She'd gone. He ate on alone, not caring tuppence really. Tortoni was brought him, and he poured steady gouts of the red ketchup over that, too. Then he stayed drinking till the club closed. Hadn't been so pie-eyed as this for years. In all solicitude the mess sergeant helped him out to the head of that pompous stairway down. Stevens took minutes navigating this and when he'd reached the hallway at the bottom he found himself on all fours silently contemplating the statue of the cestus-holding boxer above. He realized that he had carried down with him, clasped to his breasts like a baby, the gobby bottle of ketchup. With a chuckle he straightened and smeared the motionless boxer with it in a vital spot, stood for a second watching the bright red substance trickle down those muscular thighs in ironic desecration, then heaved a sigh and mooched out into the night. Below the belt, he told himself, rotten trick.

Outside the air was like a blade. He sobered slightly. The night was a dark one and no one was about. Crossing the bridge he re-entered the town proper. Implanted by the Germans, the habit of curfew died hard in the local populace, although the Allies were far laxer about the whole affair.

Fear fingered momentarily down his spine when he thought of the hours he'd spent in his sodding camp commandant's office, reading through Army law tracts in an effort to find some sort of statute of limitations in the matter of crime in H.M. forces. There didn't seem to by any. Once you'd blotted your copybook, that was it. For keeps. The only thing you could do was somehow leave the bloody Army. Get bloody out. Then, after several years, and with a bit of legal luck, they couldn't nab you too easily, so it seemed. His own seven and four had just about elapsed by this date, thanks to hostilities, and when he got back to England he was already determined to shed all military attachments just as soon as he mucking well could.

Stevens stopped in his tracks. Where was he? By now he imagined he knew Loretta bareback. But it was dark as hell. Not that he was afraid of being nicked by the poor old guaglioni; it would be biting off a sight more than those pathetic alley-rats could chew to cosh a lieutenant-colonel and Stevens was just aching for them to try; he'd give his right arm to be able to use his old .45 again. All the same, these chilly deserted streets looked different somehow, filled with tension, drawn on a ruler.

He asked the way. A scared man pointed, made off. Stevens walked on, swaying mildly. He tripped on a pile of rubble and almost immediately lurched up against two helmeted figures in olive-drab and leggings. He saw the blue and white M.P. brassards, the single chevron below, heard one gently say, "Evenin', Colonel," very courteously after the salute. Yank M.P.'s were still M.P.'s, however, and Stevens hated peelers with his life. He stumbled on, thinking: Now Giulia's out, I'll take another squiz at those old photographs. He chuckled. Yanks pretty good at keeping the ginsos off the street, he thought, but he'd like to see them in the line. Some said to have been pretty good at Anzio, however.

Over towards what was in daytime a thriving central market several bars were open. Figures banged out of flapping doors. Just like assassins, he thought, wondering if it'd ever been any different really—and suddenly, as he knew where he was, hating, hating, hating the whole sodding, mucking life.

Then from a doorway of wet sawdust, dimly lit and quickly closed, a man came towards him walking purposefully, a cigarette in his mouth. This wiry fellow with the shock of hair had something in the way he moved that took Stevens' immediate attention. The walk wasn't Italian somehow. You could always tell an Army tread. Then again, as a fighter, he'd found he'd observed the way men moved more than anything. And this walk was definitely familiar. He drew into the wall.

The man was dark, angular, with close-set eyes and beaky nose. He had on unpressed trousers and a leather workman's jacket. As he came past Stevens received a blinding image. It was an excruciatingly acute picture that flashed alight in his drink-sodden mind as the familiarity crystallized. He felt his breath coming fast. What he saw was a pair of brown canvas Army P.T. shoes twisting at each other in the bottom of a boat. The man was Corporal Marrow.

Stevens gasped, as if hit physically. It couldn't be, of course. That was what he at once told himself as, pulling himself together, he followed that rapidly failing shadow while it moved along the walls. Bleeding heaven, but it can't be, was what his pelting ribs told him as he began to run—the bogger had black hair, saw it plain as a pikestaff. But in this light…

Up two streets, across a square, down an alley. The other was walking fast. Practically a trot. Stevens hung about ten yards behind him. Then by a stroke of luck his quarry stopped at a tobacconist's shop still open, so that the weakened light fell athwart his face under the paper shading. Pressed into an angle of that ancient wall Stevens felt the old sickness swarm upward from the pit of his stomach. It wasn't fair. He'd done his best. But surely this was Marrow. That blade of nose, all right. Or, was it? After all, it was only the bastard's profile he could see.

"*Nazionali*," said the man in Italian and Stevens heaved a sigh of relief. Couldn't be. Marrow's English was bloody limited, let alone speaking anything else.

The fellow paid, took his packet, pushed off. Stevens found difficulty disengaging himself from the pursuit as he'd have liked.

I've been seeing things, he told himself. White elephants next. He was glad the blighter had disappeared now. Definitely too much to drink. Then he thought—*Marrow*! If that swine's really alive he could have heard things. Say he'd been faking in all that blood in the hallway—after all, that sort of thing had happened before—he'd have heard me ordering Loran and Ridgeworth to get out. What's more, the jerries might have told him Ridgeworth's body was found with a dirty bastard of a dum-dum in the back of the head. Close range, too. A butcher's job.

Stevens walked slowly on to the end of the street, where a barber shop formed the corner.

A voice inquired in English, "Following me, mate?"

He danced back from the figure in the doorway, his right hand moving instinctively towards his gun.

"Marrow!" he got out. "You're Corp Marrow, aren't you, by Christ?"

But the other, after one horrified stare, had darted off in a flash. His heels beat drumlike in the direction of the river. Stevens gave chase, lumbering along the uneven alleyways, occasionally crashing unfeelingly into walls, skidding the corners.

"Marrow!" he shouted. "Come back, you bastard!" He ran on in silence. I'll get you, laddie boy, he told himself grimly, if it's the last bloody thing I do. Reaching the river, however, he became convinced he'd lost him. Stevens cursed himself for being so bloody pie-eyed. Now he'd never know for sure.

The river moved unexpectedly swiftly. In spate. They'd pulled out a shaven-headed girl with a lot of whip weals on her upper legs from that muck only a few days ago. "*Part-igiani*," Vincenzo had explained, making a picturesque gesture across his throat and pointing with popping eyes to a single-barreled shotgun of an inordinate length in a corner. It was the bloody longest piece of personal artillery Stevens had ever seen in his life, but he knew the local rentiers were scared rigid of the partisans. He gazed moodily, breathing heavily, into the muddy swirl of water now.

"Christ!" he cried aloud.

A figure was running some fifty yards down the low stone surround banking the river. And he was running for dear life, there was no mistaking that.

"Marrow!" he yelled.

The runner seemed to put on pace. He was making for a Bailey bridge on the other side of which Loretta disintegrated into a muddle of dozens of side-streets and old steps. He was making his get-away all right.

"Listen," Stevens bawled in the eerie stillness over the river, "if you don't stop and give yourself up, someone's going to get their bastard teeth blown down the back of their throat, understand?"

It didn't stop the man and Stevens drew his .45. His hand was trembling. Dear God, let me hit low, he was praying. I don't want to kill him. Not yet. Not till I. . . .

"Pack it in, whoever you are. Or I fire."

The fellow was on the bridge, nearly halfway across. And running like hell. Stevens aimed off for motion, aimed low at the legs and with tears in his eyes squeezed the trigger slowly but firmly.

The shot smashed into the night. Missed? That was his first thought, and his first reaction was frankly to curse himself for carelessness. He didn't usually miss. The fleeing figure had stopped, staggered, then seemed to run on again, then falling or diving doll-like in a sideways motion, the man had plunged into the river. Stevens even heard the splash before he started running. But by the time he got to the bridge there wasn't a sign and voices were shouting in the darkness.

Stevens started to panic. Looking down now at the desolate, darkened Adige he couldn't help feeling that in his drunkenness he'd made some dreadful mistake. Perhaps brought down some perfectly innocent pedestrian, hurrying to get home. But why the English?

He began pounding back the way he'd come as a whistle was blown and footsteps sounded, running. That washout police force of theirs, he thought, and he kept on going. They'll probably think it was partisans, with any luck. If they recover the body that's what they'll put it down to, all right. But my God you're a mutt, he told himself as with trembling fingers he urged the key into the lock of his flat door. He was in a sweat. Panicked. He knew that. And every time he panicked—trouble. Oh, bloody roll on death, as Wright would have said.

He lay down on his bed. It was a bare small room, and like all the rooms he'd inhabited since the desert it looked constitutionally unfurnished. Even in his palatial El Biar quarters Stevens hadn't felt comfortable spreading himself. All his possessions in the world could be packed into a couple of small suitcases at a moment's notice, any time. Since life in the P.E.D.G. he'd come to prefer it like that.

A frenzied despair twisted him on the bed for a minute. His palms twitched livingly. He wanted very much to die. Just when he was making good. Probably about to go home. Shutting his eyes, he seemed almost immediately to see Lucy beckoning from the doorway. He thought of her letters, letters he'd never answered. He had to lose her. Had to, that was all.

He tossed on the bed. In this state of drunken half-sleep a conception came to him he found impossible to throw off—Marrow had been in the Military Police. Not killed in the raid on Dark Horse, Marrow had been sent back to a p.o.w. camp, had escaped, then turned in the true story of the affair to M.P. authorities once he'd got back. As a result of this, M.P. had decided to put him in plain clothes, dye his hair, and send him—as often enough was their practice—to exert surveillance over their military suspect, this time in Loretta. It was a fantastic tale but it hung together and it wouldn't leave Stevens' mind. That sort of thing happened. With the sodding, M.P. anything happened, muck it. Surprised by the barber shop, Marrow had then realized his quarry had recognized him and had accordingly run for it. The appallingly tantalizing thing was he'd never be able to tell himself for sure whether he had or hadn't killed the blighter.

Stevens woke in a white fever. The entire thing had been a dream—Marrow's face, Lucy beckoning, everything. Or had it? He went on churning on the bed, making the broken springs creak complainingly. Perhaps it had all been a miraculous warning, you couldn't entirely escape those supernatural ideas in Italy. Stevens' vague idea of God was got from those early days at school when chapel had been compulsory twice a day and boys who talked in their pews were beaten. There, as the compulsory Kipling hymns had been sung, God had assumed a dim face that, for Stevens, was a cross between an intellectual Bulldog Drummond, George V and the rugger coach. To which, he supposed, the schoolboy nowadays added the voice of Winston Churchill, "good old Winnie" with his soft underbelly of the Axis. Of course later you laughed at it all, but those habits of mind, of awe for abstractions, bred so early, bit deep—just as had the cane, if you came in late for evensong.

Weakened by this facile undirected spiritualism that had so prepared the groundsoil of generations of English schoolboys for guilt, a bitter consuming regret laid hold of Stevens now. In the darkness of dawn he rolled off the bed and put on the light. To his horror he saw that the front of his battle dress was bloodstained. He saw himself suddenly as he'd been on that raid, all splashed in gore from that awful pajama-ed German. He hurled himself into the wretched bathroom. In that bleak light he saw that the stains were simply from the bottle of tomato ketchup he'd hugged against himself. He tried to laugh. At the same time, he filled the bath and when it was full chucked his battle-dress top into it, to wash off the stains. Something made him do so.

He thought: God blind it, I've got to get out of the Army. Quick. But was he right? Had he simply made another mistake? Had he really seen some face as it were behind a window pane and mistaken the dream for reality? Then, turning over his pistol, he knew it was true. Too damn true, by Christ. He wiped his gun lovingly with his handkerchief. Left it too oily, that Evans. But a shot had been fired all right. Only five rounds in the chamber and the barrel was black, black as his very soul. Stevens recoiled with horror against his brass-knobbed bedstead.

He put on another blouse and went out into the night again. There was a church nearby he had been into once, because a young officer in his organization had said there was some mosaic work attributed to someone called Torriti and Stevens had remembered Loran. There had been a kind of reverent odor and quiet and Stevens had dropped to his knees and tried to pray that Loran was in heaven. Tonight, even at this hour to his surprise, a priest was conducting mass in front of an altar above which there was a glass case containing the yellowed shinbone of some martyred saint. Stevens had no idea what religion ought to mean, but the place had a kind of air of sanctity that he found vaguely reassuring at the moment. This was broken somewhat by the priest, who was badly shaven, tossing a missal casually across the altar.

Stevens knelt down, bent his head, and tried to pray. He could not. There came to his nostrils the smell of fish and, glancing up self-consciously, he saw that the woman beside him, about the only other person there, had come in with an oozing parcel under one arm. This won't do, he thought of his own behavior; I'll attract attention. What's more, I haven't cleaned my old .45 yet. Must go and do that at once.

He rose and walked to the door. Behind him the susurrations of the priest continued. Whatever he's saying, Stevens told himself, the more ways I look at this the more likely it seems to me I may have killed another man.

PART THREE
THE RETURN

CHAPTER TWELVE

"I must say we're sorry as anything about your resigning your commission, Philip. Of course, it must be good to be back after all that time."

The time was March, 1945.

"Well, there's a lot of unpacking to do, sir."

It was something Stevens had got into his head. The colonel of the regiment looked like a paper-knife, with a face that might have been pressed in a book. On his upper lip a smattering of grey bristles stuck outwards. His service dress was adorned with several pretty, faded medal ribbons, many dating back to Northwest Frontier campaigns.

Indeed, the whole place stank of Omdurman, the Khyber Pass: so Stevens thought, watching cannily. Directly he'd first returned to regimental headquarters the entire business had taken on the flavor of some gorgeous anachronism. His hands shifted on his lap.

"So soon after the end of hostilities like this." The colonel was staring vacantly out the window. "We need all the old 'uns we can lay hands on, Philip." Despite the use of his first name Stevens didn't know this blue streak from Adam. The regimental colonel at the time he'd gone out had retired, and now collected butterflies in Kent. "I say," said the present buffer who now held sway in the famous room overlooking Monk Terrace, "I say, won't you have a glass of port?"

"Thank you, sir, I will."

Might as well pick up a free drink, he thought. I'm going to need a few on a major's pension. He watched the colonel potter to the sideboard. The thimbleful of wine eventually produced as a result of his ministrations with decanters seemed to Stevens virtually insulting. But it gave his hands something to do to hold onto the glass.

"Thank you, sir." They liked to be called sir.

"Of course you chaps did awfully well out there." The colonel resettled himself with a surreptitiously larger measure of port behind the desk on which, in fact, no relics of Army activity at all could be seen.

"We tried to keep our end up."

"And you did, you did." While the colonel slipped off inconspicuously into a lot of rammel about Italian wines and the First World War Stevens' eyes strayed over his head. A framed parchment, dating from the eighteenth century. A letter or something about some member of the regiment then. He read the words: "... was in the fight at Oudenarde and he behaved as Englishmen usually behave upon such occasions. ..." Stevens' hands crisped at his side. A havering whine was coming from the colonel now, a noise not dissimilar to that given off by a radio when just turned on. "Yet you're determined to leave us, heh, Philip?"

"I'm afraid so, sir."

"Of course, you're perfectly entitled to, after all your service. But you realize that if only you'd stay with us a little longer—I know you're a C man now, it'd have to be the holding battalion—well, I mean to say, some promotions will be going. I can't promise anything, mind," he hastily footnoted. "Still, a lieutenant-colonel's pension's worth a sight more than a major's, as you know, m'boy. Matter of fact, I personally opposed the idea of your having to revert in rank on rejoining but the War House weren't having any. But your mind's made up, eh? You insist on leaving us for what they call, I understand, Civvie Street."

"That's right, sir."

"Well, damn good luck. And let me know if I can be of any help." Abruptly he squinted up. "Precisely what was it you did out there with those P.E.D.G. boys, Philip?"

Stevens couldn't help a smile. The old boy had asked it in the manner of someone inquiring after a prodigal son's offside acquaintance. "Sworn to deathly secrecy on that subject, sir, to tell the truth."

"Of course you were." The colonel chuckled as if he'd made a point. "Just like this Court of Inquiry thing they're holding into some show you chaps staged out there. They've asked me to instruct you to attend it."

Stevens stiffened suddenly. "What's that, sir?"

"Do you know, they wouldn't give me a hint as to what it was about. Me. One of me own officers. I mean to say."

"What's this Court of Inquiry, sir?"

"Nine-thirty in the morning. J.A.G. show. No instructions as to dress. Typical. Place in Edwards Crescent. Color-sergeant outside will give you all the details."

"Just what's it in aid of, sir?"

The colonel's brows shot up. "My dear fellow, don't ask me. J.A.G. have left me totally in the dark. They've simply required me to have you down at Edwards Crescent at oh-nine-three-oh day after tomorrow. Don't ask me what you lads in P.E.D.G. have been up to. I mean, I wouldn't know, would I?"

Watching the silently chortling colonel, ruddy with port, Stevens felt sweat starting between his shoulder blades. When it was over. Just when it was all over like this....

"I don't think I quite follow, sir. I'm to attend a Court of Inquiry the day after tomorrow. I must be able to find out something about it first."

"Ask the color-sergeant," whispered the colonel, through his laughter. "Though he won't tell you any more than I have, Philip. No, no," and the colonel drew himself together, stood up, held out his hand. "We'll put you on strength here till final papers come through. Tell 'em next door, do."

Stevens took the outstretched hand, an unexpectedly firm grip, saluted, turned to his right, and fell out. As he left the room he saw the colonel toddling to the port sideboard at a half-run. Perhaps it was nothing after all, he thought, just imagination. Routine inquiry into some minor incident. Would Wilf be there, perhaps?

The orderly room across the passage from the regimental colonel's office presented a contrast to that gracious chamber. No "genuine Bokhara, m'boy," no Bohemian decanters here, by Christ. Steel PENDING trays of a type very familiar to Stevens by this time, antiquated typewriters, piles of Army training pamphlets (*the tip of the blade of the foresight in line with and in the center of...*): such were the military incunabula that littered tables bitten into by burns from well-smoked fags. A color-sergeant came forward, feeling his buttons.

"Excuse me, sir, the colonel told me to be sure and give you this before you left."

Stevens glanced through the memo. Copy of the J.A.G. instructions to report for Court of Inquiry. Years of English training, both at school and in the Army, made a summons of this kind automatically ominous. Stevens shook.

"Just what's all this about, Sergeant?" he asked casually.

The man shook his head. "Really can't say, sir. Come through a week ago but with you on leave I couldn't get hold of you. ..."

"Yes, I know you couldn't," Stevens cut in. He'd purposefully obfuscated his address to the regiment while on leave. Wanted as little contact as possible. But they caught up with you all right. He added bitterly, "It doesn't matter anyhow. I'm leaving the reg, you know. Done the best part of twelve years hard by now, and I reckon I've had it." He tried to smile. The best part? Or the worst part? "I'll give you the dope for all the forms. By the way, you wouldn't be able to tell me what became of a batman from the regiment I once had, would you? Name of Wright."

The color-sergeant thought. Then his eyes lit. "I remember the man, sir."

Watching him closely, Stevens thought it bloody funny the old sweat didn't have to turn up any records to get at this information. Why did he remember that particular name, out of the thousands that must have passed through the files of this office?

"Wright's already demobbed, sir. I recall him clearly. One of the early B releases. We had to fill in some very special bumf on him."

"A B release? But I thought that was only open to the brainy ones," said Stevens, resentment creeping into his tone. "This cove—Wright, I mean—was a former milk roundsman from Leeds. Frankly I don't imagine he ever had too much in the tank. You've got the wrong fellow, Sergeant."

"No, sir. I remember him. He even mentioned you, come to think of it, when he stopped in here to pick up his papers. Seems that before the war, even though he did have this milk job you mention, sir, Wright had an old unused scholarship from one of the grammar schools to a university. Well, the Ministry of Labour has been letting these school boys out early under B, if they go up to a university. Interrupted education, like."

"I see."

His eyes fell. That bogey of cleverness again. He went quickly to the color-sergeant's desk and gave him the details for preparation of papers for leaving the Army. The other accompanied him to the head of the stairs down.

"Good-by, Sergeant, and thank you."

"Best luck, sir."

Stevens went down the staircase and out, forgetting even to acknowledge the salutes of the sentries on the gate.

At first he stood uncertainly on the pavement, feeling strongly superannuated. "Oh, sorry," he said needlessly, when a child bumped into him.

"*Noos, E'nin' Stan-ar*," a boy was calling. "*Stan-ar* and *Stah*."

And here was a woman pushing a pram, occasionally leaning forward to glug at the white mite within. Stevens started to stroll.

"*Paradis Massacre*," he could hear the newsboy persistently crying behind him now. "*Readahlabahtit* ... seek German general ... Norfolks bayoneted ... prisoners machine-gunned ... *readahlabahtit*!"

The vision of that soft, swaddled shape in the pram had disturbed Stevens somehow. He went into a park. Green trees. A woman throwing a dog a rubber ball.

"Rough, Rough, get it, Rough," she was calling.

Seek German general.

But there couldn't be, could there now, after all these years, something wrong? Dear God, not now. After what he'd been through. Should he say he was ill, refuse to attend the Court of Inquiry?

Anger started to seethe inside him. All the loneliness of the past years in various base headquarters, keeping his trap shut, watching his step, avoiding his fellow officers, fading into the wallpaper—those years of near-despair had taken their toll of his spirit, he knew. His fingers shook easily nowadays, too. Once or twice he thought he'd detected what the docs would call a heart murmur, but you couldn't be certain, of course. He hadn't had it checked; he didn't want any chance investigations into his category, into his arm, at this stage of the game, no thanks.

In the sunshine of the park he shut his eyes. He would have to gather strength to return to the little Cromwell Road hotel he'd just moved to. There was virtually no unpacking to be done at all. Just a few old map-cases. Boots. His gun. Those photographs. When he opened his eyes they fell on what appeared to Stevens a bafflingly exotic scene, a nursemaid throwing a few swans some pieces of bun.

CHAPTER THIRTEEN

He knew he was in for it as he advanced into that airy chamber over Edwards Crescent, brought his heels together and saluted smartly, and saw the man with the important-looking neck smiling up at him. They always smiled, the winners did—before they kicked you in the teeth. And this one had so much stuff on his shoulders and chest he might have been a wop tram conductor out of a job. Looked about as tidy, too.

Stevens knew it, too, because the first thing he'd seen on entry had been that face wrung out of his past. There'd been a fraction of time before full recognition had come, then he knew there was no turning back. This was it, all right. In fact, there'd been a sensation akin even to relief. There was absolutely nothing more he could do except stop bobbing and face the music. And with this realization it seemed suddenly plain that any life was better than the one he'd recently been leading. After killing Marrow.

The M.P. officer Ellis, who had come to interrogate him in 13C with the Adj and that Major Taylor, stared at him unsmilingly from behind the gleaming table. Major's crowns now shone on his shoulders also.

"I'm extremely sorry we had to send for you under such secrecy." The J.A.G. lieutenant-colonel spoke with that confident bonhomie of men gifted with a good deal of avoirdupois in the evening of life. "But the conditions of operation of your former unit, the Personal Engagement Desert Group, require this er . . . approach as much as anything. Will you smoke? No. You must have a good deal to do now you're back home at last, eh?"

"Well, sir, there's a certain amount of unpack—"

"Good, good." Charles Russ-Sykes cut him short in a manner that showed he hadn't really been listening to his own question. Stevens felt a redness rising behind his eyes. Keep that anger down. Then the fellow drew his fingertips gently together and, as he watched, Stevens found a coffin-like hollow being scooped inside him. So clean, so shiny, those clever little yellow nails.

"Matter about which we want you, Major, is a rather unusual one. It has to do with a certain patrol, ostensibly put out to try to capture the now celebrated war criminal General von Schultz in a house in North Africa. A patrol on which you were sent, am I right?"

"I commanded it, sir," said Stevens sullenly.

"Of course you did." The lieutenant-colonel laughed. "Now, look here, you mustn't think we're going to try to grill you, anything of that sort at all. I simply want to get everything aboveboard between us from the start. This is a Court of Inquiry; I do have to warn you that anything you say may be taken down and held in evidence—" from the corner of an eye Stevens saw that the single C.I.D. man had a pad upon his lap—"but beyond that the whole thing's informal. We'd like you to feel quite at your ease."

I'll bet you would, thought Stevens grimly, at the end of a nice stretch of rope. Jolly decent. And he sat hard on his already shaking hands. Ellis was scrutinizing him closely. The mucker wants to take it out on me, he's bloody dying to, Stevens thought, that time he ducked under the table before the bomb, made himself as scarce as hen's teeth, right there in front of Wilf and me... Wilf! He wondered if they'd had Wilf up yet. If only this sod with the fingernails would let him have some clue as to where he stood.

"I only wish you'd got him, Major," someone said.

"Who?"

"Von Schultz, of course. The War Crimes Commission is unearthing new atrocities by that swine almost daily. But they haven't winkled him out yet."

"We're here to find out about a man on that patrol, a man who went with you, Major Stevens."

"I understand." He tried to fix his eyes on the table legs. He saw that the claw-feet on one leg were missing. But his gaze kept slipping to the top of that glossy table, on which lay the papers of his invigilators.

"You do realize that everything passing between us is strictly confidential?"

"Oh yes."

"We didn't even inform your regimental colonel about the nature of our investigation."

"I know."

"I think it made him rather cross. The truth is," and the lieutenant-colonel folded his arms with care, "we have to find out all we can about a member of your patrol reported missing."

"Who?"

"A certain Corporal Marrow."

Stevens didn't shift. He was gazing at the parquet flooring. But with those words he seemed to hear surf in his ears, like the clashing of glass; he'd listened to it with Lucy, over and over, in the back of the P.U. For a second the memory of her moist flesh, those dragging lips, came back to him in this decorous London room with all the shock of irrelevance. He hadn't been getting his greens lately, come to think of it.

"To be quite frank with you, Major," Charles Russ-Sykes was equably continuing, "we're a bit up a gum-tree. You see, this man has been missing in the true sense. And permanently."

Her step down the ward. What in blue blazes was he thinking of, visualizing Lucy when his own number was bloody up like this!

"What exactly do you mean, sir?" he asked thickly. He clearly remembered that Ellis, saying goodby at 13C, had noticed his big .45. Now Marrow's body had been discovered. Someone had hauled it out of the Adige and handed over the swollen corpse, with its great telltale bullet splash through the middle, to whom it might concern. Eventually British authorities. Spread-out .45 slug found in body. Q.E.D. Too Awfully Clever.

His questioner had ignored his own question, however. "Am I right, Alec?" he was saying.

Alec McCole, the C.I.D. man to whom Stevens was now cursorily introduced, was busily writing on his fairly greasy pad.

"Yes, that's correct," was all he said, scarcely glancing up. And when he did condescend to do so it was with a glance that seemed to be trying to read the small print on Stevens' backbone.

Stevens said quickly, "I saw Marrow killed. Hit point-blank. What's so bloody mysterious about all this? There couldn't be the slightest doubt about the man's being bumped off. It was full in the hallway of the house. When we left he was still absolutely out cold, in a pool of blood. You should have seen it. . . ." He concluded, "That's what I told Captain—I mean, Major—Ellis back in North Africa. It's all I know."

The M.P. officer nodded briefly. "Don't think I forget your evidence on that occasion." Stevens grew hot: evidence, was it. "But we've since interviewed prisoners, including a certain Feldwebel, a sergeant who was actually on duty at what your P.E.D.G. liked to call Dark House. He said Marrow was later found alive."

"I can't see what that proves."

Ellis said, "Marrow lived. Definitely wasn't killed in the raid. We have evidence he was sent back to a prisoner hospital in North Italy."

"You see, the odd thing about it," and the J.A.G. bloke spoke almost cheerfully now, "is that neither side seems to own poor Corporal Marrow. There's reason to believe he escaped from this hospital of his, probably when under supposed sedation, but there's no record of his actually joining our own forces on t'other side."

"In short," Stevens said, his breath hissing softly, "the man was a deserter."

There was silence in the room. He could see that this wasn't the first time such a thought had crossed their flicking minds and he calculated hectically: No one can prove the contrary till the bastard turns up in person. Unless they'd got him somewhere—and if so, why all this song and dance? It perfectly explained Marrow's leather jacket, his running from an officer who recognized him in Loretta, his lack of evident surprise at being shot in the effort to effect apprehension. It explained the hair; it could have been dyed.

Stevens gently shut his eyes. That was it. The hair. He'd try 'em, see if they knew.

Charles Russ-Sykes was staring down at his shining nails. He replaced in his briefcase a Swiss edition of Nerval's *Aurélia* that had somehow strayed out onto the table and which Stevens had automatically put down as a mucky book.

"That's what we're rather afraid of. Even so, we'd like to know what became of him. He's never been found, you see."

Stevens rubbed his boxer's nose. "I seem to remember him as a cove with red hair." He looked square at Ellis but the other's eyes didn't flicker. "Surely that'd prove a spot conspicuous, eh?" But not one of them bought it. Then it was all right? The first thing was to learn how much they knew. He fenced for time. "Course, I rather liked old Marrow. Been out with him before. Good bloke on a do."

"And yet," Ellis interjected coldly, "I recollect your telling the adjutant and me that he showed signs of fear that night."

"Well, that's right. It can happen to the best. Marrow was in a funk."

"Any explanation for that?"

"No, not really." Stevens stared hard at the floor. The parquet throbbed before him. If it were true that Marrow had never been found. But perhaps they were all lying. Decoy. He got out a large silk handkerchief, one Aunt Edie had sent him only last Christmas. "A good bloke all the same," he persisted.

"Despite the fact that he was showing signs of cowardice? I would have thought, I mean, in the P.E.D.G...."

"Anyone can show signs of fear." He drew himself up. He'd snapped. Keep your head, chum, above all show your nous. But how many of these smoothies had seen a boche fall backwards, his face all suddenly... "In a scrape like that, well, it was a mess," he concluded.

Russ-Sykes conferred in a whisper with those nearest him. He turned up some notes, moving with that assurance Stevens feared and detested. No doubt which side this blighter would always be on. He turned to Stevens, smiling now, as if about to extend some cordial invitation. "According to your report in North Africa you said that this poor man Ridgeworth, the soldier you started to carry, was hit in the head."

Stevens extricated a hand from under his buttocks. For a second he pressed on the balls of his eyes, with fingers and thumb, as if to drive out the very faculty of sight there. When he opened his eyes, however, they fell on Charles Russ-Sykes' fingernails. And he was all at once reminded again of that natty figure in pale mauve pajamas tottering down the stairs towards him in Dark House. As long as he didn't remember Ridgeworth's... He felt sick.

"Sorry if these memories pain you, Major."

"That's all right, sir. It's just that, well, frankly I don't remember everything that happened too clearly."

"We know all about that, too. From your hospital. And please believe me—we commiserate."

"Yes. I'd say Ridgeworth caught it somewhere about there. Around the back of his head, I'd say."

"You dropped him then?"

"I believe so."

There was a silence.

Then Ellis put a question, Stevens answered; Ellis dried up, and the C.I.D. man asked another; Stevens answered that. It went on. The inkstand, the sheaves of papers on the tables, Marrow's face on a photograph there, Marrow's face, Marrow's face. . . .

"The German sergeant we interviewed said they found him in the shed, you know."

"Did he now." Stevens pulled. himself together. This was the C.I.D. larker again. "Ah, inside the shed. I see." He sounded puzzled. "Well, yes, he might have crawled there right enough. Ridgeworth caught it just as I was carrying him outside. If my memory serves me correctly."

"That's precisely what we expected you to say," Russ-Sykes threw in. "There remains, however, the slight problem that Private Ridgeworth was found with most of the back of his head shot away."

"I can't explain that, sir." At least, Stevens was frantically calculating, unless they're damn sight smarter actors than I give 'em credit for, at least they didn't find a .45 in the blighter's bitching cranium. "You get odd physical symptoms in battle."

"No doubt," said the C.I.D. man icily.

"I mean," Stevens plunged angrily on, "I've found a man yards away from where I saw him hit. Chicken reactions, kind of. Anyway, that jerry you interrogated is only talking from memory of years and years ago by now."

"From clinical memory," Ellis amended. "That Feldwebel happened to be in their medical corps."

"And what does that prove?" Stevens came back. But he knew this was the wrong note. He continued dully, "How do I know if Ridgeworth crawled or didn't crawl, or even if he bloody took off? Maybe I put him back in the shed myself. I tell you I can't remember everything just then. It happens. Since you seem to have checked with my hospital so thoroughly, you can probably verify that, too."

Some feet beneath the table shuffled. Ellis said, "I'd have thought you might remember. Ridgeworth must have been shot from pretty close to, in order to lose most of his head like that."

This time Stevens squeezed shut his eyes in a mental wince and sat on his hands. He could feel them crawling under him, trying to get out.

"And on that point," Ellis went on, "you recall telling me you were hit in the arm as you ran from the hut after dropping Ridgeworth, right?"

"Yes, that's correct."

"The M.O. who examined your wound when you got back to P.E.D.G. has also stated that it seemed to have been inflicted from close to."

"And what does that prove? That it wasn't inflicted from far away? Something like that?"

"You told him you got it in the hallway. What have you to say about that?"

"I don't know." Stevens rolled his head. This goes on and on, he thought. "I can't say. May have been wrong. That's happened before, too. It may have been that the burst of fire that caught Ridgey then hit me too. In the confusion I just don't know. Besides, that doc saw me years ago—can he remember the case exactly?"

He left it at that. To his surprise it seemed to satisfy them. After swapping a glance with Charles Russ-Sykes the C.I.D. man said, "Someone put a field dressing, British, on Ridgeworth's thigh. Can you explain that?"

"Perfectly well. I put it on myself."

"You put it on while he was lying in the shed after being hit in the groin?"

"Right." He could feel genuinely indignant now. "Lieutenant Loran held the johnnie's legs while I fixed it. But it was a waste of time. Hopeless. He'd all but had it."

They couldn't get Loran at any rate, Stevens reflected with hostility. Not now, by Christ. When he saw the J.A.G. man looking uncomfortable, Stevens suddenly decided the man hadn't seen action. He'd play on it.

"No, you see it isn't much fun to have your balls creased for you like that, you know. I was in dock with a chap who stopped a piece of shrapnel in the arse. He's got to carry a bag about with him for the rest of his life."

Charles Russ-Sykes did indeed hold up one white, exquisitely manicured hand. "We're all most grateful to you for what you've told us, Major. This is definitely all you know about this Marrow, then?"

"Definitely all, sir."

"The last time you saw him was lying in a pool of blood in the hall of Dark House."

Stevens' eyes gave a brief blink. "Correct, sir."

"And that's really what we expected you'd say, too." He pressed the tips of his fingers slightly together. "I was dubious about holding this Court in the first place. But the thing got beyond my personal jurisdiction. Now, as its President, I am equally unhappily compelled to go through certain final formalities. Do forgive me, won't you?"

While I stab you in the back, Stevens thought hotly. He didn't trust this wappy bastard an inch. But they guzzled up an attitude of deference, that type did, so he put in respectfully, "Any way I can help, sir, though I'm afraid that's about the lot of it. I'm pretty dense at the legal angle, of course."

"We shall in all likelihood conclude as I anticipated we would conclude," continued his interlocutor in an unruffled manner and Stevens saw he hadn't touched the mucker.

"Look," he said. "It seems to me cut and dried. Marrow escapes from his prison hospital and, since we knew back in P.E.D.G. he was cracking up, he deserted."

"Possibly had personal reasons to fear you too, do you think?" put in a voice down the table.

Stevens went on, "Possibly. Certainly he showed his funk in the boat. He knew his control had gone and that if he did get put in a spot like that again he might break down altogether and find himself in proper hot water. Court-martial, all that sort of lark. Let's assume it, at any rate; it seems sensible to me." It did. His voice gathered confidence as his exposition went methodically on. "Anyway, he didn't show. Put down as Missing, Believed Killed. Personally, knowing the Italy of that time as I do, I'd guess he met a sticky end with the partisans or some such." He paused. The sun, previously streaming into the room, had gone behind a bank of cloud. "The trouble with this Court of Inquiry, gentlemen, is that there ought to be someone else here from that Operation Cabbage."

In the gentle silence that ensued Charles Russ-Sykes said, "But there is."

Stevens stiffened slowly. "What do you mean, sir?"

The other laughed. "Now look. You mustn't think you're under interrogation, anything like that at all. No hidden tape-recorders here, I believe."

"Thank you, sir, I don't. But..."

"Well then," and he smiled, easing his Sam Browne out another surreptitious notch, "to keep the whole thing completely above-board between us, Major, I arranged that our last witness in this matter will appear here in your hearing. The rest we've seen privately: your former adjutant, Major Taylor, so on. But this seemed the fairer way about it now. We haven't anything against you, but M.P. are insisting on everything being absolutely tiggerty-boo in this affair, I mean. In fact," and he grinned amicably at Ellis, "I'd say they've been making a damn nuisance of themselves all round."

"You said another witness." Stevens couldn't seem to think. "Very decent of you. But someone who..."

"After all," twinkled Charles Russ-Sykes blandly, "you were his superior officer."

"Eh?" A visceral nerve twitched somewhere; his consciousness seemed to go on guard. At the same time his skin seemed to shrink, the seat became suddenly too small for his body. One hand inched itself out and passed, crawling, over his forehead, and he got the impression that he had in some grotesque way become too large for normal functioning.

All at once he was hurled into a distant dream, a schoolboy nightmare of being on stage in the middle of an elaborate Elizabethan tragedy, among a number of perfectly trained professional actors. His turn to speak would be on him any moment, the actors were all exchanging splendidly rhetorical and perfectly rehearsed speeches, but he himself didn't know a word of what was to come. What was worse, he was slowly but surely growing bigger. Second by second. Petrified that his fellow actors, rather than the audience, would notice his change of shape, he waited for a cue he didn't know. And for the scornful faces that would follow, the shouts of derision, the collapsed performance, the deadened lights. . . .

But this was no dream, he now realized, although the sun had momentarily gone out. The whole thing was dreadful fact. He had just seen the J.A.G. Lieutenant-Colonel, his elbows on the glistening table, nod to one side. "Alec?"

Alec had risen and gone to the door. He had opened it and someone, who must have been waiting very close by outside, came forward into the room.

At first Stevens couldn't see properly. The parquet seemed to billow, a mist was drawn off it as he watched. This had to be a nightmare, there had to be some mistake. But they were all smiling at him now, waiting for him to obey his cue.

The figure limped. A tall, thin figure in a well-cut gray suit and with a pallid face that made the scar driven down the left cheek stand out with appalling vividness. He'd always looked young enough, yet now somehow younger than ever, as if he'd grown backwards, and Stevens wished that stranded lock of hair thrown off the face would hide at least some of the cruel welt. But it didn't, and there wasn't, he knew now, any mistake at all. Holding up one hand and smiling in a natural manner, as if he were entering his club, Loran moved straight to the chair in the center of the room.

CHAPTER FOURTEEN

Everything above-board from the start, thought Stevens with bitter flushes of resentment. And now they spring Loran on me. But how could it be true? Those pale eyes were far too old, of course; the contrast with the skimpy body was now intense. Otherwise the man had changed probably less than Stevens himself had. The dark hair still cut much too long. Same long ears, too. And he looked altogether more impressive in plain clothes; despite the leannes underneath that Sackville Street suit you could now believe the man was a judo expert.

Then social repression writhed in Stevens as he noted the dark tie with the lighter stripe he had always detested so. He could never see it without annoyance. And on Loran here…

"Hallo, Phil," said the ghost. Perhaps it was simply that unexpected use of his first name—it was all so hopelessly unreal anyway—perhaps it was the hellish scar athwart Tom Loran's left cheek. Whatever it was, Stevens told himself he'd known all long they'd had more to go on than they'd given out. Swine, he thought briefly. But he wasn't surprised.

"Hallo, Loran," he said huskily. He was standing up.

Being in plain clothes Loran didn't have to salute. Yet as he turned to the table he came to a kind of shambling attention in front of it, smiling still. Oh, Stevens wished he wouldn't smile so much, it stretched that sleek scar so. Moreover, Russ-Sykes was smiling back, in confident agreement with another member of the clan.

"Please have a seat, Mr. Loran, do. We're awfully sorry to have effected this reunion between you two gentlemen in this rather abrupt manner, but it was the element of surprise, I'm afraid, in which we were interested. At least—should I say—one of our number seemed to think it essential to our general purpose."

Recovered now from some of the nakedness of that pure shock he'd felt on seeing Loran coming through the door, Stevens realized the C.I.D. man was watching him. He loosened with fear. His teeth came hard together. His hands. How he hated this world. It was a world, he felt as he studied Loran's mucking tie, that had misused him from the start. He hadn't asked to be sent into Operation Cabbage, he'd only…

He couldn't look at Loran's eyes. He was afraid to find in those limpid depths the expression of the adversary in victory that had so haunted him in the ring. Yet he had to look. Oh yes. And Loran was still smiling away, before the kill. Stevens shivered in his fat.

"So you do see, Mr. Loran," the J.A.G. clown was now coolly continuing, "we asked you here in all good faith, to answer a few questions for us in front of Major Stevens here. First—I don't really have to ask you this—but you do recognize the officer you have already greeted as the one in charge of the mission to capture General von Schultz in which you were wounded and taken prisoner?"

"I do, sir." Loran's voice rang clear and confident and Charles Russ-Sykes smiled back at it.

"Only wish you'd got him, there's more evidence of his atrocities in today's papers. Frankly, I couldn't read them. Now this was the first patrol you were sent on with P.E.D.G., right?"

"That's correct."

"Would you, very briefly, in your own words, tell us what happened during that patrol."

Stevens cut in, "Is this really necessary, sir? I've just…" But he shut up once he caught Ellis' eyes.

Russ-Sykes made a polite sign and Loran pitched in. First, the business of losing three men prior to their entry. That took some time. Then the killing of the waiter inside the house. The death of Goddard. Stevens sat with his hands underneath him once more and this time he quivered as if he had the ague. But it tied in. And yet it didn't. Everything tied in with Stevens' story of the attack on Dark House, all right. At the same time, gradually—through the fog of his anxiety—Stevens became aware that Loran was building him up as a hero. Slowly he raised baffled eyes. They'd reached the point where Marrow had been killed.

"He was shot from the head of the staircase, sir."

"Quite sure you saw him fall, Mr. Loran?"

"Yes, absolutely."

"And it surprised you to learn he lived?"

"Of course."

Ellis asked, "Did Marrow seem to you to be cracking?"

"He did seem rather odd in the boat, yes."

But Loran was beginning to invent, Stevens could see, to improvise as well as to emphasize points he himself had already brought up in the course of his own story. Yes, there wasn't a bleeding doubt about it, Loran was dropping hints to the effect that Stevens had acted as a hero. It was uncanny. Now it was Stevens who had overcome the jerry staff officer in the room the three of them had entered. It was Stevens who had pressed them to go on.

"Did he seem to you, Mr. Loran, to accidentally take this brigadier for the general, by any chance?"

"Not for a minute."

Someone said, "Then who suggested you leave Dark House?"

Stevens blinked up. Loran appeared to study his fingernails for a second. Apologetically he answered, "I'm afraid I have to confess, sir, that by this point in the operation I was extremely scared."

"That's quite understandable," soothed Charles Russ-Sykes. "It was your first patrol, after all."

"No, but I don't mind admitting—now that I've been invalided out, I mean—that I kept on trying to persuade Major Stevens, Captain he was then, to call it a day. Leave the house, actually." His eyes fell. He hung his head. The performance was bloody perfect, Stevens considered. And he felt very frightened. Then he heard Loran say, "It was only his extreme heroism that drove us all on."

"I see. So Major Stevens attempted to persuade you to stay in the house and continue to seek out the general, is that what you're trying to tell us?" inquired the C.I.D. man. "While the others, Ridgeworth and yourself, that is, wanted to chuck your hands in."

Loran swallowed. "You could put it like that, I suppose."

Steven's hair began to crawl. He stared at Loran, but the other wouldn't meet his eyes. The J.A.G. man cleared his throat.

"Ah well, I'm sure that's nothing to be ashamed of. After all, it was your first time in action."

"It was Major Stevens' spirit that kept us at it, sir," Loran repeated in the same doggedly humble manner.

"After you'd suggested you leave the house and effect a retreat," Ellis came in coldly, "didn't you consider it rather odd that the officer in command of the patrol should elect to go first?"

The swine, thought Stevens. He was growing conscious of a smell, then he placed it. Loran's hair-oil. Briefly he thought, in North Africa the unlovely wog used camel urine for his hair dressing.

When Loran spoke again. "Actually, I asked if I might go last. You see, I could guess that whoever went first might run into a trap. It was Major Stevens who volunteered to do it for us. He'd just killed a German officer." Loran added quietly, "Frankly, I'll always feel he saved my life."

What's his game? Stevens thought hotly. He felt speechless, raw-tongued in front of this cunning. Then they were leading Loran on, on to the final tragedy in the hut.

"When you picked Ridgeworth up, you say he was badly hit in the genitals?"

"That's correct." Loran moistened his lips.

"You put a field dressing on him?"

"Yes."

Ellis said quickly, "Put it on yourself?"

"Yes, I think that's right."

"But Major Stevens here tells us it was he who put the dressing on, while you held the man's legs. Which is it?"

"I think." He paused. "Yes, that was correct. My mistake, sorry. It was all pretty confused, you see. My memory must have slipped just there. I held the man's feet while Major Stevens put the actual dressing on."

"Let's keep these things straight, shall we," the M.P. officer said in a surly tone, but it was obvious he felt a social inferiority to Loran he didn't feel with Stevens.

"You then left the hut first?"

"Yes, that time I asked if I might run for it first. We seemed to be clear of most of the Germans. About then ..." Loran broke off once more. It was, Stevens reflected, watching in a sick fascination, a really bloody marvelous performance. "I'm afraid my behavior doesn't reflect too much credit on me, does it? But you asked for the truth and it's the truth I'm giving you, gentlemen."

"That's quite all right, Mr. Loran. We do understand." Charles Russ-Sykes spoke more than tolerantly. "There's one final point, however. When you ran out of the hut you left Ridgeworth behind, to be carried by Major Stevens?"

Loran only answered this after a long wait. "Yes, sir."

"Didn't hear any shot behind you, anything like that?"

Loran closed his eyes.

"These are painful memories, I know."

"Well, no, sir. I simply ran out and seemed to get hit straight away. It all happened at once. You'll appreciate it was very brave of Major Stevens to try to carry the soldier in the first place. After that you know my history. A German military hospital—I was damn lucky not to be executed because of my double Norwegian citizenship—then demobilization back here a few weeks ago."

It was conclusive. There really seemed nothing more to say. The J.A.G. johnnie was looking about him. Glad it's over, thought Stevens, who sat frozen with fear. As always, when flummoxed by something intellectually beyond his grasp, he started coldly perspiring with apprehension. Like being called out to con Livy at school . . . a cut with the cane for each mistranslation.

He looked at Loran in agony now. To his horror Loran was gazing at him with an admiringly deferential smile. Stevens' body felt twice its normal weight on the flimsy chair and his hands had become obstreperous again.

A voice said, "One last point."

"Certainly."

Ellis asked: "To the best of your recollection, was Major Stevens wounded during any of the fighting?"

In the silence that followed this question Stevens sought recourse from the dread that was dogging him in a reasonless detestation, a flooding-up of all his soul in hate. He forced himself to see Ellis in the Nissen, ducking under the table. He felt he had by this time renounced all security, every tie; it was as if he didn't exist at all in the room and they were discussing an impersonality, that cipher he had once so longed to be.

Loran spoke carefully. "There was quite a bit of blood on his battle dress, I remember, after that German bumped into him, you see. Actually, it was so long ago it's pretty hard to sort it out properly now."

"But you must remember something as important as that. Surely you'd recall whether he was or was not shot."

"As I say, he was in a bit of a mess. We all were." Stevens was glad to see Loran growing irritated with Ellis, too. "He was being pretty game and for all I know he may have been hit by the man at the top of the stairs who got Marrow. It was Major Stevens who shot him."

"But even with a minor bullet wound, surely you'd have remembered. After all, he carried Ridgeworth out of the hut."

Loran didn't say anything.

And Ellis made his one mistake. At a nod from the C.I.D. man he slumped in his seat. "Doesn't really matter. I think we can say we're satisfied over the Marrow affair. More or less. There was a slight discrepancy in Major Stevens' story, you see. When he got back to his unit he told the M.O. there that he'd been shot in the hall. As I've shown, he later claimed this was leaving the shed. However, since he suffered concussion, we can take this under the heading of legitimate margin of error, I think. We aren't here to pick holes in an old sore. I'm referring to the moment," he concluded quietly, "when Major Stevens was hit on the head in the hallway."

After a second Loran said, "Oh yes."

Then they were summing up, all smiling like mad, there was a moment of literal eclipse for Stevens, staring straight ahead into his opening hands. Loran was getting up.

"Before I go, sir—" again that deferential smile, the look of the swab at school—"I'd like to say how much I owe to Major Stevens." Stevens heard, "splendid leadership ... his inspiration alone responsible ... held the patrol together." Then very softly Loran added, "I had to put my life into the hands of this officer. I know, as no one else can, the reward he deserves."

A respectful silence coursed round the room after this. Stevens went white. He thought of the absoluteness, the totality of Loran's longing for revenge on the jerry general in Dark House. Now ...

"Yes, thank you so much." Charles Russ-Sykes was actually pumping Loran's hand. "Major Stevens was indeed mentioned in despatches for his role in the operation. I only wish you had got hold of von Schultz. Thanks so much for your candor and your—ah—your co-operation."

The others said goodby to him equally cordially.

Someone said: "One of 'em copped it in his pajamas at any rate. Jolly good."

Another added: "And damn good luck in Civvie Street."

"I'll need it," Loran answered ruefully.

Laboriously Stevens rose to his feet. "I say, Loran, could I see you afterwards for a minute?"

"Yes, we won't need you much longer now, Major," said Charles Russ-Sykes. "A few final details for the bumf experts in the War House, that's all." He wound up, "The whole thing's rather rum, you know."

Loran said softly: "Good-by, Phil. I'd like to say publicly, some day I hope to repay—"

Stevens cut in quickly, "I'd like to see you when I'm done with this lot. Would you wait downstairs a sec?"

Loran nodded gravely, half-smiling, and limped slowly out.

Resettling himself behind the gleaming table, Charles Russ-Sykes heaved a sigh of relief. "Well, that's that. Poor devil. Perhaps he'll help you with all that unpacking you say you've got to do, Major Stevens."

CHAPTER FIFTEEN

He wasn't there, of course. Stevens had scarcely expected him to be. The whole affair had come far too close to one of his nightmares for that, for after all a nightmare, when all was said and done, was essentially the failure of some basic assumption about the world—you woke up under water, you sank through solid ground. And he had assumed Loran dead.

Stevens found himself late for lunch when he got back from the court and crossed the barrack square to the mess. Life here had changed very little, he found. Two officers he remembered from his first days as an ensign dozed as usual in their customary leather chairs, one protected from the flies by a copy of Country Life. Behind the big screen, depicting with bloodthirsty realism a seventeenth-century battle, khaki-clad waiters were already clearing the table. Two old gaffers with antique medal ribbons sat opposite each other, each behind an array of salt cellars and pepper grinders.

"Enemy were there," Stevens heard, "we were here. Imagine whizz-bangs going over, all that. To get there I realized we would have to evacuate here." The man looked up with pleasure at his ancient aperçu. "It was my idea to ..."

"Heave over the mustard, would you," Stevens called, settling himself at the only single place left further down the table. One of the officers, a short bald major, glared down at him from eyes muzzy with port. And suddenly Stevens realized he had committed a mess gaffe: no one was allowed by regimental custom to join the table after the port had circulated once.

And it clearly had done so, he could see the decanter—almost empty—back at the last place, or where it had been. He took no notice. The waiter served him sullenly. Shortly the two officers pottered off. "Young generation these days," Stevens heard, "no respect for. . . ."

Once the other side of the screen, however, the twin buffers seemed to imagine that they automatically couldn't be overheard. Stevens caught stentorian whispers.

"Who was that?"

"Chap called Stevens. Heard he was back on strength."

"Oh. And what did he do?"

"Wasn't he in some sort of commando thing? Y'know, knifing people by moonlight, all that sort of business."

"I agree, I can't say I saw much point in it. Playing pirates, I called it frankly. It merely ended up in the boche taking reprisals on our ordinary infantry. No consideration."

"What school was he at, d'you know?"

Huffing and puffing they sauntered out. The mess resumed its afternoon torpor. Stevens realized he was back in that world he had tried to escape from in P.E.D.G., that little universe of privilege and position where a gentleman, one of the winners, could still count on being called "sir," "sahib," or "bwana," and where outward appearances of social position were symbolized in silly contrivances, such as the occupany of a chair or the carrying of a certain kind of stick on parade.

After lunch he sat down at a writing table and tried to compose an account of "My Years of Service Abroad" that his old school magazine had just requested of him. It took him a long time to write even a line. Nearby, an old officer snored away, his nose in correspondence columns about queen wasps, blackbird mysteries, and cruelty to trees, no doubt. What did it all mean? What in blue heaven had that twerp Loran meant just now? He felt frightened; it was inexplicable really. He tore up the paper and started out.

In the doorway a bluff, apple-cheeked captain, a sort of stage training officer, stopped him.

"Stevens? Like to congratulate you. Just been over with the adjutant. And I'd like to congratulate you."

"What the hell on?"

The other prodded him with his cane. "Look, you don't get a Mention in a show like P.E.D.G. for nothing. No, come off the modesty, old boy, I've just been listening to a young chappie in there givin' a stirring account of your personal bravery in action."

"To our adjutant?"

"Yes, personal friend, it seems. I was in there at the time. And privileged to hear, I'm glad to say, for the honor of the reg...."

"Chap with a limp?"

"Yes, that's right. Dreadful limp, poor chappie. And that scar. Still, very neat rig. Grey suit. You must have put up a rattlin' good show and I'd like to stand you one, if I may. For the regiment, I mean."

"Is he there with the adjutant now?"

"Ah no, gone some time." The other's brows went up. "Believe he had some appointment or other. Anything wrong, I mean?"

His scalp prickling, Stevens ran over to the Orderly Room. But Loran had gone. What was more, the adjutant had gone too.

Stevens went back to the mess and sat gazing straight in front of him for a time. After a while the two officers he'd been at table with returned and reshuffled their array of salt cellars and bottles of Worcestershire sauce.

"So, jerry was here, we were there, see. I decided that to knock him for six...."

The snoring officer flapped ineffectually at a fly and, still without opening his eyes, continued hectically to flap long after the fly had flown away.

Stevens went back to his room in the Cromwell Road. But there was nothing to unpack. He looked out of the window at this alien world he had returned to. People were getting off buses and walking busily up the street. At a corner a queue was forming outside a local Odeon. He watched them with a mixture of amazement and fascination. All these people, he thought, and they really look as if they're going somewhere. Suddenly lost and frustrated, he sat and oiled his gun.

CHAPTER SIXTEEN

In those few last days in the Army Stevens found himself excused of all duties after a perfunctory nine A.M. parade. Actually he would have enjoyed doing more marching, that sort of thing; at least it took his mind off it all for a few hours.

But the regimental colonel proved adamant. Stevens was treated with special esteem. In the mess the young officers deferred to him in a disgusting manner. Even the two old fogies who refought their First World War battles with cruets muttered grudgingly at him now. The bulbous, ruddy-cheeked Captain who'd first congratulated him gave a small party at a fairly fashionable nightclub the night before his demob leave began.

He felt scared stiff of Loran, but at the same time he felt he had to find him. The War Office wouldn't play with any information, however, when he went there. Nor would Loran's esteemed regiment divulge any addresses. Once, one lunchtime, Stevens tried the Cavalry Club in Piccadilly. The bulldog behind the panel there was most carefully impolite. Then on a brainwave, his last day of service, Stevens tried the Ministry of Pensions. Loran had said he was invalided out during the Court of Inquiry; with a limp like that he'd have been bound to get pension. He spent about an hour and a half being shuttled about by a lot of nonentities who'd probably never been near action in their lives. But, nothing doing.

Thirty days, Stevens thought dully, watching the crowds from his hotel window. Thirty days, then out—out for life on a major's pension, me bucko. Not so bad. He'd go away. The Channel Isles were said to be a literal paradise. Just fade into the wallpaper for thirty days. Dead quiet, like. If only Loran weren't alive.

But Loran was, all right. And even that first evening out Stevens knew the man was watching him.

Stevens had in fact no unpacking to do at all. He had his one tin box containing his sum total of valuables, which he stared at uncomprehendingly from time to time. And from time to time he moved things about a little in his room. (Once he'd awakened, bright-alert in the night, imagining he'd heard a soft scuffling sound outside the door.)

He was happiest when his room most nearly resembled his tent in North Africa: that first evening he went out and bought a tin of bully, finding there was something comforting in the old desert fare. When he came back there was a copy of the evening paper in front of his door.

At first he thought there'd been some mistake. The headline read—WAR CRIMINALS RISING GERMAN GENERAL SOUGHT. Above this had been scribbled in scarlet ink: *There is something that will interest you at page 3.* On page 3, he found, back inside his room, a column had been marked. It was a gossip trifle, purporting to give information about the doings of celebrities, of the kind Stevens sedulously ignored. He saw his name there. *Night Out at Clio's*, he read. His first reaction to seeing his name was one of slightly shocked guilt.

With the beard-and-sandal boys in North Africa Major Stevens won an honored name. In the course of time, when so many cards don't have to be held quite so close to so many chests, the exploits of the intrepid Major, celebrating his discharge at a table last night, will be written up, it is hoped, with appropriate élan.

What the hell. Jesus, he didn't even know what that last word meant, you needed a frog dictionary these days to read most English newspapers. He immediately telephoned the paper.

A sub-editor was evasive, he couldn't get anywhere with the mucker at all.

Stevens sat down on his bed and began clasping and unclasping his hands, as a kind of numb futility took hold of him. Loran was there at Clio's, eh. He might have known it. This meant the blighter was definitely after him, in earnest. He felt exhausted, his mouth drooped like a child's. His shoulders sagged. He badly needed a drink.

The local pub had the WYBMADIITY sign up and he suddenly thought of the red fezzes, the shaded terraces, the great flame of sun on the desert out there, all that world of color and clarity. A world where the rules had been simple. And he had broken them. Sitting at the counter he butted the pad of his forehead with a fist and groaned, "Sorry, sorry," aloud.

As the drink coursed down him his self-pity increased. A dreadful craven remorse, a feeling he despised with all his soul, crept into his mind. He went and called up his mess, got onto the rubicund captain who had thrown the farewell party, hoping against hope that it was he who had passed on the story to the paper. But he knew before he began that it wasn't; the regiment was very strict about dealings with the press.

"My dear old boy, you don't seriously imagine that I... yes, yes, I can well understand your feelings but after all, dash it," the other had concluded coyly, "a war hero, you'll just have to face up to that now, y'know. After all that bubbly we...."

Stevens rang off. In any case, that "at page 3" rather than "on page 3" smacked of an intellectual refinement of language all too reminiscent of his new-found enemy. He sat on, drinking, pounding his brain for some way out. Use your loaf, old bean, he exhorted himself over and over again, use your loaf, for Christ's sake, man. By closing time he'd decided that if this was going to be Loran's little game he'd have to dodge him. He'd also discovered the delights of oblivion via the bottle.

Next morning he moved to a miserable hotel in the Bayswater Road. There he put on the suit and hat he'd been given on leaving the Army, a gray pinstripe affair and a brown felt. But in the mirror he looked more of a bruiser than ever, mouth wider, the nose flatter, hopelessly wrong in such duds. What's more, although he'd chosen it carefully, the suit now seemed far too small. All in all he made the sort of bloke, he thought bitterly, whom coppers looked at twice.

But this change of clothing, after so many years, represented a considerable transference, and more than ever he felt it psychologically essential to emphasize his connections with the only life he'd really known. He ate bully in his room out of a mess tin, washing down the oily pressed beef with a few cornflakes mushed in watery milk. And he started drinking heavily. At night he lumbered back from The Pig and Whistle pub nearby and slept in his clothes. For several days on end he drank steadily, starting with brandy after breakfast—when you can really feel it, he told the saturated reflection in the mirror, bones and all. But it didn't help, for once again he knew Loran was watching him.

This evening he'd been bingeing in a Services Club in Kensington and had stopped for one for the road in his local before turning in. But tonight the publican of The Pig and Whistle, a man with vaudeville mustaches and cheeks of the correct varnished red, greeted him with a peculiar smile.

What's up now, Stevens wondered, his faculties sharpening as he ordered. When he dug for change to pay, the pub-keeper grinned openly. "Don't want none of that ternight off of you, Major. On the 'aas, please."

Stevens said, "What's so special about tonight?"

The man's face went solemn. "Dun' min' telling you, Major. Na, I los' a boy out there, min'."

"Out where?"

"My oldest. T'anks."

"What the hell are you talking about?" He collected himself. "I'm sorry to hear that."

"Seems long ago and done wiv' now, of course. On'y, when that gen'leman come in again ternight and tell me as how 'e'd bin out there in North Africa with you." The varnished cheeks contracted in the proper stylized wink. "Describe you purfick, sir. To a T. 'Tain't every day as we get customers come in oo've risked their ruddy necks to cop a jerry general, what! Na, na, sir, y'aren't. Y'aren't paying for this lot, sir. Not ternight y'aren't. Not if I knows it, sir."

Through his teeth Stevens said, "Tall, lean, dark. Too much bloody hair, eh? Did he have a scar? Limp?"

"Ah, ah." The man was chuckling now in a copybook succession of publican nods. "Purfick, sir. To a T. Like I say. Arty-looking type. 'As bin in once or twice lately. Spoke very 'ighly of you. Ah."

"Did he say where he could be found?"

"Na, na. Simply said as 'ow he owed you quite a bit for what you'd done out there and fer me to tell you 'e'd get even. Yus, 'at's wot he said, 'at's 'ow he put it, Major."

But Stevens had left, accompanied by a final protesting "Sir … on the 'aas!" Back in his room, he knew he was breaking. He tore off his clothes, put on a pair of striped pajamas, lay down and tried to sleep. But no bagging it deadly for Philip Stevens now. And every nerve in his body seemed to quiver, exposed, as the ring at his door sounded several minutes later.

Slowly Stevens swung himself out of bed. His pajama top had slipped off his left arm and he caught sight of the pinkish blob of flesh where the bullet had entered there. For some while he listened, aching. Someone was standing in the passage, he felt sure of it.

"Loran?" he called softly. "That you? You're there, aren't you?"

There was silence. He wondered if he could smell perfume or something. Hair-oil. Trumper's, sure to be.

"Listen, Loran," he pleaded, "I'm coming out swinging, I swear to God I am…"

All at once, deafeningly close—Trrrling!

Stevens opened the door, his hands on guard. A police sergeant stood there. His heart went worse than ever.

"Sorry, officer, never know who it might be at this time of night, do you?"

What did this blue eye want? For some reason the man's right hand seemed to be covered in rings. A duster? Or his imagination? Always hated bobbies. That last drink…

"You left this behind in the pub, sir, I believe." The constable held out a hat. He spoke in a cultured voice.

"Ah. I see. Thanks." Stevens took it, asked, "How did you cotton on to where I lived, incidentally?"

The other grinned. "Followed you home, sir. Didn't want anything to happen to an old P.E.D.G. scout, and you did look, if I may say so, sir…"

"Yes, I know. Under the weather. But how did you know I…"

The sergeant's accent dropped a trifle. "It is your titfer, isn't it?"

Stevens studied the hat. Just the same. Initials. Everything. "That's it, all right. Demob version. Thanks awfully"

"Well you know, sir." And he leant forward confidentially, as one non-gentleman to another. "See, my name's Pryde,

sir."

"Is it now."

"Course, the others rag me. Pride of the force. All that sort of thing." Stevens could have sworn he had on several rings. He considered that this smiling individual had a bad face. It confirmed all his dislike of the bobbie. "Now I reckoned you were entitled to a spot, after what you've been through, sir. That young gentleman who was in earlier, he came back directly you'd left the pub, you see, and pointed out how you'd forgotten your hat. In fact, it was him who gave it me, sir."

"Go on."

"Praising you to the skies he was, of course."

Suddenly Stevens held up a hamlike hand in front of the constable's face. "Stop speaking, please."

"See, I always wanted to get out there myself, sir. Yes. I'd have liked to have had a go."

"Please. Enough." He began closing the door. But the sergeant wanted to stay and chat, it seemed.

"Pryde, sir," he called through the closing door. "Any time I can be of help."

The door shut. Stevens threw the hat onto a chair and sat down on the edge of the bed. He wondered if he could detect a mild heart murmur in his chest. Daren't go and see a doc till he was safely out...

Next morning he found a letter from the Conservative and Unionist Association, saying they'd heard he might consider standing for Parliament and, if so, would he care to arrange a meeting. With his war record... Stevens packed up his tin trunk and moved into new digs, a small hotel near Victoria Station. A few days after that he knew he was cracking in earnest when he got back from a bar and found himself staring into a smashed mirror in his room. Glancing down, he saw bloodied meat. He moved again.

Hours spent in the British Museum checking on extradition laws. He had begun to concoct elaborate fantasies about flight overseas and actually put in train an application for a passport. He picked inevitably on South America and made hopeful enquiries about immigrant fares. He was still systematically lifting the elbow, all right, and once—anything to forget—he decided to have a woman, so he'd followed a beefy, discontented-looking prostitute up to her quarters in Maddox Street. Look her over well, boy, he'd told himself during the pickup, there's more to a stove than the burner. But when she stripped, he laughed. Jesus God, this slut was a bag. It was all just another fraud, all rubberized girdles and that kind of muck; why she practically tripped over her tits when she walked.

There was no question of any desire. He groaned at her once or twice, shook his head, and started weaving to the door. That was when she screamed at him. Stevens slapped her and she went down on hands and knees with a puzzled expression on her face. He stood there watching her for a second, studying his degradation.

"Sorry," he mumbled. An officer and a gentleman. He realized he had hit her far too hard. Blood seemed to be oozing out of the old whore's right ear. He felt suddenly frightened, then saw that his slap had torn an ear-ring out or off. He threw all the money he had on the floor and ran for it, panting.

When he got back to his tired room the words WAR HERO had been scrawled in pink chalk on top of his trunk. Despite furious and frantic enquiries from the tawdry hotel help no one seemed to know anything about it and so he shifted off again, this time to an hotel in the Baker Street district. But he could feel Loran watching him every minute of the day now; it was uncanny. And so he wasn't surprised when the telephone went his second morning there.

"Loran?"

"Is that Major Stevens?" inquired an exceptionally pleasant voice at the other end of the wire.

It turned out to be a publisher asking him if he'd be interested in penning some memoirs of the "Westarn Desart."

"How did you know I was staying here?" Stevens asked him.

"Wa-a-arl," drawled the polite voice, "shall we say, a source of information ..."

Stevens saw he wasn't going to get any further with the man. "Afraid I'm not the literary type."

"That could be taken care of all right, Major. Our editors are excellent at rewrite jobs. From what I hear you have a magnificent story in that desart business and the War House is bound to relax these secrecy regulations soon."

"I'm sorry. I'm supposed to be writing about My Years of Service Abroad for my school mag, but I haven't got any further than the first sentence." It was true. He hadn't. When he'd rung off he stared at what he'd written so far once again: "As we look back through the years, and see how our team did things, we can say: Some people have all the luck, others do not." It had seemed to him when he wrote it, and it seemed to him now, a profound statement of fact. He sat on his bed and pasted some Marmite on dry bread with his penknife. He'd have to move again, he supposed. But it was getting hopeless, really. Loran had him by the shorts.

Two days later he was coming in from an afternoon drink when the hall porter took a copy of The Times out of his pigeonhole together with his key.

"Wrong number." He handed the paper back.

But the porter was adamant. "Oh no, sir. Young gentleman come in with it for you. Said to be sure to give it you, as there was something that would interest you in it."

"Give his name?"

"No, sir. But he was a tall, dark gentleman …"

"With a scar."

"Right, sir."

While the hall porter gaped Stevens crammed his upper body over the desk. "If you ever let that man in my room I'll cream you, so I will. In small spoonfuls."

Up in his room it was some time before he found it because this time the paper wasn't marked and his hands were shaking very badly. Lot more about war crimes. Names like Schmidt, Denkmann, Kaltenbrunner. Paratroopers handcuffed and shot down in cold blood. Awful, he thought, what if that kind had taken me and Loran red-handed that night. Sod it, he cursed suddenly as he searched, I'm just playing the bastard's game for him. There was nothing in any of the news items so far as he could see. Then he tried the face of the paper, the voluminous

Personals. And sure enough, there he was: BRUTE STRENGTH AND IGNORANCE. *Even Steven. War Hero or Plaster Saint?* Wait for it. TACL.

Stevens crumpled the paper and flung it at the wall. Despite the deliberately distorted spelling of his name there he most undoubtedly was. Courtesy, Too Awfully Clever Loran. He shivered again. I'll get you, my friend, he told himself, fingering his pistol. Eton and Bloodyall, you just see if I don't. But this time he didn't change his hotel; he knew it was useless; he'd been run to earth at last.

When the telephone went a few nights later he simply watched the instrument throb intermittently for a while. There'd been too many callers lately who'd just silently replaced the receiver after he'd picked up his phone. This ring seemed to fill the room.

"Who's that?"

"This is Tom Loran," the voice equably replied. "Remember me?"

Blood leapt like a fish in Stevens, listening. "That's not you, Loran."

"Oh yes, it is."

"Listen, have you gone mad? I don't know what the hell game you think you're playing. . . ."

"I want to see you, Philip."

"You put that Personal in *The Times*, didn't you?"

"Ah, highly confidential," came the so-U answer back. "Anonymity of advertisers. After all, you did try *The Times* yourself, didn't you? How did you like it, by the way?"

"I told you to wait for me after that Court of Inquiry. You didn't. Why not?"

"Unfortunately you aren't my senior officer any more, Philip."

"How in hell's name did you find out where I've been bunking all the time? Where are you now? Why've you been following me around like this?"

Loran gave a laugh. It made Stevens cringe. "Oh wouldn't you like to know? Listen, take this down." He gave a number in Poland Street.

"What the devil's that?"

"You'll find out." Another chuckle. "It's called the Honey Bee. A day club, actually. You know the sort of thing, you've been lifting the bottle in quite a few recently. I want you to meet me there tomorrow night at ten-thirty sharp."

"What if I don't show up?"

"I'd advise you to. After all, I do have one or two things on you, don't I, Philip? Please don't be late. I hate to be kept waiting."

"Hey!"

But Stevens was listening to black bakelite, a beetle blank and hot in his hand. This isn't real, he told himself, not happening. And as he reached for the golden smile of Johnnie Walker he thought: I must remember I'm alive. Free. Free to do whatever I like. I'm here, he said to himself a moment later, throwing wide his arms. But the big fists recoiled on their own, as though they'd touched the bars of a cage.

CHAPTER SEVENTEEN

It cost a packet to get into the Honey Bee. Having shed the necessary notes Stevens waded into a muggy lounge with elaborately Gallic décor. A speaker behind the bar relayed from what appeared to be another part of the establishment the nearest thing to Gabriel's music Stevens had ever tuned in to. Some classy-looking couples were listening with all the reverence and respect more normally found in a church.

That kind of place, he thought sourly, and looked quickly for Loran. But he himself was anxiously early and he couldn't spot the tick yet. He told himself he needed a drink. Strictly speaking, he didn't, but he had to have one. Behind the bar a buxom blonde was holding forth in black velvet, swivel-hipping about and displaying her figure as she reached for the requisite bottles. Among these, absurdly enough, stood several jars of honey, and he now saw that replicas of bees were worked into the fixtures. A rum-and-honey drink was announced as the specialty of the house and Stevens felt in no mood to refuse it.

He ordered. Lamp her, he thought as she turned and, bottom-tight, reached. This was one post-war minx not made by Hillman.

"I admire your gownless evening strap," he told her when she'd mixed the drink. "How much is the Strychnine Special, if you please?" She duly dimpled and asked him for seven shillings and sixpence.

Stevens sighed and paid. Dozens of these silly little clubs, useful to drink through London afternoons in, and God knows they made you drink, had sprung up in Soho lately, but this price was steep even by their standards. These places were strictly purposeless: Stevens mentally contrasted them with the bars in Cairo or Alex or Algiers where the drinking, though equally heavy, was somehow morally exonerated by the war. He wondered why Loran had picked this spot in particular, told himself it must be one of the semi-posh places where debs and young Guards officers adjourned to hear the stomp and sputter of "progressive" jazz and occasionally get up to dance new steps with absurd names.

He downed his drink, and made for a table at the back, from which he could watch the room. These days he'd come to feel more comfortable with a wall behind him somehow. Yes, it was typical of Loran to have chosen home ground: this place was social all right. He hailed the nearest waiter, an anemic youth who seemed deliberately to ignore him until Stevens shot out a foot as he was going by and tripped him. He ordered another.

Oh yes, this place was snooty. You could tell that, not only by the number of noses that looked as if they had very bad smells just underneath them, but also because the music now gave way to a monodic banter about feuilles mortes and amours perdues and a lot of similar bilge in a feline purr, and the society faces moved together in even greater solemnity as the dilatory accents poured through. Phony, he told himself, shifting his feet, oh phony as all hell.

He remembered the simplicity and brutality of relaxation after duty in the desert, and he was suddenly reminded of a column of infantry singing a song. And the singer's words Stevens heard now reverted to the old ballad:

Look around the mountains, in the mud and rain—

You'll find the scattered crosses—there's some which have no name.

Heartbeak and toil and suffering gone,
The boys beneath them slumber on.

It had been sung to the tune of *Lili Marleen*. Stevens' head suddenly fell. Battle-scarred veterans. Bottle-scarred veterans. Battle-scared veterans.

"She call that singing, son?" he asked the waiter when the boy eventually came back with his drink. The price had mounted to nine shillings now.

"Strite from Saint Germin-day-Pray," came the offended answer.

"Saint Vermin, you mean," said Stevens, paying and at the same time prying loose the boy's made-up bow tie. "Don't you give me any of that, lad. Here you are, and next time look slippy when I call you, see."

There was an empty glass of the hock variety standing on the table. Stevens put two fingers inside it, lifted it onto the expectant waiter's tray, and with the mildest pressure snapped it in pieces. The boy goggled, made worriedly off. Stevens sat back. Better for that. The action had restored his humor and the second drink was beginning to dispell something of that fear which was like anguish in him nowadays. But dammit, the rum smelt. Nasty oily stuff. It stank of Bren guns.

He contemplated a group making for the entrance into the basement quarters—you had to pay a second time to enter this holy of holies, it appeared—and he thought bitterly again, All phony, tell that lot it's a frog and they'll lick the floor she walks on to get near her.

"Hello, War Hero," said a voice.

He straightened like a hinge. He hadn't been watching and so Loran had come up beside him wearing, for some reason, very large dark glasses. His scar, as he smiled, seemed to throw out a livid accusation at war itself.

"What's your game, Loran?" Stevens said hotly and seized his arm; it felt ridiculously frail within his grip.

"Steady, there." Loran carried a drink. He put it on Stevens' table and sat down. "As a matter of fact, I rather think we were on rum the last time we drank together, eh. Very appropriate." He cocked an ear while sipping his drink. "Who's the damsel with the velvet tonsils tonight? It must be Marguerite, isn't it?"

"Stop jawing," Stevens said, "and come to the point."

"But I thought you used to drink Younger's. I seem to recall something about a garden in Kent, surely. Grass, hammock, so forth. Anyway it was nice of you to tip up. I'm very glad you did." He added, "For your sake, actually."

"You've been following me, haven't you?"

Stevens bowed his head. "Tell me, you bastard," he whispered, "or I'll hide your bloody hair-oil for you, so I will." When Loran said nothing he added, "What's the bleeding score, man, what are you after with me?"

But Loran only continued to hum to himself. Stevens wished he could see his eyes. He'd begun to tremble and he was afraid it was visible. Winner and victim, he thought, and he knew it showed.

Then Loran said gently, "You have been hitting the bottle rather just recently, haven't you?" He raised a hand and instantly the waiter appeared at his side with a deferential bow.

After they'd reordered Stevens said, "You needn't think you did that. I just put the fear of God into that kid." He glared at Loran's well-known tie. "Listen, you realize I could take you out of here and smash you up into bloody kindling, if I wanted to." Or could I, he thought suddenly, remembering Loran's judo.

"You're in trouble, Philip, aren't you?"

There was silence while the waiter brought the round.

Stevens said, "Why did you lie to that Court of Inquiry? That's a pretty serious matter for a young officer, you know."

"I couldn't get hold of you beforehand, that's why," Loran retorted coolly. "Nobody seemed to know your whereabouts on repatriation leave. Besides, I had my reasons."

"What do you want from me?"

Loran drank. Stevens noticed that he did so almost greedily, too. "You're right, Philip. There is something you can do for me. I hope you're ready to now." He paused, then brought out softly: "You shot Ridgeworth after I ran for it, didn't you? After they hit me, I mean."

"I don't know what the hell you're talking about, man."

"Yes, you did. I heard the shot, Phil."

"You can't have done. There was firing all…"

"It silenced, after they brought me down. No, I heard it all right, lying there waiting for them to come and get me and thinking of them executing me later on. Direction of the shed. There wasn't any doubt. They told me what they found, you know."

Stevens said, "You're crazy, Loran."

"You even came to the door of that hut and covered me, didn't you? Oh yes, I looked back, all right."

"Listen," he said, his voice shaking as he spoke, "even say one of us had killed Ridgey then, you know as well as I do it'd have been an act of mercy. His aorta was bloody severed. You should have seen him at the end."

"I remember all right, Phil. Everyone in the patrol done for but you and me." He stroked the scar on his face as he repeated, "You and me. For you gave me this, didn't you, Phil, and this." He extended his leg.

Stevens looked at him horrified. "What do you mean?"

"Oh, I ran from that hut just as hard as I knew how. I was scared stiff then myself, anyway. It was only later thinking it over in the hospital that I realized you must have known I was running straight into a bunch of boche. You sent me in that direction, remember?"

"I swear I didn't know." He slumped forward over the table, his voice strained and flat. "I swear to God…"

"Oh, it all suited your book so well, didn't it," Loran continued wearily. "You imagined they'd do your work for you. No one left. And I'd be shot if captured, anyway. Only, it didn't work out quite like that, did it?"

"Please—" Stevens was grappling with the accusation, trying to dredge up some arguments to refute it, convince Loran. "Whatever you do, you mustn't think I..."

"Dear boy, you're in too deep, much too deep by now. I managed to get a word with that German Medical Sergeant they were interrogating at the Court of Inquiry. If was he who actually handed over Ridgeworth's corpse to the Army doctor. The Court didn't choose to pursue the matter any further. They were principally interested in Marrow. But that doctor could be unearthed. Why not?"

"How do you know he's even survived?" said Stevens, hopelessly following the drift of Loran's argument like some mesmerized rabbit.

"It might be possible to collar him via that Feldwebel, say, and let him give evidence on the state of Ridgeworth's cranium. The Court is rechecking some ex-prisoners now, as it happens. I seem to recall," he concluded suavely, "you ported a big Colt and slit your rounds. Rather conspicuous in its effects, you know, Philip."

"But you can't go back on your entire story in front of that Court now, man."

"I don't see why not, after what you've done. I should think I could extremely reasonably plead fear of intimidation."

Stevens' head dropped in his hands. "You're insane, Loran."

"I do sometimes wonder. When I wake up at night, I mean, and relive all that awful Operation Cabbage again. You were in a pretty bad way, I know, but what possessed you, just what possessed you to go so far?" He drank deeply, abruptly, went on, "Afraid, weren't you? Well, so was I. But you didn't get concussion, my friend, you weren't hit in any hallway or out of it. All that happened to you was that you gave yourself a nice clean self-inflicted wound in the left arm. Well, my wounds were neither nice nor clean."

When Stevens raised his head he expected Loran to be baring another appalling scar somewhere on his meager person, but in the morbid lighting he was holding up the speckled photo of a man. A wiry man with a shock of unruly hair, beaky nose, and features he recognized all too well. Stevens recoiled with a moan.

"Thought so." Loran had been studying his victim's face with care. "I suspected you knew something more about our Corporal Marrow than meets the eye, Phil. Perhaps it'd be a good thing to re-open that Court of Inquiry after all."

"God's teeth, he was shot down in Dark House; you saw it, didn't you? That's all I know. Now leave me alone." But his head would keep turning from side to side and now his hands had started crawling on their own. "This isn't going to get you anywhere, Loran, you needn't think it is."

"Marrow's widow's suspicious. She got in touch with me."

Wailing came through the speaker overhead. The singer was completing her so-called song.

"You can't prove anything," Stevens got out quickly. "Any of this cock-and-bull you're spinning. It'd be your word against mine and don't forget who's senior officer."

Loran said, "A pit of quick lime. My father had to dig himself. It was very cold. I watched from a window, you know."

"There's one thing, old chap," Stevens' voice was begging now. "Whatever you think about me, I mean, I didn't send you into those boche. I wouldn't have wanted ... you can't think that. You mustn't. Please."

"Follow me"

Loran stood up and made crookedly for the lower rooms, in which the dancing was taking place. At the entrance to this velvet-lined armpit a man in dirty livery sat at a ticket counter.

"This lout knows me," Loran said. "Emil knows me, too."

He would, Stevens thought, standing behind him and catching the whiff of expensive hair-lotion again. They were smilingly invited over the throbbing threshold. I've got to stall, he thought desperately, stall for time somehow.

"It is Marguerite, what did I tell you!"

By a trick of optics Stevens first saw the blonde songstress reflected in Lorna's dark glasses—hair like a helmet, tight black sweater, slacks and slippers. A final bow to bursting applause, then she slid off the maple strip that comprised the stage.

"What did you think of her, Phil?"

"Nice. French, I suppose."

"Marguerite spent most of the war in a concentration camp. You wouldn't think it to see her now in these infernal regions, would you?" He moved back to let another couple enter and chuckled to himself. "I'm afraid Marguerite's become a very ruinous jewel of late."

All over this low-ceilinged cellar the moths were getting up to dance. Stevens saw another bar on the far side, supplied with several of what he'd now learnt to be, in dives like this, the customary "hostesses." Made you order sherry glasses of weak tea for them at five and sixpence each. I've got to play it light, he kept telling himself foggily, how the blue blazes did he find out about Marrow too?

"I bet you get to know your partner pretty well in a spot of light fantastic like that."

Lorna nodded. "Yes. A new one. It's called the Fish. Some people call it a form of mass juvenile delinquency." He added without transition: "You know they're trying to find von Schultz?"

"I wish we'd got him. That bastard was evidently one of the nastiest of a very nasty bunch of war criminals. Quite apart from what he did to your pater, I mean."

"I know. The swine's gone into hiding somewhere or other."

They were both still standing by the door and couples coming in took Stevens' bulk for that of the chucker-out. He duly responded to their japes on the subject. But he had that feeling he'd known in the ring, that gasping solitude after being hit in the solar plexus when every fiber in the body seemed to turn into spaghetti. There was one idea he grasped at—Loran wanted something from him. Maybe Loran himself wasn't dead straight. A chink in the armor. Everyone had it, really. If only he could see his eyes.

"Makes me feel old."

Loran nodded again. "Did you have that feeling when you came back home? Of being out of touch? Nobody seemed to be living. Say what you will, there was something about Africa."

"My God, there was."

The dance had ended, the couples moved back to their tables. A smear of sax went up and the lights dimmed. Loran said, "Let's watch this one. Angela can be fairly inspiring if she's in the mood."

The act connoted by the well-bred name was about as far from what came up as anyone might have desired, even that lubriciously inventive officer in the bed next to his in 13C, Stevens reflected. The charming girl who had come onto the stage in Mayfair tweeds had begun to slither into a peeling act of unequivocal candor. Her quasi-surprised demureness gave an amateur air, and thus a freshness, to the whole thing that strongly underlined its sexiness. When she was starkers but for something in front (embroidered with the ritual bee) Loran said, "Angie's the daughter of an earl, but got fed up with crumpets for tea, so broke loose."

"She certainly did. I thought she wore those tweeds rather well."

"Personally I don't think she does badly in a G-string, either. Just how far she'll go now much depends on the local political situation. Angie can make it fairly raw. I do hope they told her," and he shook with silent laughter, "that you're not a policeman."

"Me," said Stevens wonderingly, "me."

The girl had started to writhe. She wiggled her mammary muscles in a positively legendary manner and then proceeded into a bump-and-grind that threw a sheath of sudden silence over the male spectators applauding at the back. She flipped her derrière like flagging a bull.

“Angela has to be fairly careful. Only one or two of us know she works here, as a matter of fact. She’s just sixteen.”

Stevens watched, thinking: typical of Loran that he’d be of the “one or two” who knew the inside story. Always on the inside. But as the girl progressed with her act, becoming ever more exotic, Stevens felt an irritating sensation of revulsion and pity squirm up inside him. It was totally unexpected. Why the flaming hell should I feel sorry for that brazen sliver of flesh, he asked himself. But there was something in the contrast between such purity of limb, those adolescent articulations, and the engorged male eyes pawing up at her through bluish smoke—something nasty. He turned his head. Clapping of a ferocious quality, greedy clapping, told him it was over. Couples got up and resumed the Fish.

“I wanted you to see that.” Loran spoke thoughtfully.

“Thanks. Nifty. Frankly, I thought it ran rather near the knuckle.”

“I remember in the boat…” Then he interrupted himself—“What’s wrong with your hands?”

“Hands?”

“Yes. Look. They seem to be behaving oddly.”

Stevens angrily thrust his fists into his pockets. “I’m all right,” he said. The boat, he thought, my hands. Then Loran saw…

“Remember how you said you’d like an English girl in that garden of yours, Phil? Thin frock, all that sort of thing. I think I’ve found her for you, too.” And he was pointing, pointing across to the far bar and to one of the hostesses standing there.

“The hostess with the mostest, eh,” quipped Stevens. “You mean that size twenty model over there?”

She was indeed a big girl, close on fat, with her back to them, the fleshy shoulders furrowed by the straps of her cocktail frock which was thin enough all right, peering Stevens thought, it might have been put on with a spray-gun. A man had an arm slung round her neck.

"She also came from a goodish family, Phil."

"Well, I don't understand what you're driving at."

"Think she'd look well in your hammock in Kent?"

"Wouldn't withstand the avoirdupois." He was determined to keep the tone as light as possible. "That girl's got a great deal behind her, you know."

"That's what you like, isn't it?' Then his dark glasses glittered. "I found her, Phil."

Hating the plumbless depths of those twin discs which now were Loran's eyes, and hating, hating above all staring at that hypnotic scar, Stevens turned again. This time the girl—a grown woman—could be glimpsed in profile. Another man pinched her upper hip. She wriggled slightly.

He heard Loran say, "You have to be pretty hard up—or a psycho case—to take work in dumps like this. They don't give you much for it, you know, only the drinks. It's a hardish life."

Then Stevens moved. Cat! The word nearly burst out of his mouth. The recognition came as the hostess wrenched herself free from the man fondling her like a butcher handling meat and his arm dropped from her neck—that pure round nape he'd once thought good enough to chop through with a chiv. There was no possible doubting it when she turned. Something stirred inside him. He felt weak and incoherent. Thankfully, through the haze, she hadn't seen him. But it was Lucy, all right.

"Let's get out of here, Loran."

"Why? I rather like it."

"Out."

When they'd resumed their previous table upstairs Loran leant forward, his glasses winking. "You see, what did I tell you? I did find her, didn't I?"

"You had no need to do that."

"Like me to call her over?"

It wasn't any use pretending he didn't know her. Loran had done his work too well, had been too perfectly thorough, for any further dissimulation to be possible. The game was up. That guilty-schoolboy quaking took hold of Stevens again so that all at once he said, "I'll do what you want."

"Ah. Good. Frankly, I thought you'd see it like that. Actually it was quite hard tracing Lucy, you know. Of course I checked on all the hospitals you'd been in but, still, it wasn't easy. Eventually I got in touch with a rather nice doctor who seems to have been responsible for boarding you out of 13C. I explained that I'd been with you in P.E.D.G. and here's where I fear I spun what you'd rightly call a bit of cock-and-bull—about your being missing. Wanting to find out about you, so on. To cut a long story short he told me the person at 13C who'd seen most of you—in all senses, it now seems—was a certain Sister Matson. So the search for Mattie began." Loran sighed, smiling. "Lucy was returned to the U.K. fairly soon after you took off for that Amgot job. Incidentally, how did you wangle that, Phil? Somehow, dear boy, I could never picture you as an Amgot wallah."

"Go on," Stevens said.

Loran shrugged. "There you have it. Lucy began to break up fairly fast. Bottle, men, everything. They shipped her around, to one or two of the remoter places, even posted her to duty in a mental home in Wales to try to straighten her out for a while, but it didn't work. You know, Lucy liked you quite a lot."

Stevens said, "I hate you, Loran."

And yet it wasn't true. They sat facing each other, knowing it wasn't true. In this light the flesh of Loran's facial scar looked shiny and new and Stevens found his eyes slipping back to it again and again.

"Finally she was sacked, Phil. And drifted here. I found her in rather a bad way one night, escorted her home. No, I didn't, you needn't think." He held up a hand, a mocking hand, to Stevens, sitting ill with fear. "But she told me everything. Listen, Philip:

duly sobered and made sensible, Lucy could damn you to hell and back for your behavior in 13C. Evidently you were perfectly able to lift that arm of yours when you wanted to. In short," he said, clearing his throat, "you faked."

"Let's get out of here. I feel sick."

"You did fake, didn't you."

"Shut up," Stevens said, "or I'll bash your bloody naffing teeth through the back of your throat. Personally."

Loran spoke quickly now, prey to some excitement of his own, it was plain. "Ah no, I wouldn't do that if I were you, I wouldn't do that at all, dear boy. I've got far too much on you by now and you know it. Anyway there's already a discrepancy in your story on the record, to begin with: as that Ellis observed, you've given two accounts of just where you picked up that nick in your arm, in the hall and outside that shed."

"Ellis was a sod. He came and ..."

"I couldn't stand him either, agreed." Suddenly Loran laughed, raucously, shockingly. Several tables looked round. "In the hall, by Christ! Do you realize they found no less than eleven bullet wounds in me?"

"Please." Stevens groped for Loran's fragile arm. "Don't. I swear to God almighty I never knew ..."

"You must have seen I was going straight into those Germans." Reaching into a pocket before Stevens could protest further Loran produced several stubs of gouged metal; two of them looked like Roman coins. "See? I still carry some of the lead around for luck. It was a miracle I came through. All the doctors said so. God knows why they took so much care of me. I need a drink."

Stevens said, "Look, I may have been yellow that night, but I swear I never sent you into those boche knowingly."

"So if I reopened the case with what I've got, Phil, you wouldn't stand an earthly. Now, would you? No matter how senior an officer you were. Do you really imagine you could stand up to protracted cross-examination from that M.P. blighter? Why, I remember you'd been drinking before you started on that patrol, hadn't you? I could smell it on your breath. . . ."

All at once Loran broke off, leant back his head, and smiled. A lock of hair had strayed down his pale temple which was, Stevens could see, quite damp. That scar again. Hard to look elsewhere. His world was caving in, bit by bloody bit. He wondered what was coming next. And then he knew.

Aus dem stillen Raume, aus der Erde Grund
hebt mich wie im Traume dein verliebter Mund.

Those plaintive accents burnt a film across his eyelids. An unbearable, bursting anguish grew in him with each note. He wanted to scream. His fists crept, balled.

"Yes, I requested it," Loran said. "Old times' sake. Marguerite puts a lot of feeling into the ballad, don't you think? Perhaps understandably."

"I told you I'll do what you want, man."

"I knew you would." The scar, the entire lean face, tautened as he leant across the table now. "You have still got those photos, haven't you, Phil?"

"What photos?"

Loran ticked. Again Stevens wished he could see his eyes. But the fingers of Loran's right hand were drumming on the table now. "The photographs you took off that brigadier I killed."

The face dashed into Stevens' mind as the other spoke—thin hair, rimless pince-nez, the features of the society-sanctioned assassin. "I didn't say I have still got them," he answered cautiously.

"You didn't," Loran patiently conceded, moving his glass round and round the table. "But that ugly mug of yours, Brute Strength, is a shade too transparent, I fear. You were born to be an Achilles, not an Odysseus. You've got 'em all right, haven't you?"

"How do you know if I have and how do you know if I haven't?"

"You're methodical, you keep things; Army training dies hard. Even if that's not sufficient explanation I distinctly recall that some of the maidens in those pictures had very delicious real estate out back, and such was always your penchant, wasn't it, Phil? No, as Sister on your ward, Lucy went through your things when you entered 13C, you know. She found that German's papers and the photos and then later on, during one of your beach outings, she chanced to search your battle-dress pockets for a smoke. She saw that for some reason you'd destroyed or secreted all the other stuff, including the fellow's driving license, but hung onto the smutty pictures. In those days she wasn't caring much. Well, I reckoned that if you'd kept them that long, chances were you'd hang on to them for good. It was a risk I had to take. But it's paid off, hasn't it, Phil, for you do still have those photos, don't you?" He ended breathless.

Stevens watched him, perplexed yet relieved at Loran's present nervousness and impatience. He said quietly, "Those photos were of paintings you owned, weren't they?"

"What if they were?"

He couldn't be sure but he felt that Loran answered with his eyes shut.

"I'd like to have known a bit more about art, honestly I would. Now you take those women, somehow you never get tired of them, do you know what I mean?"

"I need those photos rather badly."

"Listen, if the jerry's copped some of the pictures from your home then it stands to reason you ought bloody well to have them back."

"Yes, yes, let's say I want the snaps back for sentimental reasons. My mother would like to have them very much."

wie einst Lili Marleen
wie einst Lili Marleen

Stevens swore. “I wish she’d stop that song.”

“You will give them to me, won’t you, Phil?”

“And if I haven’t got ’em, what then?”

“Why then,” Loran answered after a moment, “then I think I’d have to turn you in, Phil.” He paused. “But if you can give them to me, quite soon, I mean, then I won’t say anything. I give you my word.”

“The word of a gentleman!”

“Not of a gentleman.” As he spoke Loran laid a slender hand on Stevens’ left knee. “Don’t forget I’m a foreigner here. It’s the word of an outsider. And it’ll be kept.” After a second he added, “Anyway I’m on oath in front of that Court for what I’ve said so far. Don’t you see it’d be far easier for me to leave things that way?”

Lili Marleen suddenly stopped. As if by some common consent they both stood up. Stevens said, “They’re in my duds. At my hotel.”

“Thank you so much.” Loran pulled back his shoulders in a high-strung motion. “You can count on me to keep my contract. Anyway I won’t be living in England too much longer. There’s just something I have to do first.”

On their way to the door out—waiter bowing low to Loran—Stevens caught a last glimpse of the rites within, powdered flesh and some more nihilistic eurhythmies going on amain. Loran donned his hat, a dark brown Anthony Eden with a strong curled brim. The blonde at the bar waved them good-by. In the taxi outside Loran said, “I’ll be glad to get involved in some sort of action again.”

“Action?”

“There’s something I have to do, let’s leave it at that.” He turned and smiled at Stevens. “Sorry if I was rough on you in there but I really thought you had sent me into those Germans. I now think I may have been wrong.”

“You were.”

"You must accept my apologies." Speaking in this formal manner there was a slight accent, Stevens thought, in Loran's voice. "Listen, please don't think I'm unaware of the strain you P.E.D.G. people lived under for a long time. You mustn't use that word about yourself again. You shouldn't have gone out that night. That sort of thing can happen to anyone. Take Marrow, for instance." Then he leant forward and rapped out to the driver, "Here, can't you go any faster than this, we're in a hurry." And the driver, Stevens observed, stepped on it at the voice of command. His Master's.

They went into the hotel past a bleary-eyed night porter and walked up hurriedly, disdaining the lift.

Once in the room Loran limped straight over to the tin trunk as if he'd seen it several times before. He was clearly excited. "Now then."

"Half a mo'," said Stevens, fumbling with his keys. "By the way, how'd you get in that other place of mine and write on my trunk, if I may ask?"

"Come on, hurry up, do."

"Bribed the skivvy, eh? Well, it must have cost you a penny, she wouldn't tell me a blooming thing."

"Open it. Please."

Kneeling beside the box Stevens threw an irritated look back. Loran was wringing his hands.

"Look, if jerry's swiped your paintings, I say, we've got to get 'em back." There was a smell of mothballs and webbing in the trunk. Suddenly he whirled. With a curiously grating tone the telephone had begun to ring.

"Who's that?"

"I don't know." Loran also looked tense. "Give me the photos, Phil, and I can get out of here and leave you in peace."

In peace, thought Stevens. "But no one knows I'm here," he said. "That is, no one excepting you."

"Don't answer it then."

"But I must."

"Why?"

"Well. It's ringing."

"Oh, leave it alone."

But though frightened Stevens felt he had to answer. That so aggressively anticipatory sound fairly demanded completion. He doggedly crossed and took the receiver off the hook.

"Hallo."

"Hall porter here, sir."

"Woken up, eh. What do you want?"

"That gentleman you bring in registered at the hotel, sir?"

"No."

"Then I must ask him to leave, sir. At once."

"Go and get stuffed, will you. Oh, O.K., O.K., he'll leave." Stevens grinned as he replaced the instrument. "Hall dogsbody. Thought you were my nancy boy. For the night. Imagine."

"God!" Loran tried to laugh but his bony hand was already opened for the photos. When Stevens gave them to him he scanned all five rapidly and said, "Do very nicely, very nicely indeed. Thank you very much." He turned.

"Hey, wait a sec'," Stevens called, "how do I know…"

But he didn't. The door had closed and he was a man alone, talking to an empty room.

CHAPTER EIGHTEEN

The solidly constructed specimen of British womanhood who turned off into Poland Street some days later did not notice the man under the lamp-post on the opposite pavement. A big man, wearing a plastic mackintosh against the London drizzle. As she high-heeled past a Crippsian poster—WORK OR WANT—towards that small red door, a brief body perception made her realize her emptiness. She hadn't had anything much to eat since yesterday morning. The thought of a drink was very good. But a drink cost money, dammit. Work or want.

With her hand on the door she hesitated. I told Tom I wouldn't go back but hell, I've got to earn some cash. Anyway it's probably safer in the Honey Bee these days than in some of the staider sections of London town. She shrugged her heavy shoulders and went down into the darkened rooms. Alex, she thought, those clear days, blazing sun. . . .

"Wot cheer, Lucy," called the dance-floor barman as she finally teetered down the velvet steps into the club cellar. "The cohort of the damned come back for more, eh."

"Double, Harry."

The barman reached pokerfaced for the bottle. She glanced at herself in the mirror. Mechanically she tugged at her black wool dress, inspected her eye-shadow. Then she winced, tossed down the drink.

"Good to see you back at the old stand again, Lucy. Emil will be pleased."

"Double please, Harry."

As easy as that. Behind her the club began to fill. The manager came over to have a word with her, stood her another drink. One young couple were fooling around with an oversize bee, hung dustily furry from the ceiling. It was then she saw the man.

At first she couldn't be certain. Swinging on the stool she put a hand to her creamy forehead. It couldn't be. She should have kept away, as Tom had told her. But there was no ducking out now. He came to her anxious and doglike; he'd put on weight since those days, all right.

"My old Roman soldier," she whispered.

"Lucy."

"Still built like a brick wall, aren't you, Philip?"

"A bit too much mortar these days," he ruefully replied.

"Well, I wonder what brought you here. Nothing good, I take it."

He gripped her arm. She blinked. Forgotten just how strong he was.

"Luce, let's sit down somewhere and have a drink. I want to talk to you about something."

She led him to a wall table. He sat down heavily. Even in this light she could see how exhausted he was and thought: I mustn't be touched. A waiter came up.

"Pink gin," she said briskly.

"And make it genuine or I'll break your dizzy neck, Bob," he told the waiter, who looked petrified. "I'm testing it personally, see." For himself he ordered the rum-and-honey hooch. "How've you been, Lucy?"

"Mustn't grumble, must we?"

"Why not?"

A couple of the other hostesses glanced at them and in rapid succession a flower girl, a girl selling Turkish cigarettes, a girl selling chocolates and one selling small dolls and teddy bears (Buy British—Export Or Die) approached their table. Stevens bought silently. Eventually he said, "Tell the next one to peddle her coconuts elsewhere, would you, Luce?"

"All right." His shoulders were hunched and sagged and a sadness she was unprepared for drove a groove within her at the sight of his old frown as he calculated the change. "You don't have to worry; they'll bring me proper booze in here, all right."

"Cat, do you remember?"

"It's too late, Philip," she said. "You hurt me too much. You never loved me, did you. You just used me."

"That's wrong," he protested thickly. The waiter brought more drinks. He paid again. She raised her glass.

"Good luck, Phil."

"Cheers."

The new drink brought another unexpected surge of pity for this huge man slumped in his chair, mouth open, broken and lost. She realized more than ever that she should never have come back.

"I did love you, cat, you know."

"You just used me."

He said, "If only the clock could be put back."

She started drinking steadily. As always she got tight quite quickly, then stayed in that stage for almost as long as she liked. Sixteen-year-old Angela passed their table porting a hat-box and smiled at her before she vanished back stage. Lucy saw him bite his lips.

"I hate to think of you here, Luce."

"It's a little late to feel sorry for me, isn't it. You realize that once I lied for you, didn't I?" She gave a burst of laughter. "I jeopardized my career."

"Let's get out of this place. I mean, it's a bit fierce in here, isn't it?"

She took a breath. She had to stop this feeling of pity for him. "You. What did you do? Where did Captain Philip Stevens go?" she asked him curtly. "As if I didn't know."

"Loran told you, didn't he?" He crowded forward over the table at that. She thought she'd never seen such a big man in her life before.

"That loony bin in Wales wasn't any fun, Philip, I can assure you." She remembered it all suddenly, so far away from all this bad velvet, these grieving singers. "You never answered my letters, did you?"

"Didn't know where you were." At her ironic smile he added, "I heard you'd left the service."

"That's rich." She gave another open laugh and extinguished her cigarette, heavily circleted with lipstick. "Left the service, oh my God, oh that's good."

His shaking hand slopped the drink as he said, "Listen, Luce, if it'd be any help, I'd like to try to provide for you a bit. I haven't got much. But there's my pension. If…"

"Please," she said harshly, turning aside her face. "You don't owe me a thing."

"I've got to find Loran, cat."

"So that's it. I might have known you were after something."

"It's not that, Luce. I…"

"Well, Tom Loran doesn't come here much, I'm afraid. But it's true he did come back to see me and he told me he'd informed you of my frightful fate. What did you think of it, Philip?"

"You do know where he is, don't you?"

"Do I?"

"It's almost ten days since I met him here."

"As long as that." She started another cigarette. What was he up to now? Turned scared after giving Tom the photos; realized all of a sudden that Loran had the only evidence of the truth on the raid? That would be typical. The trouble was, this great crumbled facade of a man didn't know how dangerous he was by half. If only she could keep remembering how much harm he'd done her. She said sharply, "I knew you inflicted that wound on yourself, you realize. I'd seen too many of them. Oh yes, even back here at home, before we went out."

"That fellow Loran who was with me in Africa," he was mumbling into his drink. "He's half-crazed, you know. Ought to be locked up. Got some fantastic ideas about me. You must help me find him, Luce. I've searched everywhere. Every day, all over town. You don't know what it's like."

"What?"

"Waiting," he said.

Without watching the stage she heard the blonde songstress start up about the Boulevard Richard le Noir. She saw him curse. Then he grasped her hand.

"Oh."

Dozens of men had held her hand since those days in North Africa, but this touch was frightening. His hand was shaking in hers.

"Luce, I must stop this idea you have."

"What idea?"

"That I swung the lead, I mean. Got myself past the board; all the rest of the bilge Loran's been thinking up." He paused suddenly. "You know, the odd thing was, I was somehow glad to see him again."

"Malingering's a serious offense," she tried to say bitterly. "I suppose I'm an accomplice before the act, or whatever they call it now."

"Let's get out of here, cat."

He still had her wrist and this time she cried, "Ow!"

"Sorry."

"Look, don't you want to hear Marguerite?"

"No."

"Well, I ought to stay a little longer," she said uncomfortably. "I ought to tell Emil."

"Who's Emil?"

"Manager. He's given me an ultimatum. This is my first night back." How much older than him she felt then, watching that void of desolation that was his face. I mustn't, she kept telling herself as she ordered another drink. I simply mustn't feel touched by him after all he's done. She began humming: "'There was a young lady named Lou who found her love-life in a stew'—remember?"

He was drumming his powerful fingers on the table. Fear flickered through her almost voluptuously then. She was getting very drunk. A girl selling large jars of honey came up to their table, looked at them, went quickly away. Marguerite was summoned for an encore and began pitching into a song that made him come to life with the relaxed alacrity of the born athlete. This time he took a roll of her flesh between finger and thumb as if she had no feeling there at all.

"Phil! That hurt!"

"I can't stand that song. Played it last time I was here."

"Lili Marleen. It's very popular now."

"Not with me. Let's get out."

"But Emil…"

He half-dragged her from the table. On the steps out Emil indeed appeared, with his greasy hair and greasy eyes, and seemed about to interrupt their exit, but Stevens pushed him aside as a man does a coat in a cupboard.

Lucy shivered as she passed to lead the way outside. She knew his eyes were on her as she walked and on the last step to the street, before putting on her mack, she smiled at him. "Always were one to admire the back of a girl's lap, weren't you, Phil? Alas, I fear I've far too much of it at present."

In the taxi he kept folding and unfolding his hands in a queer way and half-toppling off the seat. She reminded herself that in fact he'd been really ill. She experienced a flicker of panic. Why in heaven's name had she half-consented to this? Was it true what Tom Loran had told her—that Philip had probably killed a fellow soldier in cold blood? She stared at that harshly silent, ferociously tormented face and felt deeply afraid herself.

Her two-room flat, shocking them both with light, somehow completed this sense of horror growing inside her. Closing the door behind him she saw it—all the dusty chi-chi smartness—as a suddenly second-rate film set. The curtains strained inadequately across the grimy London windows when she drew them, and there were far too many clever things about: a wrought-iron table that had absurdly caught her fancy once, an ashtray like a fiddle she'd picked up in a drunken moment from a seedy boutique off the Edgware Road, some tired ivy trailing (in deference to some idiot women's columnist) from a bracket on the wall—the whole had the impermanence of cake icing; and as she sank onto a button-back settee and kicked off her shoes she was all at once vividly reminded of the places where he and she had met before.

"Oh damnable, damnable," she said. "I think you ought to go." She stood up to get a drink. "You laced my liquor once, now I'll lace yours."

He was seated awkwardly across the room from her, his pinstripe suit stretched taut. On one knee he had what looked to her to be a filled sponge-bag, with the zipper of which he was fumbling. There was the density of absolute saturation, misery like a ruin, in his face now.

"What is it, Phil?" she asked sharply.

Then she saw he'd taken out of the sponge-bag a large .45, the one he'd had with him in Africa. She straightened her back slowly and tried to concentrate.

"Look, I can't tell you where Tom Loran is. I promised I wouldn't. Now don't try to make me."

But she heard the tell-tale quiver in her tone. Hold on, she told herself.

"Do you realize, cat," he said with slow deliberation, "I'm free, free to do anything I like in the whole wide world."

Then to her alarm his bruiser's mouth writhed slightly at the edges and he began to cry. His face went hot, he gulped and choked, tears inched down his cheeks which she noticed now were very lined. Words wandered out: "Tried ... you don't know what it was like ... raid after raid ... in the army ... at school ... the right thing."

She watched him with repulsion, fast followed by pity. He had ruined her life but she felt no desire now to ruin his. Oddly she felt no venom for revenge.

"Please tell me where he is, Luce."

"No, I can't."

He pressed his head to her knees, his shoulders heaving. She bit her lip.

"Cat, I've got to find him."

When he looked up she saw his dead face crumpled with tears. She had known this man more intimately perhaps than anyone had ever known him, he had hurt her and she had no responsibility towards him whatever; all the same, she was helpless when he looked at her like that. They'd shared something, after all. She couldn't add to the wreck of all his life.

"Your eyes, cat. They've gone gray. Remember?"

"Phil," she began, "I ... look, you don't have to force me." Lurching once, half-wondering at what she was saying, weeping with vexation at her clumsy fingers on the buttons of her dress. She was glad, glad when finally she stood before him that she'd picked the coffee-lace slip today. For some reason he was somberly unscrewing a jar of honey that some lunatic had once brought back with her from the club.

PART FOUR
THE HUMANISTS

CHAPTER NINETEEN

Loran arrived at the place at the dead of night. Bells rang out from the sleigh. The coachman made a slow, circuitous waving and the air exploded in front of them. The horse strained up a black slope between topless pine trees. It was all suddenly like Norway.

He could barely believe that only an hour before he had got off the Magdeburg-Halberstadt train at Pohlde, walking painfully over to that deserted branch station with his single bag and the specially long "scholar's" grip, the leather case in one hand, expecting any moment to trip and sprain his ankle on the smashed streets, to run into a wall, break his weakened leg in some fiendish pothole, most likely.

The tired train had been waiting. An equally war-weary official had punched his ticket and, with a hand extended before him, Loran had steered himself like a somnambulist, or someone walking under water, down the blackness of that empty carriage. Empty! He had started at a movement in one of the last seats, but there didn't seem to be anyone there, after all. Eventually he'd awoken out of a doze to hear a man running down the side of the train, calling out "Nordbühel, Nordbühel" in a strange sort of nasal süddeutsch he scarcely understood at first. Odd how different this all seemed from England. Another world, in fact. Well, it'll make my own accent all the less conspicuous here, was what he thought.

It seemed that no one else had got off the train and Loran only just had time to jump to his feet, grab his bag, and limp for the door, when the engine plunged on, ejecting him onto the snow on all fours. By the time he'd risen, shaken himself, the rear of the train was winging away and a man in a black coat was standing holding his case for him in the silence.

Loran reached for it. "*Danke.*"

But hopping after the man past the group of huts that comprised Nordbühel station to the single waiting sleigh, Loran had thought to have detected a hesitation of curiosity as the other had tested the big briefcase's weight before returning it to him. So long, so empty yet! And the dark glasses... that scar. Loran understood such peasant suspicion perfectly.

Altogether it was a Germany of suspicion, he'd considered as he had stepped up onto the sleigh, the driver babbling on about the unprecedented snowfall in the village these past few nights while tucking the heavy furs about Loran's sides, then got up himself, barked, cracked his whip, and they'd started jerkily off. The cold matched that icy determination in Loran's mind; it had been like a core that had held his being together all through those long prison years.

Suspicious faces at Tempelhof. M.P.'s. Loran had never liked them. Odd-looking civilians. Watch-sellers. Obvious crooks, caricatures really. Then, that moment passing some compound of bleak barbed wire, command cars, kitbags, during the drive from the airport and hearing *Defaulters* blown (You can come to De-*fault*-ers as much as you *like*; as *long* as you *get* there on *time*). Yes, he'd surprised himself by a brief nostalgia for those old bonds the Army had provided and which poor old Stevens had so worshipped. That sense of unity in the P.E.D.G. You couldn't deny it. He thought of Stevens. How little that poor devil whom he'd had perforce to torture in the nightclub would have guessed the pair of them shared identical attitudes to the English code. Ambivalent love and hate. Loran remembered the years at that English school, the bullying he'd undergone for being a foreigner, an outsider: "Dagoes begin at Dover," as his tutor had told him. The British terror of losing caste. Consequently, at school, university, in the Army, that constant social score-board you were tacitly measured by. The Englishman's constant question—"What school were you at?" For of course they were all still at school, all still indulging their puerile enjoyments of special ties and badges and colors, their protective screen against the world, their exclusiveness and xenophobia. Yes, Stevens had suffered from this, too, if in a different way.

Loran glanced down at his briefcase. He had to play his cards very carefully, indeed. The case had been measured exactly when he'd bought it. Just big enough to take the larger one, the Tanz, unframed. And he'd taken it out of its frame. If, that is, the picture could be found. If it was still there, intact.

For a minute these thoughts occupied him as he huddled in the vehicle. He wondered what it was in his psychology that had made the killing of his father such a turning-point in his life. But it undoubtedly obsessed him, his longing for revenge had become a wick of light in his soul. Splashes of orange from the twin lanterns struck out at the equine shanks in front as they climbed. He had expected snow early in the mountains, but this was colder than he'd imagined. Quite like the Northland. He thought: Best to start showing my hand soonish.

"Excuse me. I want to find somewhere to put up in Nordbühel. Is there an inn?" His breath steamed out. "Not too expensive, you know. I'm only a student."

"Ah, a student, a student." The cap of mangy fur turned round, revealing a profile really out of Cranach. "Die Drei Mohren, sir. You're from the North, eh? You've been here before perhaps?"

"Never."

"It hasn't changed." With a snapping of whip and reins he urged his nag up a steep ascent. "They say Germany's beaten to her feet. But no. Oh, she isn't. Not here. *Sehr schnell aufgebaut.* You won't find any bomb-damage here, sir. Most peaceful. You would be visiting as a student, then? For some research, perhaps?"

Precisely the question he'd been hoping for.

"*Ganz richtig*," he agreed with cordiality, leaning forward in the bumpy seat. "I'm hoping to be able to examine the collection of manuscripts at the Schloss."

"At Schloss Canossa, sir?" The voice was dubious.

"Quite so. From all I could ascertain they've survived safely, haven't they?"

However, at this the driver simply shrugged and shook his head. "I don't know, sir. I don't think that nowadays the Schloss ... well, here we are, sir."

They seemed to race into a deserted square. Loran imagined that the impression of speed the sleigh conveyed was due to the fact that, as in Norway, the passenger was seated relatively low, close to the ground. He caught glimpses of gabled houses. There was the smell of smoke. The driver helped him out. The packed snow rang underfoot.

"*Lieber Herr*," the driver was saying in a solicitous voice from the horse's head as Loran, in the light of the lanterns, counted out some money. "*Lieber Herr.* You must stand away from her feet." The man reached down and caught up a hoof in his lap. And Loran remembered—spiked, for the snow. "If she stamps on you with that ..." He grinned, a yellow snarl. "There's no beaten-down Germany here, sir. You'll find it very quiet. Thank you very much, sir. *Danke sehr.*" He pocketed the tip as if in a hurry and fawned a moment at his cap. "*Danke ... danke ...* There's been no one to the Schloss, sir, not from the north, at least, not since. ..."

"Well, I'm English." Loran saw no reason not to admit it; he knew the inn-keeper would see his passport in a minute and the news be spread. "*Bin Englander*," he said, the remark forming a German pun on horseflesh which the driver duly took.

"No, sir, Nordbühel was most quiet. Very peaceful indeed. One bomb." He gestured. "Over there. But who knows who dropped it? Germans, Americans, you English, the Russians. What I say is, we were all poor devils caught in it together."

"You haven't had any visitors here since the war then?"

The driver shook his head. "No, sir. But all *Engländer* will be welcome at Nordbühel from now on, you'll see." He bent forward in a confidential manner: "There are people in our quiet village who never knew there was such a thing as the National Socialist Party of Germany at all. Goodby, sir. Yes, *danke, danke*."

Loran watched this sweetened travesty of *Gemütlichkeit* and *Alt 'deutsch* drive gently off, those spiked horse's hooves biting neatly into the snow. But why was it as they did so that he couldn't help remembering that such hooves had been used to ride over the bodies of Jewish women? Newspaper knowledge now. So neat.

As he registered he flipped briefly back through the book. Not a sign. The trouble was, he realized as he was shown up to his room by a peasant girl bursting out of her bodice, it had taken far too long to get started out of London after he'd got hold of the photographs. If only he'd still been in the Army it'd have helped. That was the irony of it. West Germany was very much a military zone, it transpired.

The room he was shown into was small but cheap. An advantage. Currency restrictions made it impossible for him to stay long for his task in the village. Even had he wanted to, which he didn't, for fear of possible future recognition. That was why, too, he kept these big dark glasses on. No. he had to work fast, no one knew that better than he himself did.

Later he found an excellent meal awaiting him downstairs. The coachman had been right. It was obvious that everything was being done to show him the war was over, that bygones were bygones. After eating he strolled up to the manager.

"Schloss Canossa's not too far, is it?"

Loran thought the man hesitated. "It's a little way, sir. And with your leg. I don't think you'll find much of interest in that direction."

"Oh, but it's always been quite well known to Renaissance scholars, you know. About half an hour's walk, isn't it? Through the woods." It was a mistake. The manager's eyes came up in surprise at this knowledge.

"About." He lingered dubiously on the *um.* "*Etwa um*... I really don't know, sir. You see, I've scarcely ever been up there myself. I've only once been inside the Schloss."

"Well, you certainly don't seem to encourage visitors to the place." Loran laughed.

The manager squinted at him, seemed to reflect for a minute. "I'm sorry, sir, if I seemed like that. You see, we have recently had some American troops here. It was only a brief visit to our little village but we would prefer not to undergo it again."

"What were they doing here?"

"To be frank, sir, investigating the Schloss. Searching for, well..." He lowered his eyes. "Former members of the Party, we presume. In any case, they found nothing and went away quickly in their fast cars. But it's an experience we'd prefer not to repeat."

"Of course I'm not interested in anything like that at all," Loran put it hastily. He thought: So they've been. Does that mean I'm too late after all? In the disappointment he continued mechanically, "It's simply that the shelves at the Schloss were last catalogued in the Twenties, it seems, and I'd like to know if the library there still contains certain holdings. The truth is, I began my studies at Oxford just before the war and now I've been demobilized—thanks to this." He waved at his leg. "I've gone up again and started picking up the old threads."

These "revelations" clearly set the manager at ease.

"I understand, sir."

"My tutor's a great Renaissance man, you see, and of course knew all about the Canossa collection. The trouble is, no one was allowed to visit the place after the Party took power, it seems. At least, no one from outside. It would be a great feather in my cap if I could sort of penetrate the mysteries, as it were." He smiled as engagingly as he could and, as he spoke, produced a number of mark notes which passed with a rapidity amounting to legerdemain into the manager's right hand. "I need to get some facts on a Codex I'm following up. It's for my B. Litt., you know."

"Then I wish you much luck, sir." The manager now seemed reassured. "It's true that the State left the administration of the Schloss to a group of savants in the field. I don't think it's been quite decided what is to happen to it now, and certainly we don't see anything of those wise men down here. Frankly, the people around..." He threw out apologetic palms. "Why, our peasants think they bring bad luck. No one goes that way now."

"I'd heard that." Then Loran asked cautiously, "There's evidently no telephone, is there?"

"Absolutely no connection with the outside world at all, sir."

"Of course, I wrote in advance." At the foot of the stairs up he added, "By the way, you haven't had anyone else except those Americans investigating the Schloss collection, have you? I mean, no one has come here from England recently?"

"No, sir, not that I know of."

"Thanks. We scholars have to be so careful, you know."

"Then, I trust you'll sleep well, sir. Goodnight." And he pottered off, mumbling, "So, so."

The following morning Loran awoke to green mountains and the scent of peat in the room. He had indeed slept well, after some dark moments wondering if he was really too late.

He went to the window. The snow had been cleared by the rising sun. The evergreens stood clear. The air was of an intense purity, still and translucent, the atmosphere, he considered, of utter innocence. He could scarcely believe he was really here, on this sinister mission. But he would go on and on, even after he had found the pictures, until he had got von Schultz. Or someone had.

The village truly seemed untouched, a fairytale world in which it was impossible to imagine evil. Timbered chalets and log huts dotted the lower slopes. A piney sunlight drenched the scene. Over the potted plants on the windowsill Loran stretched sleepily, liking what he could see of this little hamlet more and more.

Staring at himself in the shaving mirror a few minutes later, he considered he looked nicely untidy. The "savants" in the Schloss would have no difficulty taking him for a student, lean and floppy-looking. And that had been the trouble at school, too, of course, not only that he had been a foreigner but—much worse—clever. Yes, if that poor devil Stevens had felt an outsider because of the social snobbery in English institutions, Loran himself had learnt that one of the outward forms of "playing the game" was a steady detestation of intellectual pursuits. He had suffered from his cleverness at school. His tutor, an erstwhile England cricket cap, had been a fool and proud to be so; the last thing that trim-mustached figure with the cardboard carriage would have wanted thought about himself was that he was clever.

Loran hummed as he picked up the stack of note-cards he'd prepared as a result of those hours in the British Museum, and went down to breakfast.

If all the good people were clever,
And all clever people were good,
The world would be nicer than ever
We thought that it possibly could.

So he sang mentally to himself throughout an excellent breakfast served to him by the pig-tailed, drindled maiden who looked positively better-built than ever this morning. And as he ate he snapped off the rubber band securing the cards and began to flip through them. The one on top, for instance, read as follows:

CODEX DONATI lib. fam. 31

Francis I's Ambassador to Venice—Guillaume Montpelier—Jacques Claude of Avignon—1793 the Swiss, Herr Pampaloni, acquires from Meerman collection Copenhagen.

1824 presented to anon. Ger. collector

Curator Ciceronian ms Czernin coll. refers to it end of c. in archives Schloss Canossa, Nordbühel, nr. Pohlde, Thuringia.

Yes, he knew enough about the Donati Codex to deceive them now, he thought. At the back of the packet were the photographs, and he glanced at the top one only fleetingly. He knew it by heart, had always known that picture by heart since the earliest awareness of his youth, and now its setting had been revealed to him—that long corridor adorned with the tell-tale insignia of crabs. For close on centuries now the old Canossa family crab had defined the Schloss for scholars in the Renaissance, who had not failed to joke over the symbol at learned meetings. Loran had spotted it from the start, from that distant moment in Dark House after he had killed the brigadier. Von Schultz must have taken the paintings there as much for positive identification as for safe keeping. The point was—were they there still?

He extracted one last photograph, that of a man, all open-necked shirt, bush of hair on end, the snap of Marrow he had thrust in front of Stevens at the Honey Bee. It had been a bluff, of course, a long shot indeed, he himself had no idea of what had really happened to Corporal Marrow. But somehow, for some reason, it had done the trick. It had worked some trigger of terror in the conscience of that great hulk of human flesh, and the man had given himself away. Loran smiled wistfully. No one could have accused Stevens of the vice of cleverness at school, surely. It was lucky, as things turned out, that Mrs. Marrow had lent him the photo in her pathetic unshakable conviction that one day, somewhere, her husband would be found. Perhaps, Loran reflected as he put the snapshot away in his wallet now, perhaps it'd been no more than the memory of Marrow's fear in the boat, an unholy funk all too reminiscent to Stevens of his own, whatever it was, the sight of that picture, coming on top of Loran's following him round London, had undone the fellow in a trice. He had caved in shortly after that. Strange how effective the war-hero stuff had been, it'd worked even better than Loran had hoped, playing on Stevens' guilt, the poor blighter was such a simpleton. Now Loran decided to be just as deliberately direct once more and chance his luck, for it had held so far. He would go straight up to the Schloss unannounced. But not too early. No impatience, please.

Accordingly it was after ten before he set off on the white track that scrunched up into the fir trees. The sun was growing warm. He could smell resin. Huge laricio pines pillared his path. At first he passed one or two peasants in local jackets and *Lederhosen*, driving a cow or so with sticks studded with *Stocknägel*, but these decreased as he ascended in the deserted southwesterly direction he had been instructed by the manager to take. It was quiet in these woods. The needles deadened his halting steps. He could hear only the murmur of some distant weir, once some sawing. All the same, he had that strange sensation of being watched—he felt certain of it somehow.

Then he saw it. First the strangely shaped tower of the Schloss that he'd seen in so many pictures of the place. The whimsy of a bibliomane. As he drew nearer this tower appeared to be of grey granite, obscured from the sun by the endless fir trees, the approach to its high and sullen walls being by a single gravel track.

At this point he lost his path. The track through the firs bifurcated oddly and as he wandered back on his path he again had the impression of being watched by human eyes. He stopped. The silence was exact. Finally he found the correct path, and as he limped along it the sharp odor of resin now seemed mingled with another smell, a faint fragrance of incense or old wax. Suddenly he saw the high bell-tower riding under a cross set grotesquely on the back of the stone sculpting of the immense crab, which itself formed the well-known cupola of the place. An addition? Loran certainly didn't remember it from any of the pictures of the place. And it would have been odd to have added such an explicit symbol of the Christian religion during the Hitler regime.

On inspection there appeared to be one door set in the walls, which were absurdly monumental and covered very thoroughly with spiked gaffs and bits of broken glass—in a manner to make an Oxford proctor envious, he considered. He smiled down at his leg and thought: I suppose I felt special resentment against that poor devil because Operation Cabbage half-killed me while he got himself down-graded to the cushy jobs.

He tugged suddenly at the iron bell-pull. About two seconds later, it seemed, this produced a rolling note that traveled to his marrow. He stepped back a bit, startled by that nineteenth-century knell, and glancing up imagined he saw a shadow move in the tower above. He got out his note-cards in preparation. No one came, however, so he rang again. This time, he reflected, those delayed reverberations should jolly well have shaken the old edifice from crucifix to pit and, sure enough, he heard footsteps shuffle on the stone within. He felt immensely excited as the oak door, bound with staples, opened a crack. Someone resembling a cleric blinked whitely out at him and nodded at once in a brief, businesslike manner

"Akademie?"

Loran made a sign of agreement. "I wrote a letter." He started to explain, but without waiting for him to complete the sentence the other shut the door behind them and hurriedly led the way down a chilly passage lined with marble statues, his soutane-like robe swishing as he went. And suddenly Loran's heart struck at his ribs: he saw the crab insignia on the walls; it was identical with the photograph. But so far nothing yet.

"Bitte, schnell," his guide threw back over one shoulder as Loran limped after him in a virtual half-run. He had no time to explain himself; in any case all he could think of was his good luck to this date. This place fairly stank of the Renaissance, or at least its parody.

"Started," the monk figure ahead called out, as he scampered down a flight of steps and along more corridors past marble and terracotta busts whose features were all cast in a similar timeless calm, and many of whose foreheads, Loran noted, were crowned with the green of living laurel. He wondered how many of these casts had been plundered. It was possible that the von Schultzes of Germany had gone in for this sort of thing pretty thoroughly.

By now, however, they had reached a doorway over which was engraved the ritual red crab and it was only then, catching up with the other who held the big door half-open, that Loran observed that the man's tunic carried the identical symbol on the left breast.

He found himself in a spacious but barely furnished chamber in which about fifteen men were seated in a semicircle. It was cold and smelt stale, the air tinted with incense, and in front of the semicircle was an altar-piece hung with some sort of antique damask, on which had been arranged several volumes of old pigskin, some parchments mounted tenderly between glass, a quill or two. It was somehow all of a piece, thought Loran, his eyes running rapidly. No pictures. Then—Am I in a nuthouse? he asked himself as he saw the absorbed, quasi-mystical resignation on the faces of those present. Practiced expressions, as it were, yet expressions which precisely reflected the prevalent atmosphere of blight, that sense of worn stone and book wax and dried leaves and decomposing pages.

"Good morning," he said pleasantly in German. It sounded fatuous. No one moved. Then all at once he noticed one or two faces that seemed out of place, utilitarian, seamed, modern and different. All but three or four of the assemblage wore dark coats and badly pressed trousers, many of these striped. The exceptions were seated in the center and had on what seemed to be white sheets, embroidered with the scarlet crustacean. In the very middle of them all sat a queer creature with sunken cheeks, wearing the replica of a Roman toga under a marble bust that Loran could have bet his bottom dollar was of Cicero.

He took a step. "I wonder if you had my letter, sir."

A voice said, "Who? A member?"

"I've come to see the Donati Codex, if possible." This was the moment he had been rehearsing in London libraries. But at the statement the central figure gave a start as if struck. The rest remained rigid, looking fixedly at Loran now.

"I say, I'm terribly sorry if I've interrupted some meeting or other." He tried his most winning smile. "You see, I was brought straight in here. The thing is, I'm involved in some research at Oxford. Greats, you know. I wondered if you might possibly permit... liber jocularis, that is... I'd be happy to read under supervision, of course. It's the last chance I'll have to collate it for completion of my study. I only got here from England last night."

The wrong thing to say? Something was now going very wrong with the play. His words literally hung in the air. Prepared as he had come, Loran still felt strangely frightened. It seemed to him as if he'd been raving aloud. What on earth had he run into here?

The man in the center leant forward, his thin lips screwed to one side, like someone in agony attempting to smile. On a temple of that slender skull the dark blister of a vein beat rapidly.

"*Barbar*!" It was a spit.

"Plautus!" exclaimed a voice, not unmusically. Someone stood up. Loran saw the central figure being clasped by two men. There appeared to be tears on those papery cheeks.

"Sorry," he was saying now in a sort of speechless whisper, as if he were being strangled. "*Schuldigen....*"

Astounded by this reception, Loran turned to leave.

"Eccard! Eccard!" they were calling.

A powerful, almost merry tone carried into the somber corridor outside—"*Ec*-card!"

The clerk who had led Loran in appeared at his elbow. Evidently he was Eccard. His face was filled with alarm. Anxiously he hurried ahead to the main portal out. They went just as fast as Loran's leg would allow. "I thought, sir, I understood … and your dark suit, you see, round here … well, the way you spoke too." He tried to gasp out something else but the great door had slammed in Loran's eyes and he found himself locked outside.

At first he took a moment to recover from the odd scare the place had given him. He stared up at the vast crab sprawling over the bell-tower and beneath it the words inscribed, SCHLOSS CANOSSA. He ran a finger under his collar. Then for a second it all struck him as gruesomely funny. Hilarious, really. He returned to Nordbühel, in fact, more irritated than anything else.

CHAPTER TWENTY

That afternoon Loran dozed in the westering sunlight on his balcony. His thoughtful host, now quite friendly, had placed three books in the otherwise unfurnished shelves beside the bed: W. Grimm's Die deutsche *Heldensage*; the *Düringische Chronik*; and a small, battered *Evangelienbuch*. A little "escape" literature for the scholar, Loran wryly supposed, as every now and then he dipped into the copy of Joyce's *Dubliners* he'd brought with him. And every now and then his eyes would look up and gaze ahead into the numb silence of those woods. What in God's name had all that mummery meant? One thing seemed certain. The devoted crew of infatuated "monks" up there were Renaissance-lovers all right; Loran recognized the breed instinctively, they had visited his family's house so often in the old days, that type. He wouldn't find any Von Schultz here. But would he find the pictures, and so take the first step in his awaited revenge?

Actually Loran's hope was high. That kind of librarian hermit would find it literal agony to part with those acquisitions von Schultz had brought from Norway. The thing was, to get in the place, use the library and, if possible, move around a bit. In any case, it was good to be involved in action again. If he felt one thing in common with Stevens over the Army it was a detestation of the base-wallah existence. There'd been a unity of conception back there in the desert, no one could deny it. And in England the spirit had gone, or was very hard to find. Making money was merely a habit, it wasn't a philosophy of existence.

The following morning Loran was cashing a traveler's check in the tiny Nordbühel bank when all at once, behind the glass window next to which he was queueing, he caught sight of the face of one of those who had been seated in the ring around the fellow with the Roman toga. He was sure of it. The man glanced up, gave a look of recognition, smiled, beckoned Loran behind the counter.

By the time he had left the bank some twenty minutes later his earlier theory seemed to him to be corroborated. After the American visit Schloss Canossa was "sensitive" about its collection. He learnt that the Abbot—"old Plautus" as the bank clerk affectionately dubbed him—was now extremely distressed about what had taken place the day before, and wanted Loran to receive an explanation as soon as possible. The "academy" that met there was a humanist group, "lovers of the classics," drawing membership from the neighboring villages and towns. Only during official meetings, such as Loran had accidentally stumbled into, were the most valuable manuscripts brought up from the locked crypt and, well, poor old Plautus (the bank clerk wagged his head in amusement) lived in mortal terror of losing one of his verfluchte parchments. Yes, he took the leadership of the Schloss very seriously indeed. Well-nigh fanatical, you might say. And now they wanted to apologize for what had happened. The porter at the door had simply taken Loran for a member, a latecomer—no other individuals went up to the place these days, and by chance that very day the pride of the Latin collection had been brought up, and set out for the group to inspect and, ah, to savor. Plautus had been about to deliver an oration on the Codex, as it happened, when Loran had been shown in. Now with the possibly—might one say?—rather arbitrary powers of possession exercized by certain occupying forces ... well, the bank clerk did hope the visiting Herr would feel entirely free to avail himself of the Schloss library at his leisure.

Loran positively chuckled as he crossed the square. So that was what it was. Limping slowly up towards the erstwhile old monastery once more, his heart was racing in his chest. He could get in. By their very desire not to show suspicion he could gain entrance. How well he could imagine it all. Old Plautus sitting, meeting after meeting, cold as an eel and wearing a Roman toga, under the marble bust of his master—scared absolutely stiff of any pillaging being found out and the treasures that had become so dear to him removed. Beyond anything else he had looked the type whom the intoxication of the book, the poison of bibliomania, had filled with its irresistible and quasi-divine afflatus. Now they would be prepared for him, Loran realized. But they didn't know the singleness of purpose with which he was after those pictures. If only they were there....

This time, as he turned up that last path shut off from the sun's rays, he heard the great bell ringing joyfully. A breeze caught those confident carillons and brought them to him antiphonally. Was there the sound of voices in a choir? When the walls eventually emerged from the monotonous firs he was scarcely at all taken aback to find the door wide open and the clerk who had answered it before standing there smiling with servility.

"I am Eccard," he said gaily. "I am—we are all—so sorry about what happened yesterday. A most dreadful mistake." Inside the building he added in a humble tone, "For which I have paid, in penance." Loran glanced at him sharply but there was nothing but the utmost solemnity in the other's face. Then the man went on brightly as before: "You were in the bank. Plautus has been expecting you to call. Won't you come this way, sir?"

Loran stopped. "Excuse me, but that's odd. Have you got a telephone here?"

The man smiled as he shook his head and then hurried on as previously. Loran caught phrases—"Our local group, a modest affair, the Summum Bonum ... you must forgive us ... pure research ... Plautus presides, yes, a most ardent humanist. In fact, sir, you will find us all," he added proudly in a vaulted passageway, "all ardent humanists here."

They went through what seemed to Loran to be a sort of sacristy, then he was fully engaged in navigating a winding wooden staircase, at the head of which he was ushered into a study where the figure he had first seen in the center of that crazy semicircle rose from behind a high desk and bowed with a stiff smile. Loran took the lean hand of "old Plautus" himself.

"Apologies are due to you for what occurred yesterday," he said with awkward haste. "I gather you have received some explanation at least. Now please let me provide you with a glass of wine." He had on a brown monk's robe ornamented only with the crimson crab on the left breast. His study was littered with papers, Loran noted rapidly, its naked walls decked with medieval arms. On a marble console table lay an antique hunting-horn. There was something excessive and unsavory about this chaos of taste and period, with its admixture of the valuable and worthless. Loran felt the skin grow taut between his shoulder-blades. Quickly his eyes flicked over the walls for pictures. None here. Nothing. The "Abbot" motioned him to a dark green Empire chair of dubious cleanliness under a plaster cast that must have been the death-mask of some Latinist. Correctly sinister, Loran thought, taking ing the glass of wine offered him. Indeed, this whole study was like some lifeless scrap left over from the Middle Ages.

"I've really come about the Donati Codex," he began, extracting his impressive stack of cards.

Plautus' eyes went to these, then mournfully he moved his bald white head. "I received your letter, but there hardly seemed any point in replying. I do fear we have nothing of Cicero here. I only wish we had."

"But I made practically certain. The Bodley list ..."

"Mistaken." This time the interruption was sharp enough to be out of character. The Abbot gently corrected it. "The Ruccellai," he went on. "Bernardo was the real culprit. Pilfered the lot. We've hardly a thing left from the master. It was shameless."

"I see." Was there some faint smell of ambergris? At his elbow Loran observed an hour-glass slowly spending its sand. All at once, on another table, he caught sight of a small piece of precision machinery. He wasn't certain what it was, but it lay there with a kind of menace, shining with oil, and the skin on his back tingled again. Another big N on a chair. It was all of a piece. He felt certain that these scholars could be thieves. Or conquerors of the Napoleonic brand. He averted his eyes. "All the same, I should be glad to avail myself of the hospitality of your library for a few days, if I might, for the purpose of my thesis."

The old man again shook his head. "I assure you, sir, we have very little. *Ciceronis liber jocularis nunquam repertus et in lucem editus.* I'm most sorry. They made so many sales."

Who "they" were, Loran had no idea. "But you'd permit me to make some notes," he persisted. "One never knows, things you people don't value unduly often seem to us others ..."

"You may come when you wish." Once more he spoke with a surprisingly sharp intonation, a voice of command, and once more he corrected himself. "But I assure you we are barren. Just one or two trifles that might be ... Augusta Vindelicorum ... very little Greek now ... *Habemus pontificem Dominum Othonem de Colonna* ... you are sure you do not mind working under supervision; one has to be so careful these days."

"Of course not."

"Eccard will show you our little library." He opened the door and there stood Eccard waiting on the threshold with—so Loran considered—a look that was now a peculiar mixture of adoration and terror. How devoted these Renaissance curators could become, to be sure. "Your dark glasses, sir?" inquired the Abbot with a rigidly kindly smile.

"I'm afraid I have weak eyes." Loran touched his scar. "An accident."

"How unfortunate. By the way, you didn't drink your wine."

The Abbot held out phthisic fingers and down the hairless and finely articulated back of this wasted hand Loran saw a black vein throbbing excitedly. "We're naturally most interested in English scholarship, but with the mark as it is..." He shrugged. "So, come when you like, sir. But I fear we're barren."

Eccard escorted Loran the way he had come, dropping back cheery comments as they went. "At Oxford we had members once... the late Horatian expert, Tide, you may have heard of him, yes, he was one of us...."

Loran was keeping his eyes skinned about him. This time, traversing the sacristy, he thought he heard a susurration of voices. The library turned out to be a large hall, divided into sections, on an upper floor at the end of further complicated passages. He was presented to another evident brother of this strange order, an individual who sat poring over a framed parchment and whose raw, tough mug—when he raised it—seemed savagely out of keeping with his rôle. Their bulldog, Loran thought. This time they're making no mistake.

All day he "worked" in this library, and by the time he was shown out by Eccard he had counted paintings on the walls by van der Weyden, Petrus Christus, Moroni, Bellini, Carpaccio, and others of the ilk. Yet although his heart beat high he was fairly certain that these were already officially attributed to the Canossa collection. They wouldn't be such fools as to hang a stolen Bosch on their walls, not at the moment, at any rate, not until the heat came off.

During dinner at Die Drei Mohren the manager hurried up and informed him there was a telephone call from London. Loran had to cross at once to the post office. He found excitement and confusion in that bare room on the far side of the square, where he sat down to an ancient, crackly instrument. A faint female voice cut suddenly through: "It's Lucy. Yes, me, Tom. I had to get you. Listen, I haven't very long." A pause. "Are you being overheard?"

"Very much so."

"Listen. Please get this carefully, Tom. He's found out where you are."

"Everything? You didn't tell him everything, Lucy?"

"No, just the name of the village. He left after that."

"It's quite enough."

"Oh Tom, I felt dreadful after doing it. You know, like giving birth to piebald mice or something. But I had to. Seeing him again at the club did something to me; I can't explain it now. Besides, I'd had far too much to drink."

"Oh Lucy, I did ask you to keep away from that place, you know. I felt sure he'd be watching it, and he obviously was. I only hope to Christ he didn't beat you up or anything; he's quite capable of it in his present state."

Loran was surprised to detect a chuckle. "Course not. Only, he did pour a jar of honey over me."

"What on earth for?"

Another giggle. "It was silly, really. He wanted to pour it all over me, you know, in my slip."

"Did it hurt?"

"No, but it was dreadfully sticky. And it smarts in the eyes, honey does, so I've learnt. I cried badly. Oh what a mess, Tom. I am sorry I did it, but he's a man who gives himself to that sort of lark, you know." She added with a laugh, "Once he wrote his name in lipstick on my tummy. Now listen, there's something you ought to know before they cut me off. Something I never told you." Loran waited. And it indeed seemed to him as if a thousand ears were listening to that distant voice, so unlike Lucy's robust person. "You see, he may be slightly balmy. He may have gone over."

"What do you mean?"

"Yes, when he left… what I'm saying is, he did have narcolepsy in hospital out there."

"Are you quite certain you aren't simply trying to defend this man again, Lucy?"

"No, no. He thought he didn't, Tom, but he did. You know what he was like on that patrol."

"He was in a bad way, the poor devil."

"He should never have gone out on it. I really don't think he's safe now. Do please be careful. And be careful of him. Get him to a hospital, if you can. God knows what he'll do if he finds you, I dread to think." The voice faded fainter: "He's armed."

"I know. I saw that old pistol in his trunk." He spoke calmly. And was suddenly cut off. It was an odd cut. Quite dead. He thought of trying to get her back, but had no idea whether she had called from her flat or from the Honey Bee or even somewhere else. The point was, when had Stevens forced Lucy to tell him? How long ago? In any case, he would surely have a few days in the clear, with travel restrictions what they now were.

But T.A.C. Loran was wrong there. Very wrong indeed. He realized as much the next morning when he'd barely started on his way towards the Schloss and the man came out of the trees, carrying in one hand a small fiber suitcase and in the other a .45 pistol.

CHAPTER TWENTY ONE

That wrinkled pin-stripe suit, so tight it looked as if the man inside it were inflated—Loran recognized it all in the first shock of seeing the figure emerge from the firs. He remembered, too, that hulking walk, body thrust slightly forward, yet balanced: like many athletes, Stevens had agility rather than grace in motion: Loran recalled watching him move through the Honey Bee and half-expecting chairs and tables to get knocked over. What he wasn't prepared for was the look of pain on Stevens' face.

"Dear boy," he tried as gently as he could, stopping in the middle of the track and striving to hide his fear. When he was so close—for this to happen, it was cruel. "You don't have to wave that thing at me, you know."

"Hands above your head, Loran, and no bloody rammel about it, see. All right, now get off the path. Double quick. Over here. And don't call me dear boy."

When they'd gone a little deeper into the forest Loran said: "Look, I really don't think you need to cover me with all that ironwork." He turned, lowered his hands. If only he could get near Stevens. But it was extraordinary. The man looked as if he hadn't slept or shaved for at least two days. Lucy was right, he appeared stricken to the point of collapse. "Dear boy..."

"Stuff it."

"I mean, with my leg. I'm scarcely a threat to your safety, am I?"

Stevens sat, or dropped, onto the bole of a tree. He put down his case and ran his free hand across a brow that glistened with dampness. "I know you judo experts. Sit down there, Loran. Facing me."

"And a very pleasant place for a cozy chat, too. The countryside round here's staggeringly beautiful, don't you think?"

Stevens was really shaking, running his hand over his head. "I'm hungry," he uttered sullenly. "I ran clear out of money. That last taxi fare cost the earth. You haven't got anything, have you?"

Loran tossed him a Kit-Kat and Stevens tore at the tinfoil and munched the chocolate in silence for a while. "What wouldn't I give for a damn good kedgeree," he stated finally. "Some Heinz Tomato on top, eh? Tell me what you're after here, Loran, and tell me straight."

"You ask me that!" Loran tried to raise his eyebrows politely. It was strange how sorry he felt for this broken creature, and yet how frightened of him at the same time. He hadn't felt quite that way before, but Stevens now seemed to be panting, his hands shifting off in that grim way they had, and Loran began to wonder how long it would be before he could get at that gun. He decided to try to keep Stevens talking. "You know why I'm here. I object to the Germans appropriating my family's valuables. I imagine you'd feel the same way in my place. There are some paintings involved—as I think you also know."

"What's all this bull? You mean to say, you think you'll get 'em up here. What is this place anyhow?" He was staring as if in a stupor. He took out a small flask, unscrewed it with his teeth, and sucked a few last drops before tossing it disgustedly away. Slowly he shook his head about. "Those photographs I kept told you where the paintings were, didn't they?"

"Where they'd been at one time, shall we say. Yes, those snaps were of Father's favorites, as it happens. He loved the Bosch."

"Think they're still there?"

"I don't know. But I'm having a try."

They sat in silence for a moment, then Stevens said thickly. "You know, I'm sorry about that, Loran. Trouble is, I've been feeling pretty dicky these past few days. Not quite myself, you know. But Jesus, I felt sorry for you about your old man. I can understand why you were keen to get von Schultz."

"Don't worry," Loran answered quietly. "I can understand why you weren't. I don't think you were well." He added, "Anyway I'm afraid we won't find the general up here. The Americans have already been over the place."

"The Americans, eh?" Stevens was still stubbornly shaking his head. Loran wondered how much he really understood. "What is that place, some sort of castle?"

"Originally an old monastery. It became quite well known for its art collection. Nowadays there just seem to be a lot of nuts up there."

Stevens cocked his head. "You got in all right?"

Loran told him about his first visit to Schloss Canossa, the weird meeting of humanists being held there, and then of the odd Abbot who presided over the place. He also mentioned the bank clerk. "Here, let me show you the Bosch again"—and he reached into a pocket.

"Steady!" Stevens' tired eyes came alert. "Don't try any flash business with me now."

"My dear fellow, it's quite all right. I'm unarmed."

"Well, you needn't show me 'em again, I remember 'em damn well." The pistol barrel dropped an inch. "Couple of those maidens were pretty classy in the sitdown, if you ask me. It was the crab sign that gave this place away, eh?"

"Canossa emblem. Lucy told you that, I suppose."

Stevens lowered his head.

Loran was watching the pistol hard. He said, "You've come to kill me, haven't you? You think I'm the only man alive who knows you killed Ridgeworth. That's it, right?"

Stevens sat in silence in the glade.

"You don't have to worry about Ridgeworth," Loran said. "I know he was dying. But I needed those photographs and I did think you'd tried to kill me off in that raid by sending me straight into the enemy."

"You're wrong about that, Loran. I didn't know they were there."

"I believe that now. I'm sorry." For a second he thought of putting out his hand for a shake but decided it was better not to risk it; in Stevens' unstable condition it might mean death at the hands of that ugly Webley.

"Looting's prohibited, you know."

Loran laughed. "I fear the Geneva Convention meant precious little to von Schultz and his ilk."

"I always warned our men off anything like that." Stevens' face flushed. "Do you realize, I can't look at a steamroller these days without thinking of it. Really. Extermination of Jews, all that sort of thing; it's all coming out in the papers now. The papers—Christ! They were getting on my bloody nerves. Did you feel like that back home? The day I left there was some stuff about SAS paratroopers. Had to dig their own graves, all that. Like your dad." He looked away. "Von Schultz's filthy clock was plastered on the front pages of practically every bloody daily in London when I left. No eyebrows. That hare-lip. They still haven't found him, you know."

"We should have got him that time."

"Yes. We should have." Stevens took out a vast silk handkerchief, stared at it. "Listen, Loran," he said, his face was pouring with sweat, "I've come to help you get those pictures back. I mean, teach the jerry he can't walk around Europe nicking other people's possessions, see. I never believed in looting." Stevens stood up at that.

For a fleeting second Loran felt a flutter in his ribs. He's faking, he's going to finish me off now. If I smile hard enough he won't kill me, it's said to be hard to kill a man when he's grinning.

"Yes, I came here to get you too. All that. God, I don't know. But you ought to get compensation, see. It's in the regs, isn't it. I mean, we ought to clear up this lot first. I'll bet those paintings were valuable as bleeding hell."

"You're right." Saying it, Loran wondered if this was a trick. Had it now occurred to that perplexed, dull brain that he could get the pictures for himself? Nick them (as he put it) himself, and light out for some foreign soil?

But Stevens was doggedly continuing: "It's only fair, isn't it? That is, if you're sure you can't go through the normal channels for 'em."

Loran's head bumped back on the bark of the tree at that. He grinned violently. "The normal channels. My dear chap, have you tried sitting it out through some of the normal channels in any of our minor ministries recently? It transpired that to get back those Bosches for my mother I'd now need an import license, an antique license, and a dozen other permits into the bargain. Meanwhile, there's some godforsaken law about possession constituting ownership after a certain time working against me all the while. Possibly those phonies up there know it, too. I finally cracked when I learnt that the Ancient Documents Inspectorate would require special crating and that the Ministry of Agriculture made it mandatory to have signed clearance from foot-and-mouth on any straw or packing used." He glanced up. His bitter outburst had surprised himself. Stevens' face had eased.

"You're right, laddie. There's far too much bloody red tape back in the old country these days."

"Come to think of it, how did you get here so quickly?"

"I'd previously put in for a passport, see." His eyes drifted off again. Loran shifted his bottom forward a few inches. "I'd been thinking, well, of getting out of it all, frankly. The Argentine," he said in an abruptly aggressive tone. "They have almost no extradition laws to speak of there. All I need is the ante for the trip."

So that is it, Loran thought quickly. A nice idea to make off with the swag. Having killed me first, of course. Yet somehow he found it increasingly difficult to doubt Stevens' sincerity.

Suddenly the man put a hand to his chest. He gasped a little. "Hell's bells, the red tape back in Blighty these days. It was just as well I was officially in the Army or I do honestly believe I'd never have got over here. Bullshit at its bloody best."

"What happened, then?"

"Needed my passport for getting back into the country. In case I spent longer over here than planned. I'm almost a civvie by this time, you know." He paused again—to laugh or for breath, Loran wasn't certain which. "Weeping bloody Judas, I'd have had that crowd slap in the guardroom at short order for supreme inefficiency in the old days."

"Yes, I'm with you there."

"See," he confided, "I broke in."

"Where?"

"Passport Office," replied Stevens with satisfaction. "They kept me hanging about for so ruddy long I felt like blue murder, I did. They kept promising and promising. Obviously didn't have the faintest idea of their own schedules. Nothing but bumf and bull and coming the old soldier on you. Then I rang up and they said it was ready. But I got round there too late. By two minutes. Traffic jam, taxi delayed. Place closed up. It was weeping awful, I do assure you. I could see the bloody thing, I tell you, staring me straight in the face through a glass door. Lying right on the top of a pile of other passports. That was last night, you understand, and me with a ticket for Tempelhof this morning and everything else booked up for months ahead, apparently. Well, I got in." He smacked the butt of his pistol. "Pretended later it was my arm. Bumped the glass, you know. But I made too much ruddy noise. Bluenose got me. Thought there was going to be merry hell to pay. Luckily there was a Bayswater bobbie, sergeant name of Pryde; that was where you helped me, sonnie. Oh yes, he vouched for me, see." A smile stole over Stevens' bashed and shining features. "Seems the reputation you built up for me worked the trick with Pryde. He did me proud, as you might say. They let me off." He mused a moment. "Funny cove. Wore rings. Never seen that before on a copper."

Loran rested back his head. Cut-outs of blue drifted high overhead. Like the pattern of a dress. So blue, so green. It was good to be alive. Keep talking, he told himself, just keep talking to the fellow.

"All the time in that prison camp, Phil, I lived on hate, you know. Hatred and despair. I ought to have got von Schultz that night." For some reason Stevens was now wrapping his large silk handkerchief round the butt of his pistol. Loran thought: he's going to brain me over the head with it then, that's it. Then Stevens slipped the gun in his pocket.

"Get up."

"It's not going to help to kill me now."

"I want to see if this piejaw of yours is correct. You were a British officer, weren't you. Then we bloody can't let jerry swindle you like this."

"Want to try some snooping with me?" For it really seemed as if he did. Loran smiled. "It might prove difficult."

"Tell the muckers I'm a fellow scholar."

"Well, I'll try if you're serious, but frankly you don't look like one to me, Phil. What are you going to do with your suitcase?"

"Dump it here. We'll call that B Echelon," he said without smiling. "Pick it up on return sortie."

At pistol point Stevens made Loran solemnly secrete the case under some brush and then mark the spot on the track with an arrangement of twigs common in P.E.D.G. training When Loran had finished he saw Stevens frowning. He was holding something shiny in his left hand.

"That's odd. An old round." He tossed Loran the spent cartridge. "Mauser. What do you make of that, my friend?"

"It is rather queer." Loran was indeed surprised. Glancing at Stevens' flattened face he caught a flush of fulfillment there.

"Well, let's get weaving then. You walk well ahead and please don't try any funny stuff, because I'm covering you every step of the way, got it?"

They slogged on slowly in silence for a while. Suddenly Stevens hissed: "Stop!"

Loran turned. Again he thought—I don't want to die here, not now when we might be so close. … "Yes?" he asked tiredly.

"You know we're being watched?"

"Funny you should say that. I felt that the first time I came up here, as a matter of fact."

"Well, I'm frigging positive of it. This was something you got in the desert very strongly, I'm not wrong." There was a genuine light of purpose in Stevens' eyes as he spoke now; his whole being had come alive. Loran himself felt it, but it seemed to invigorate the other man. "Look natural and keep going. I'll walk a little closer behind you."

A twist in the track brought them in sight of the queerly shaped bell-tower of the monastery.

"That the shop?"

"Yes, that's it."

"A bit ye olde, isn't it?"

"Mostly thirteen-century. With additions."

Then once more, still closer to the Schloss, Stevens stopped Loran in the pathway. He spoke almost excitedly now.

"See that?"

"What?"

"Definite flash of light. From the beetle sort of watch-tower affair."

Loran shielded his eyes. "Under the crab cupola, you mean? I can't see anything. Signalling?" He turned. "Come to think of it, that's interesting. You remember I told you of the Abbot knowing all about my coming up—even though they haven't got any telephone wired here?"

"Signal or antenna being run down from that cross affair. I rather think the latter. And catch that? Flash of binoculars." Stevens was squinting into the sun, he was suddenly a soldier again. "I have a suspicion that one of the local additions you speak of, laddie boy, is a distinctly twentieth-century radio set in that bell-tower. Military. Can't you feel it? Dammit, I've had that in my bones all my sodding life, it seems. I feel sure," he added more calmly, "there's enemy about in these parts. Don't ask me how I know it, man, but I do. However, since we're probably under scrutiny, just keep going forward, will you."

After Loran had pulled the doorbell they chatted in undertones in front of that massive portal.

"Man on the library, you say?"

"Yes, constantly. But it's absurd to think there's anything sinister about these crazy old humanists up here." Loran told himself Stevens was madder than Lucy had hinted. At the same time he found himself unconsciously sharing Stevens' excitement. He couldn't help reflecting how completely the wheel had come full circle. Back they were, hunting the boche—as Stevens might have put it. This very sense of exhilaration made Loran add cautiously, "The collection here's been famous for centuries."

"Look," Stevens said. "My appreciation of the sit's this. You want your daubs. You ought to have your daubs. All right. We've got to get into the place and if you ask me, we've got to recce that tower. Don't look up now but there's definitely equipment there. I can see it. What's more, we could scan the entire layout from there. Do these blighters savvy English, by any chance?"

"I don't think so."

A smiling Eccard opened the door. Loran introduced his plug-ugly of a "fellow-classicist in the field" and Eccard's eyes scurried uneasily over Stevens' unkempt bulk.

"The Abbot is unfortunately otherwise detained at the moment, sir. But I feel sure he would like to meet your good friend later this morning. If in the meantime…"

Limping after Eccard down those theatrically dank corridors lined with marble busts, Loran heard Stevens' breath close behind him.

"Who are these types?"

"Famous classical authors. Juvenal, Pliny..."

"Look a trifle constipated, don't they. Think they're swiped?"

"It's hard to tell."

"Keep going but take a dekko at that chap's boots, will you?" Loran glanced quickly down. It was true. Under the monk's cassock Eccard had on creaking leather boots of a pattern most familiar to a p.o.w. Stevens went on in an undertone, "German Army boots. Well dubbined, too. I told you I smelt enemy. There's something fishy here, all right."

They passed through the sacristy in which, amid enormous shadows, a heavy cross now lay athwart the cracked wall. It occurred to Loran then what an excellent smokescreen this sedulous object made. He felt his arm pulled back. For a second they both had a glimpse into what appeared to be a chapel. It was at least a large hall, lit with candles, from which a vague muttering or sibilation of sandals on stone made itself audible. In profile stood a gigantic statue, crowned with thorns, and they had time—before Eccard beckoned them on—to catch sight of a brother bending his knee in front of this. But the pallid luminosity shining on that hallowed, towering figure had been enough and with a flicker within him, Loran recognized the pseudo-crucified waxwork. It was somehow like touching the source of some primeval infection.

He turned back to Stevens as they plodded on upstairs. "That was Virgil's face."

"And I'll tell you something else of interest when we have a mo', laddie," returned the other in his new tone of fulfilled anticipation—but his whisper was cut short. They were being politely ushered into the library. Presenting his "fellow-classicist" to the roughneck librarian on duty, Loran now needed no words in which to phrase his own first suspicions of this dubious individual. It was an Army face, he suddenly realized. And between that face and Stevens went a sort of intraspecific recognition. When the man had resumed his place behind his parchment Loran exchanged a look with Stevens at the clunk of metal caused by something under the surplice striking that chair.

They settled at a table at the far end of the room. Stevens pointed upwards once and Loran saw what he hadn't previously observed, mirrors for the supervision of readers.

"Some pretty valuable books about here," he muttered as he drew out a heavy Thieme-Becker and a Meyers Lexikon.

He turned up an entry: BOSCH (or BOS), JEROM (c. 1460–1518). He translated for Stevens on a note-card. "Name generally given, from birthplace Hertogenbosch, to Hieronymus van Aeken." He read on: "...devoted himself to the invention of bizarre type, *diableries*." He whispered, "Bosch was involved in a strange secret society. It looks as if they had some half-baked notions in that direction at Schloss Canossa too, eh? This one's in the Lippmann collection in Berlin, by the by. I hope to God it's survived."

To his astonishment Stevens was paying no attention to him at all. Laboriously, pressing very hard, he was writing something on one of the note-cards with a bitten pencil. The result of this effort he passed over to Loran.

"Man we saw genuflexing in chapel just now GEN VON SCHULTZ."

The last word was underlined twice. It flamed in Loran's vision. He glanced up sharply. Stevens nodded slowly. His lips said, "Sure of it."

Loran felt a trembling in his wounded leg. His limbs seemed to rebel. He put a hand to his forehead and felt it damp. About to reply, he was prevented from doing so by the librarian rising and strolling past their table. Together he and Stevens pored industriously over their Thieme-Becker. When the librarian had resumed his seat, Stevens muttered, "I wouldn't be at all surprised if that weren't an ex-Sicherheitsdienst type, either. Notice the haircut, Mensur scars? No, I tell you, this dump is bloody reeking of the military. I can feel it in my bones." As if to confirm his words there came to their ears a direct metallic sound, which might, or might not, have been that of a chamber being checked.

"Are you fairly certain that was von Schultz?" Loran asked as slowly as he could. "The light was bad."

Stevens put a hand on his. "Don't you worry, son. Harelip. No eyebrows. Swear to it."

"I took that for a monk's tonsure or something."

"Well, don't take anything on trust in this place. We'll get him. Now, what's your recee been to date?"

Loran explained how little he'd been able to search so far. Still, the previous day he had—under semblance of going through the stacks—made fairly certain there was nothing he was after in the library.

"Does this codger scatter for lunch?"

"Yes. But he's relieved. At least, he was yesterday. Old Plautus, the Abbot I told you about, gave me something to eat in a refectory place. Knives and forks all crossed, drinking in three sips, that kind of business. I suspect he'll be sending to meet you soon."

"I see." Stevens pondered.

Watching those dogged eyes so full of pain and loneliness, Loran again wondered whether this was all turning into a dream, and Stevens going dotty.

As if reading his thoughts the other said, "Think I'm off my rocker? Not on your life, son, not on your bloody life. I'm sane as Saint Peter at this moment and three times as normal. Now then, you coming with me up to that tower?"

"The tower," Loran exclaimed. "Let's think this out. It mightn't be wise to show our hands just yet."

"Don't ask me why," Stevens replied patiently, "but I'm bloody convinced that tower affair is the key to this whole outfit. I know jerry, see, and he's a methodical blighter. Remember how you could set your watch by his mortars in the desert? Listen, I watched a chap sliding into an observation hole for two bloody weeks out there and, no matter how we shelled him, in he went at the dead same time every day. Then he got hit, and another chap took over. Same hole, same time of day. It got monotonous. No, they're working from that tower all right."

"Even granted they are, just how do we dodge the man in here, pray?"

Stevens began to formulate his plan and somehow something in Loran responded. Information. Intention ("We will secure missing valuables and eliminate General von Schultz"). *Method. Administration. Intercommunication.* There was no stopping Stevens now. But Loran had the impression that they were being carefully scrutinized by the lout-like librarian in the overhead mirror. To his sudden horror he saw that Stevens had so lost himself he had put his pistol out on the table.

"Own troops," he was murmuring slowly, writing laboriously on a note-card. "Disposition and size of enemy forces being unknown, we will ..."

Loran realized he could seize the weapon himself without any difficulty whatsoever, put an end to the whole crazy rigmarole that had caught him ineluctably in its grip. He was contemplating doing so, in fact, when he realized that the librarian, who must have trodden very quietly indeed, was standing over them. What was more, this out-of-place citizen was covering them with an exceedingly out-of-place but up-to-date and trim little Luger. A piece of armory, Loran reflected, exactly like the one that brigadier had leveled at them so many years—so many centuries, should he say?—ago.

Loran's throat was dry, his heart hammered with fear. This time the game was up, all right. He was about to try to nudge Stevens, who seemed neither to have realized what he had done with his big Webley nor to have noticed the figure standing behind and to one side of him at all. Then he heard him say without altering the pitch of his mutter—"I've got him, Tom."

Stevens spun on his seat like a top. Never had Loran seen such a big man move quite so fast. The Luger was sent flying without a shot, and the Prussian librarian barged flappingly backwards and fell, smashed with the most terrific blow full in the face Loran had ever conceived it possible for anyone to administer outside an abattoir. The blow could not be said, indeed, to have come from Stevens' fist, so much as from his entire being. The bunched knuckles crashed into the man's features, and the impact of bone on bone made a noise of such an utterly physical quality that Loran had a split-second of pure revulsion, staring down at that gaping mouth, at the blood seeping from the eyeballs.

"Quick!"

Stevens' whisper awoke him. Together they tucked the body behind a stack containing large Chinese yearbooks in German. The librarian, who had on Army trousers under his toga, was still breathing, it seemed. Then Stevens said, "Let's get cracking."

But at the door Loran touched his arm. He couldn't seem to get that glazed face out of his mind somehow; it was truly a distortion of the animal, a perfectly ferocious convulsion, black eyebrows, the teeth gone, a kind of pristine rudimentariness of being that suddenly, inexplicably, cut the ground from under Loran's control. He heard himself saying, "Let's get out of here."

Stevens grasped his arm. "Coming with me, lad? Mind, we're getting your pictures." He had his pistol in his fist again. "And we haven't too much time. This little nipper's due to be relieved at one, you say. O.K. That means we've got just over an hour or so before they give the hue-and-cry. Assuming the Abbot doesn't send to get me first. D'you think we ought to settle him now?"

"No."

"Let's start for the tower, then."

"I..." Loran's voice trailed off. He found himself removing his dark glasses; they were slipping off the sweating bridge of his nose anyway.

Stevens said, "Glad you did that. Can't say I much cared for the giglamps myself."

Loran's eyes slipped back to the stacks. There seemed to be a virtually sarcastic number of books in the room now. And that scent of incense. He thought he detected a tacky dribble of blood, bright as oil-slick, seeping under the well-bound yearbooks. That livid countenance. A sudden petrifying fear, a terror unlike anything he had ever experienced in his being before, overcame him as he heard something resembling a soda-siphon.

Stevens cocked his head, his eyes filled with interest at the sound. "Think we ought to bind and gag him, Tom?"

"Not necessary." Loran shook his head with great deliberation. It felt heavy on his neck. The ghastly bubbling seemed to increase in volume—in dreamlike crescendo—and he couldn't face returning to that smashed-in face. "You hit him hard enough, I think."

"I think so, too." Stevens chuckled. "Now let's get weaving, eh?"

It was with a prodigious effort that Loran followed Stevens out. He saw his briefcase on the table. He hadn't the energy to go for it. In any case he'd need both hands, in all likelihood. Courage was a queer quality, he thought. His gammy leg hung on him like lead.

The odd thing was, Stevens seemed instinctively to know the way. At the corner of a deserted corridor decorated with more busts and statuettes, yet contriving in some manner to appear martial, Loran remarked this to him.

"Comes of appreciating the situation properly," came the chuckled reply. He led Loran up an empty stair. "Manage all right?"

"Yes, I think so."

"Sure you don't need any help?"

"No, thanks." But he fell behind Stevens who padded swiftly, alertly, on to the head of the staircase and turned the corner into the new corridor. Tiptoeing up, Loran ducked like a hinge behind a cast of Chryses, mounted on black marble, at the sound of a door banging ahead of them. The inscription throbbingly confronted him as he huddled painfully there, out of sight from the passage, his tongue swelling with fear. The slam was succeeded by a thud like a pistol falling. Then, for what seemed an eternal interval, nothing happened. No sound at all. Loran seemed to be listening avidly into some titanic seashell rushing with soundless sound. At the same time he felt overcome with exhaustion. Then, a sourceless footstep.

He'd been right. He saw Stevens in profile, moving backwards, like a dancer in slow motion. His hands were held on top of his head. All at once the partner of this ballet came into view, and Loran no longer had the smallest doubt in the world.

Wearing the uniform of an Obergruppenführer of the Reichssicherheitshauptamt, the man had a sallow face barred by a sparse black mustache, and the bluish revolver that menaced Stevens was held in delicate, slim dark hands—fitting hands for the Aryan who had been personally responsible for framing the "special treatment" program in the "final solution" phase of the Jewish problem in the Third Reich.

The man covering Stevens was, in short, Krum Brandt, and Loran knew that Stevens was correct—somehow Schloss Canossa, investigated and cleared, had become a nest of ex-Secret State Police and Nazi officials in hiding.

Loran struck Brandt's right wrist a slashing, rising blow exactly where it joined the hand, as he came level.

"Ai!" A yelp of pain from that creamy skin. The gun spun like a rocket and skidded noisily down the corridor. This time Stevens dropped his man with a short clicking uppercut. There was a murderous, diabolic swiftness in his movements now, as he picked up his own pistol and, retrieving the German's, tossed it to Loran. Together they tucked this body behind the cast of the priest of Apollo.

"Thanks," Stevens said.

"Oira marble." Loran stared at that numb, recumbent face behind the bust; this one somehow didn't affect him quite so badly. "You were right. That's Brandt."

"Who?"

"Krum Brandt. His Einsatz commandoes personally cremated most of the *Nacht und Nebel* prisoners. Also about a couple of million Jews, at present count, including some of the finest intellects in Europe. Looks gentle in sleep, don't you think?"

"Shall we make it permanent?"

"Finish him off in cold blood, you mean?"

"Make too much noise. O.K. Let's get to that tower. I've an idea we'll be able to cover the whole shower from up there, to start off with. See what's on, that sort of thing."

By some architectural trick the tower was separated, squared off from the rest of the monastery, the sole mode of entry being through a trap-door at the head of the stairs underneath it. At first Stevens heaved at this without effect, shoving till he was in a muck-sweat. Then Loran noticed that it slid, easily, on the very finest German ball-bearings.

Stevens penetrated into the place first, with another of his quick leaps, Colt in hand.

"Empty, I think. O.K."

Loran got up. Stevens pushed back the trap and secured it with an iron bolt.

"Safe as houses here. Take a look at this, man."

Yes, it was fantastic.

To start off with, the place was far larger than Loran had anticipated. Further, the colossal crab suspended over the bell was raised on stone buttresses from the tower walls, into which interstices had been carved. The crab was higher from these walls than was the impression given on ground level.

The actual room, which resembled in atmosphere a small gymnasium, was lit by electricity that someone had left on. In one corner a sandbagged German radio set ticked with imbecilic rapidity. The walls were hung with red bunting and what appeared to be horse-blankets. And the bell-rope dangled ludicrously. There was also what seemed to be a bookbinding press; a couple of pairs of boxing gloves were hung on one wall; and in a corner Loran caught sight of a Schmeiser, several German rifle grenades, an old Pickelhauber helmet, and a dog-whip. A globe of the world reposed on a small desk, beside a pair of seventeenth-century compasses. He instinctively disliked this place. It was like being in the prop room for some medieval drama to be staged by undergraduates. But then what else had the Nazi mythos been? he thought. There was a musty sense of concealment which was strangely sinister.

Stevens, however, seemed more and more in his element. Action had taken him over completely. Hands on hips, he was staring at the isolated trappings around them; this time, thinking how easy it would be to hold him, armed as he himself was, Loran dismissed the thought immediately, as if it pertained to some other level of existence. He felt shocked at the depths of his own emotions in that library just now. He had never known fear could be so unmanning. His eye fell on some newspapers in Gothic script.

"What's this?"

Stevens indicated a table on which lay a binding in black Niger, nicely tooled with a swastika on the front. Loran picked it up, put it down quickly.

"This happens to be a copy of a ten-day course on corpse-burning in *deutsche Schrift*."

Stevens nodded. "And see the Altenberg Special Corps insignia? No, this is the goods, all right."

"I agree. It's explicit."

"No blower, eh." Stevens grinned and straddled the radio operator's stool. A moment later he had the earphones fitted to his head. "Remember that short course on these sets?"

"Can we be one hundred per cent certain about all this?" Loran asked it without conviction, however. He felt as excited as Stevens now.

"The evidence we've picked up so far is more than enough reason for us to contact occupying forces." Stevens twiddled the knobs as if he'd sat behind this very set every day for years. It peeped and burped intermittently. "Give me a hand up with this antenna, would you?" Loran stared briefly at the back of his head. Defenseless. "Thanks. That's got it, I think. If there's any jabbering in boche to be done, I may have to call on you. Thank God we practised on these sets in P.E.D.G. till we had 'em by heart."

Stevens worked the set with skill. With surprisingly little difficulty he crossed a voice speaking in English. It turned out to be an M.P. post at Pohlde.

"Marrow! Marrow!" he called gleefully as he struck the band, frantically tuning the knobs. Loran thought: He's cracked, after all. When Stevens had the set in, Loran took over. "And tell that sergeant receiving to get a bloody move on," Stevens said as he did so.

"M.P.? Over to you." Loran, too, began to remember the drill, and this evidently impressed the originally rather sleepy Signals sergeant who was on duty at the set. "And give that Sparks my rank and serial number," Stevens called. "I might as well make use of it, 'cause I can't much longer."

A few minutes later a P.U.-load of M.P. had been promised to Schloss Canossa at once. When Loran switched off, he became aware of the barking of a number of deep-throated dogs, and the tautness tingled at his spine again.

"Stout work" Stevens smiled from a wall-opening. "They've caught on now, you know. I just saw that cove who let us in take a look up here through glasses from the garden." He pointed down. "However, I suspect we can hold out the necessary forty minutes or so before M.P. arrive. While you were sending, I checked our arc of fire. It's as I suspected. Frankly, we can cover bloody much everything outside Berchtesgaden from where we are."

Stevens indicated a long cupboard where a veritable hedge of small arms bristled. Loran selected a perfect small automatic, wiped clean and fully loaded. He slipped off the safety catch and put the other revolver in his right-hand pocket ready. And suddenly his heart bumped. There, beside the row of guns, was another cupboard, one door of which was open. It too had a swastika inscribed on it. He looked at Stevens, dry-throated. Now the moment had come he felt queerly weak. Stevens was standing look-out, talking to himself at one of the loop-holes, keeping an eye over what he termed "buildings and grounds" with a slender Italian Beretta.

What Loran had seen inside that half-open cupboard was something familiar to any student of art—a series of long upright racks used almost universally for storing paintings. And in these reclined not the customary canvases of most modern artists, but those thin strips of wood known to all lovers of the Renaissance. He slid them out with trembling fingers one after another, then all at once he half-shouted: "God!"

Fragile as a bird's wing, the lean stretch of linden made Loran's pulse sing like a harpstring as he took it out. The exclamation drove Stevens from his wall-opening.

"One of your pictures? You've found it?"

Loran was on his knees, examining the back of the panel. There was an old cash-box and a tray of jewelry on the floor beside him.

"But that's not it," Stevens petulantly cried. "That's not one of the snaps. Why, that's a frightful hash, anyone can see that, man."

Loran stiffly straightened. But he did so with an exhausted smile.

"You got a lighter, by any chance?"

"What for?"

"Fluid."

"Going to burn it or something?" Stevens inquired, handing Loran his old lighter made out of a airplane shell.

"And that nice big silk handkerchief of yours, if you would, please."

Stevens watched as Loran soaked the fine silk and gently, very gently, worked for a second at the corner of the brassy, vulgar abstraction of swirls and splashes that covered the front of the picture. With weariness flooding all his limbs Loran said at last, "This is it, all right. Tanz auf flandrische Art. Someone's had it painted over, probably after bocheland caved in. This pigment's quite new and should be easily removed with a solution of anhydrous alcohol."

Stevens hardly seemed to understand. Loran explained in further detail—how the picture, deframed and disguised, still showed on the back the stamp of the Essen Museum from which it had been purchased by Loran's family. The size also proved on measurement to be precise.

"Matter of fact," he concluded, "this'll actually help me get it through Customs, if they prove tricky. Oh, believe me, I've studied this slice of wood back and front till I know it like my hand."

"Incidentally, just what the devil were you planning to do about sneaking the damn thing back? After all, you say it's a valuable, catalogued painting."

Loran shrugged. "A gamble. The check is said to be fairly cursory leaving these days. It's coming in that our people inspect you closely. But at any rate I'd have got it out and then, well, I simply planned to tell the truth and trust to justice."

"Tell the truth and trust to justice," Stevens mused after him. There was a touch of bitterness in his tone. "I had a theory, you know, that the world was divided up into two camps, winners and losers. Yes, I think you'd get it through once out of this place all right. Come to think of it, jerry let me bring my pistol in with me on the grounds that I was still officially in H.M. Forces. I couldn't risk being caught concealing that, you see."

For a second Loran held up that frail strip of old linden, so lovingly painted by the master, so meticulously sincere. The clou of his father's collection. It was almost what his mother needed to live again, a memento of that wise man's vigorous taste. He slipped it back into the cupboard again, now feeling oddly ashamed of his suspicions of Stevens.

"What about the others?" Stevens spoke from the loophole by which he had again taken up his stand.

"Just a second and I'll take a look."

Then both simultaneously heard an odd noise in the tower, an irregular clicking that certainly did not emerge from the radio, which was now shut off. Loran thought it might be footsteps, someone trying the stairs underneath. Then both turned. Against the iron bars of a cage, hung in the far corner of the tower, a well-fed parrot was assiduously stropping its beak. They smiled at each other.

All at once Loran said. "You know, down there just now... Hell, I was damn scared, I don't mind telling you. If it hadn't been for you, I don't know if I'd ever have got myself up here at all." He was interrupted by a smacking whine. Stevens immediately fired back over the parapet.

"Intercepted our message or found friend Brandt, most likely. They know they're for it now. I fear you and I are in for some ballistic aggression, Tom. All right," he completed, grinning. "We're right up here waiting for you, Fritz."

With a limping leap Loran made for an opening in the opposite wall. Something moved on a lower rooftop and he fired and missed. But no one, he soon saw, could possibly leave Schloss Canossa without coming under their fire—Stevens had been dead right. No one, in fact, could so much as cross the gardens to those high, gaffed walls without risk of exposure. And the main gate out was set so far back it made an easy mark. As Stevens put it in a moment of lull—"Just so long as the sods didn't construct a tunnel."

"They spoke to me of a crypt."

Even so, their view over the great forests was superlative, every path open to them for what seemed like miles. Two

Doberman pinschers prowled the front garden now, occasionally throwing up a howl or two in the general direction of the tower. Otherwise peace lay uneasily over Schloss Canossa. And the M.P. patrol was due up, in twenty minutes or so.

"That window!" Stevens shouted abruptly, as the bell, struck by a bullet, gave out a gravely sonorous tung! "Watch it, would you, old man."

"Right."

They had reverted automatically to their ranks on Operation Cabbage. All went quiet again. As the grave. They watched out from various loop-holes—fake archers' slits perhaps, changing their positions, allotting the areas to be covered between them, chatting from time to time.

"Do you know," Stevens said once, "there was a fellow back in London rang me up. Said he wanted me to write a book."

"You ought to. When we get back."

Stevens shook his head. "I've been trying to do a thing for my school mag called 'My Years of Service Abroad.' And anyway I can't go back, Tom."

"Yes, you can," Loran said earnestly. "No one knows. No one except me. And now I understand. Listen, Phil…"

Something flickered. Both fired. There was a melodramatic clashing of broken glass. In the next interval Loran added, "You realize what this means. If between us we've copped blighters like Brandt."

"Think I gave him a Visible Distinguishing Mark, eh?"

"For life, I'd say. No, you can come back all right now, Phil."

"I can't, you know." He shook his head again and from across that gruesome chamber Loran could see his eyes were wet. "No, I've had my chips, Tom. I'm throwing in my hand. Yes, turning myself in when this lot's over. I've got to, don't you see?"

"I don't see that you have to at all," Loran said hotly.

"Well, I've had it."

"But you'll be let off. You were undergoing mental breakdown, nervous confusion. I felt the same thing just now. It happens to the best. Lucy will swear..."

Another bullet nicked the tower. Then one flew in under the crab's belly and hummed in ricochet like a furious wasp. Loran and Stevens hugged the floor, both flat for a second. Yet when they had resumed their places, Loran saw tears rolling down into the bristle of Stevens' chin.

"See, Tom, I was fond of the Army. God, I hated it at times. But it was the only thing I knew."

For a few minutes Loran left him to that quiet grief. To steady his aim Stevens had placed one muddy shoe on a gold-and-white Louis XVI chair. Watching his heaving shoulders, Loran felt that perhaps some unknown transgression of his own was at stake, some secret shame for which he, too, shared the responsibility. He glanced at his watch. Not much longer now, if that M.P. patrol had got off the ground pronto.

An ominous calm, meanwhile, had fallen over the garden and outbuildings of Schloss Canossa. The view over all those motionless firs, he was thinking, gave one the impression of subsisting in another element, lifted closer to the infinite azure than man could normally endure: all the sky overhead was so splendid and so pure. Then a furrow of gray rippled through that fabric of green below. The noise only came later. But when it did so, things started happening in the monastery in very rapid succession.

They first became aware of it by shouts. Loran was watching the little British P.U. pulling lustily up the slope and smoking like mad for some reason as it climbed the widest of the white paths scarring through the trees. Then Stevens opened up. A monk racing in a most unmonklike manner across the vegetable gardens dropped behind a bank. In reply an automatic weapon suddenly began hammering at the watch-tower, firing long bursts at a time. This was serious, indeed. Loran tried desperately to locate it, then saw the man in an archery window, and fired fast without evident success.

Stevens shouted, "They're making a run for it. This is quite obviously covering fire. Don't let 'em get away."

"They can't, Phil," he called back. "I can see the P.U. this side. Don't worry, it's nearly here. They can't make it now."

"Well, let's give 'em a peal or two of welcome on the jolly old bell, shall we?" And darting to the bell-pull, Stevens gave it a couple of hearty tugs.

The sound the bell gave out seemed deafening to Loran. "Smoked-out!" was what he thought he heard Stevens say before the Beretta went up to his shoulder again, and the Spandau below started blasting at them like a pneumatic drill. Bullets whined inside the tower, and it became obvious that the gunner was a professional, aiming off for ricochet. The parrot suddenly gave a scalded squawk and turned into a purple flower lying on its side.

The noise of the approaching P.U. grew steadily stronger. Suddenly Loran saw a figure in a dark suit crossing a lower lawn at a brisk trot.

"Schultz!" It was virtually a scream of pleasure that burst out of Stevens' lips at the sight.

And Loran froze. He felt a strange weakness in all his limbs. "Look out, Phil!" he shouted. "Let me. I'll get him."

For to aim properly at the man from his side the tower Stevens had had to climb up on the wall projection nearest him, leading to one of the flying buttresses.

"No, get down, Phil. We'll find him. The place'll be surrounded in a few minutes."

"I'm not letting that beggar get away, Tom. He killed your dad. Schultz!" he screamed again.

The figure whirled at Stevens' cry. The Beretta kicked but once in those hamlike hands. The German general dropped as instantaneously, Loran considered, as if an invisible giant had tugged a cord tied to his legs. In any other context in the world it might have been nearly comic. Then the Spandau opened up once more and the stone crab spat where Stevens was standing.

"Come down!" Loran yelled. "Oh, come off, you damned fool!"

And Stevens came, obedient to that call. He came sideways, with a sob thickening in his throat, a bullet through his brain, but no cry for mercy on his lips.

As Loran knelt under the tower's lee with his old enemy's body in his arms, he noticed for the first time that the boxer's hair was gray at the temples. Both his fists were bloody. . . .

THE END

www.ingramcontent.com/pod-product-compliance
Lightning Source LLC
LaVergne TN
LVHW091122080826
845145LV00008B/2009